Also by Stephanie Garber

Once Upon a Broken Heart

Caraval
Legendary
Finale

About the Author

Stephanie Garber is the #1 *New York Times* and internationally bestselling author of *Once Upon a Broken Heart* and the Caraval trilogy. Her books have been translated into thirty languages.

THE BALLAD OF NEVER AFTER

STEPHANIE GARBER

HODDER

First published in Great Britain in 2022 by Hodder & Stoughton
An Hachette UK company

This paperback edition published in 2023

1

A CIP catalogue record for this title is available from the British Library

Paperback ISBN 978 1 529 38100 9
eBook ISBN 978 1 529 38098 9

Printed and bound in Great Britain by Clays Ltd, Elcograf S.p.A.

Hodder & Stoughton policy is to use papers that are natural, renewable
and recyclable products and made from wood grown in sustainable
forests. The logging and manufacturing processes are expected to
conform to the environmental regulations of the country of origin.

Hodder & Stoughton Ltd
Carmelite House
50 Victoria Embankment
London EC4Y 0DZ

www.hodder.co.uk

For anyone who has ever feared
they won't find true love

Inn for Travelers
and Adventurers

THE HOLLOW

Slaughterwood
Castle

YOU ARE ENTERING
THE LANDS OF
HOUSE
SLAUGHTERWOOD.
WELCOME, IF YOU ARE
A GUEST.
BEWARE, IF YOU
ARE NOT...

S S

THE MAGNIFICENT NORTH

Words of Warning

Dear Evangeline,

Eventually, you will see him again, and when you do, do not be fooled by him. Do not be tricked by his charming dimples, his unearthly blue eyes, or the way your stomach might tumble when he calls you Little Fox —it's not a term of endearment, it's another form of manipulation.

Jacks's heart might beat, but it does not feel. If you are tempted to trust him again, remember all that he's done.

Remember that he was the one to poison Apollo so that he could frame you for murder in order to make a long-lost prophecy come true—one that would turn you into a key capable of opening the Valory Arch. That is all that he wants, to open the Valory Arch. He will probably be kind to you at some point in the future, to try to influence you into unlocking the arch. Do not do it.

Remember what he told you that day in the carriage—that he is a Fate and you are nothing but a tool to him. Do not let yourself forget what Jacks is or feel sympathy for him again.

If you need to trust someone, trust Apollo when he wakes. Because he will awake. You will find a way to cure him, and when you do, trust that the two of you will find your happily ever after and that Jacks will get what he deserves.

Good luck,

Evangeline

She finished writing the letter to herself with a deep breath. Then she sealed the note with a thick dollop of golden wax and wrote the words *In case you forget what the Prince of Hearts has done and you're tempted to trust him again.*

It had only been a day since she'd learned of Jacks's most recent betrayal—poisoning her new husband, Apollo, on the night of their wedding. The duplicity of it all still felt so raw, it seemed impossible to Evangeline that she might ever trust Jacks again. But Evangeline knew that her heart longed to hope for the best. She believed that people could change; she believed that everyone's life was like a story with an ending that was not yet written, and therefore everyone's future held infinite possibilities.

But Evangeline could not allow herself to hope for Jacks or to forgive him for what he had done to her and Apollo.

And she could never help Jacks open the Valory Arch.

The Valors, the first royal family of the Magnificent North, had constructed the arch as a passageway to a place called the Valory. No one knew what the Valory contained, since the stories of the North couldn't be fully trusted, thanks to the story curse that had been placed on them. Some tales couldn't be written down without bursting into flames, others couldn't leave the North, and many changed every time they were told, becoming less reliable with every retelling.

In the case of the Valory, there were two conflicting accounts. One said the Valory was a treasure chest that held the Valors' greatest magical gifts. The other claimed the Valory was an enchanted prison that locked away all manner of magic beings, including an abomination that the Valors had created.

Evangeline didn't know which account she believed, but she had no plans to allow Jacks to get his cold hands on either magical gifts or magical monsters.

The Prince of Hearts was already dangerous enough. And she was furious with him. Yesterday, after suspecting Jacks had been the one to poison Apollo, Evangeline had thought five words: *I know what you've done.*

Guards had then removed him from Wolf Hall. To her surprise, he had left without a fight or a word. But she knew he would be back. He wasn't done with her yet, though she was done with him.

Evangeline took the letter she'd just written to herself, crossed the length of her royal suite, and placed the note atop the fireplace mantel, waxed side out—making sure she'd see the words of warning if they were ever needed again.

PART I

*A Cruelty
of Curses*

1

There is a door deep inside the royal library of Wolf Hall that no one has opened for centuries. People have tried to set it on fire, break it with axes, and pick its lock with magic keys. But no one has so much as left a scratch on this stubborn door. Some say it mocks them. There is a wolf's head wearing a crown emblazoned on the door's wooden center, and people have sworn the wolf smirks at their failed attempts, or bares its sharp teeth if a person even comes close to opening this unopenable door.

Evangeline Fox had once tried. She had pulled and tugged and twisted the iron knob, but the door would not budge. Not then. Not before. But she hoped it would be different now.

Evangeline was very good at hoping.

She was also rather good at opening doors. With one drop of her willing blood, she could undo any lock.

First, she needed to be sure she wasn't being watched or

followed or stalked by that deceitful, apple-eating scoundrel whose name she wouldn't even think.

Evangeline checked behind her shoulder. Her lantern's ocher glow chased the nearby shadows away, but the bulk of Wolf Hall's royal library stacks were nebulous with night.

She fidgeted nervously, and the lantern flickered. Evangeline had never been afraid of the dark before. Dark was for stars and dreams and the magic that took place in between days. Before losing her parents, she had constellation-watched with her father and listened to her mother tell stories by candlelight. And Evangeline had never been frightened.

But it wasn't actually the dark or the night that she feared. It was the spider-thin prickle crawling across her shoulder blades. It had been with her since the moment she'd stepped out of her royal suite on a mission to unlock this door, in the hopes it would lead her to a cure that would save her husband, Apollo.

The uncanny sensation was so subtle, at first she let herself think it was merely paranoia.

She wasn't being followed.

She'd heard no steps.

Until . . .

Evangeline peered into the library's dark, and a pair of inhuman eyes stared back. Silver blue and brilliant and broken-star bright. She imagined they shone just to taunt her. But Evangeline knew that even if they sparkled now, even if these eyes lit up the dark and tempted her to lower her light, she couldn't trust them. And she couldn't trust him.

Jacks. She tried not to think his name, but it was impossible not to as she watched him saunter out of the dim, indolent yet confident and handsome as ever. He moved as if the night should have been afraid of him.

The tingling of her shoulder blades slid over her arms, an unsettling caress that went down to her one remaining broken heart scar. The wound stung, then throbbed, as if Jacks had sunk his teeth into it again.

Evangeline clutched her lantern like a sword.

"Go away, Jacks." It had only been two days since she'd had the guards remove him, and she'd hoped he would have stayed away longer—forever would have been ideal. "I know what you did, and I don't want to see you."

Jacks shoved his hands into the pockets of his trousers. His smoke-gray shirt was loosely tucked in, with sleeves shoved up lean arms and buttons missing at the throat. With his tousled hair now golden instead of seductive midnight blue, he looked more reckless stableboy than calculating Fate. But Evangeline knew she could never let herself forget what Jacks truly was. He was obsessive and driven and entirely without morals or conscience.

The stories said his kiss was deadly to all except his one true love, and as he'd searched for her, he'd left a trail of corpses. Evangeline had once been naive enough to believe that meant the Prince of Hearts understood heartbreak because his heart had broken over and over as he looked for love. But now it was crystal clear—he was the one who did the breaking, because he didn't know how to love.

Jacks spoke softly. "I understand if you're upset—"

"*If*," Evangeline cut in. "You poisoned my husband!"

Jacks lifted his shoulders in an insouciant shrug. "I didn't kill him."

"That's not something you earn points for." She fought to keep her voice from cracking.

Until then, Evangeline hadn't realized that a part of her still held on to a sliver of hope that Jacks was innocent. But he wasn't even trying to deny it. He didn't care that Apollo was little more than a corpse, just as he hadn't cared when Evangeline had been turned to stone.

"You need to stop holding me to human standards," Jacks drawled. "I'm a Fate."

"That's exactly why I don't want to see you. Since I met you, my first love was turned to stone, *I* was turned to stone, then I was turned into a fugitive, multiple people have tried to murder me, and you poisoned my husband—"

"You already said that one."

Evangeline glowered.

Jacks sighed and leaned against a nearby bookshelf as if her feelings were the emotional equivalent of a sneeze—something to be gotten over quickly, or avoided simply by stepping out of the way. "I'm not going to apologize for being what I am. And you're conveniently forgetting that before we met, you were a sad orphan with a broken heart and a wicked stepsister. After I stepped in, you became the sweetheart savior of Valenda, married a prince, and became a princess."

"Those things only happened because they served your twisted interests." Evangeline seethed. Everything he'd done for her was just so that he could use her to open the Valory Arch. "Children treat their toys better than you've treated me."

Jacks's eyes narrowed. "Then why didn't you stab me, Little Fox? The other night in the crypt, I threw you a dagger, and I was close enough for you to use it." His gaze sparked with fresh amusement as it lowered to her neck. To the exact place his mouth had lingered three nights ago.

She blushed at the unwanted memory of his teeth and tongue on her skin. He'd been infected with vampire venom, and she'd been infected with stupidity.

She'd stayed with him that night to keep him occupied so he wouldn't feed on human blood and become a vampire himself. He hadn't, but he'd fed on her sympathy instead. Jacks had told her the story of the girl who'd made his heart beat again— Princess Donatella. She was supposed to be his one true love, but instead of filling that role, Princess Donatella had chosen another and stabbed Jacks in the chest.

After hearing that story, Evangeline had started to see Jacks as the sympathetic Prince of Hearts that she had first gone to for help. But Jacks was all broken without any heart. And she needed to stop hoping that he could be more.

"I made a mistake that night in the crypt." Evangeline banished the blush from her cheeks and looked straight into Jacks's inhuman eyes. "But give me another chance and I won't hesitate to stab you."

He smirked, flashing dimples he didn't deserve. "I'm almost tempted to test that claim. But you'll have to do more than wound me if you wish to get rid of me." Jacks pulled an intensely white apple from his pocket and started tossing it. "If you *really* want me out of your life forever, help me find the missing stones and open the Valory Arch. Then I promise you'll never see me again."

"As much as I'd love that, I'm never going to open that arch for you."

"What about for Apollo?"

Evangeline felt a sharp stab of pain for the prince and another flare of anger for Jacks. "Don't you dare say his name."

Jacks grinned wider, looking oddly pleased by her anger. "If you agree to help me, I'll wake him from his suspended state."

"If you actually believe I would do that, you're delusional." Her first bargain with Jacks was the start of this entire mess. There would be no more deals with him, no more partnerships, no more anything. "I don't need you to save Apollo. I've found another way." Evangeline lifted her chin toward the sealed library door. It was still half-covered in shadow, but she swore the crowned wolf's head grinned as if it knew that she was the one who'd finally open its lock.

Jacks took one look at the door and chuckled, quiet and mocking. "You think you'll find a cure for Apollo in there?"

"I know I will."

Jacks laughed again, darker this time, and took a cheerful

bite of his apple. "Let me know when you change your mind, Little Fox."

"I won't change my—"

He was gone before she could finish. All that lingered was the echo of his ominous laughter.

But Evangeline refused to be nettled. She'd been told by an old librarian that this door led to every missing book and story about the Valors. Although the North's first royal family was human, it was widely accepted that they all possessed remarkable powers. Honora Valor, first queen of the North, was said to be the greatest healer of all time. And Evangeline had very good reason to believe that among the stories on the other side of this door were tales about her healing, which hopefully included a way to bring someone back from a state of suspended sleep.

Evangeline pulled out her dagger, a jewel-hilted blade with a few missing gems. It was actually Jacks's—the same one he'd tossed at her the night they'd spent in the crypt. He'd left it behind in the morning, and she still wasn't sure why she'd picked it up. She didn't want to keep it—not anymore—but she hadn't had time to replace it yet, and it was the sharpest thing she owned.

One prick of the dagger and her blood welled red. She pressed it to the door and whispered the words "Please open."

The lock instantly clicked. The knob easily twisted.

For the first time in centuries, the door swung open.

And Evangeline understood why Jacks had been laughing.

2

Evangeline stepped through the door, and the ground beneath her crumbled as if her slippers had found crackers instead of stones. It was rather like her hope: rapidly disintegrating.

This room was supposed to hold shelves of books on the Valors, answers to her questions, a cure for Prince Apollo. But there was only a wheeze of cloudy air, wafting in swirls around a dramatically carved marble arch.

Evangeline closed her eyes and opened them as if she could blink the arch away and the precious books would appear in its place. Sadly, Evangeline's blinks did not contain magic.

Still, she refused to give up.

In the Meridian Empire, where she was from, this arch would have just been a decorative curve of carved rock, large enough to frame a set of doors. But this was the Magnificent

North, where arches were something else entirely. Here, arches were magical portals built by the Valors.

This arch had mighty angels clad in armor carved into the columns, like warriors on opposite sides of an eternal battle. One of the angels had a bowed head and a broken wing; it looked almost sad, while the other appeared angry. Both had their swords drawn and crossed over the center, warning away anyone who might wish to enter.

But Evangeline wasn't just anyone. And if anything, the forbidden nature of the arch made her want to look inside even more.

Maybe this arch was a gateway to the books and the cure that she needed for Apollo. If the old librarian was right about this room containing all the stories on the Valors, perhaps the angels were protecting the books from the story curse so that they would stay uncorrupted. Maybe all she needed to do was press her blood to one of their swords and they would politely step aside to let her enter.

She took another step, feeling a hopeful thrill as she pricked her finger on the dagger once again and pressed her welling blood to one of the angels' swords.

It lit up like a candle. Glowing gold veins spiderwebbed across the stone swords, the angels, the entire arch. It was bright and light and magical. Her skin tingled as the dust on the arch floated up and sparkled all around her like tiny bursting stars. Air that had been cold was now warm. She'd known she was meant to enter this room, to find this arch, to open—

Suddenly, the breath whooshed from her lungs as the thought triggered the warning Apollo's younger brother, Tiberius, had given her: *You were meant to open it. Magic things always do that which they were created to do.*

And Tiberius believed that Evangeline was created to unlock the Valory Arch.

She staggered back, hearing the memory of Jacks's laugh again. This time it didn't sound dark at all. It sounded amused, entertained, *happy*.

"No," she whispered.

The stones still gleamed with gold threads that wove around the columns. She watched as they spread across the top, lighting up a series of curving words that had not been visible before.

Conceived in the north, and born in the south, you will know this key, because she will be crowned in rose gold.

She will be both peasant and princess, a fugitive wrongly accused, and only her willing blood will open this arch.

Evangeline's blood ran cold.

These were not just words. This was—she didn't even want to think it. But pretending would not erase or change anything. This was the Valory Arch prophecy, the one that Jacks had manipulated her to fulfill. Which meant that this wasn't just another arch. This was the Valory Arch.

Panic replaced every other feeling.

It shouldn't have been possible. The arch was supposed to be in pieces. Although there were two conflicting tales about the Valory's magical contents, everyone had agreed about one thing:

the Valory Arch had been broken into pieces and hidden across the North to keep anyone from knowing what the prophecy was and to prevent anyone from putting the arch back together.

"No, no, no, no, no . . ." Frantically, Evangeline tried to wipe her blood from the stones before Jacks or anyone else could discover what she'd done. The angels hadn't changed their pose, but she feared that any second a door would appear behind them or they would move aside. She spat and scrubbed with the sleeve of her cloak. But the glowing arch didn't dim.

"I knew you could open the door."

The scratchy voice was too old to belong to Jacks. But the sound of it stopped Evangeline's heart all the same.

"My apologies, Your Highness. I see I've frightened you again."

"Again?" She turned.

The man in the doorway was almost as small as a child, but far older than Evangeline, with a long, silver beard that held threads of gold, which matched the burnished trim on his white robes.

"You . . ." For a moment she remained too nervous to form words. "You're the librarian who first showed me the door to this room."

"You remembered." Though he looked clearly pleased, the old man's smile did nothing to put her at ease. Like the arch, he almost seemed to glow, his beard turning from an ordinary gray to iridescent silver. "I wish we had more time to chitchat, but you must hurry to find the missing stones."

He looked up at the arch to where four stones were missing along the top. The holes appeared to be smaller than her palm—not the large chunks of fractured rock she had pictured. But Evangeline instantly knew *these* were the broken pieces that needed to be found to truly unlock the Valory Arch.

Her blood had not been enough. Relief swept through her.

"You must find them," the old librarian repeated. "One for luck. One for truth. One for mirth. One for youth. But you must be careful. The stones are powerful, deceptive things. And the translation—"

"No!" Evangeline cut in. "I won't find these stones. I'm not *ever* going to open this arch. Pressing my blood to it was a mistake."

The old man gave her a weary frown. "It's not a mistake, it's your destiny. . . ." His voice trailed off as smoke puffed from his mouth instead of sound.

He scowled and tried to speak again, but only more wisps of gray and white poured forth. This time the smoke formed the words *Oh bother,* as if this sort of thing happened all the time.

The librarian's beard had now gone completely to smoke, exactly like his words. His hands were suddenly transparent, same as his robes and his wrinkled face, which was now as sheer as wispy curtains.

"What are you?" Evangeline breathed, trying to make sense of what she was seeing. She'd encountered vampires and Fates, and her stepsister was a witch, but she didn't know what this being was.

"I'm a librarian," he finally managed to say, but the words came out like something carried through a gust of wind, rattling and distant. "I know this makes me look rather suspicious, but I assure you, if you only knew the truth. If I could tell you . . ."

He faded completely before he could finish, leaving Evangeline with nothing but tendrils of lingering smoke and the unsettling feeling that perhaps the Prince of Hearts was not the only supernatural force she needed to be wary of.

3

Days later, Evangeline's heart was still racing. She didn't want to think about the contents of the Valory Arch. She didn't want to wonder at its secrets. She didn't want to remember how desperate the old librarian had sounded when he'd said, *If you only knew the truth.*

"We're running out of time," Havelock said, voice gruff, as their coach rumbled down another cobbled street frosted in white-blue snow.

Havelock had been Apollo's personal guard, but now he acted as Evangeline's escort while the two of them covertly searched for a remedy for Apollo's condition. During the last week, they'd visited mystics and apothecaries, doctors of medicine and physicians of the mind. They'd opened previously locked doors and entered libraries full of fables, but none of them had offered any help. *"No one has been in a suspended state since the days of Honora Valor,*" was the general refrain, followed by curious stares that prompted quick departures.

No one knew Prince Apollo was still alive, and word of it could not get out. Apollo was too vulnerable in his current state. As far as the public was concerned, Prince Tiberius, Apollo's younger brother, had murdered him. Evangeline felt a pinprick of guilt, knowing this was false. But since Tiberius had tried to kill her, she didn't feel all that guilty.

"This might be our last chance to save him," Havelock said.

Evangeline knew that he wasn't entirely right. She could always agree to open the Valory Arch for Jacks—but she hadn't mentioned that to Havelock. She still hoped there was another way to save Apollo.

"Have you seen the latest scandal sheet?" Havelock asked.

"I've been trying to avoid it," Evangeline replied. Yet she took the rolled page when Havelock held it out across the chilly coach.

The Daily Rumor

ALL HAIL LUCIEN JARETH ACADIAN

By Kristof Knightlinger

The newest heir to the throne, Lucien Jareth of House Acadian, is scheduled to arrive in Valor- fell tomorrow, and already there are more rumors about him than I can keep track of. I've heard that when he's not building homes for the poor or finding families to take in stray dogs and kittens, he's teaching orphans how to read.

Our royal liaison at Wolf Hall has also confirmed that preparations for the next Nocte Neverending are already underway.

Evangeline stopped reading, unable to stomach more. It had been like this for the last week. As soon as she had been cleared of murder, the papers had switched to printing stories about the new heir to the throne, a distant cousin of Apollo's, Lucien Jareth Acadian. The tales were always treacle sweet, making this Lucien person sound more saint than man.

"I wonder how much of this is actually true," she mused.

"Don't know," said Havelock. "I think the only thing we can count on is that he will arrive tomorrow."

Tomorrow.

The word suddenly sounded so menacing. Even if this Lucien really was a paragon of virtue who loved orphans and spent his time saving puppies, he'd still be taking Apollo's throne tomorrow. Unless Evangeline cured her prince today.

"You don't have to worry," Evangeline said with more confidence than she felt. "LaLa will be able to help us."

The coach stopped as it reached the spires. To Evangeline, the twisting towers of flats and shops looked like stacks of snow-dusted fairytales.

This was where Ariel "LaLa" Lagrimas lived. Also known as the Unwed Bride, LaLa was a Fate, like Jacks—except she was Evangeline's friend. When Evangeline had been poisoned by

Tiberius, LaLa had been the one to cure her, and Evangeline desperately hoped LaLa could do the same for Apollo.

Evangeline had actually come to visit LaLa straightaway, but the sign outside of her flat had said *Off Adventuring!* Evangeline didn't know where her friend had gone adventuring, but she'd sent royal soldiers to watch for her return—which, according to them, had happened that morning.

Evangeline's breath came out in puffy white clouds as she climbed the steps to LaLa's. She'd never noticed before, but the railings had lines from stories carved into them. Things like:

Once upon a time, there was a girl with a furry tail that twitched whenever snow was coming.

And, *Once there was a house where laughter constantly curled from the chimney instead of smoke.*

LaLa's flat actually felt like the sort of home that unbidden laughter might float out of. The front was a cheery speckled yellow, with a rounded white door that had a dragon-head knocker.

"Oh, my precious friend!" LaLa opened the door before Evangeline could knock, a blur of smiles and warmth as she captured Evangeline in the sort of hug that made it seem as if they'd known each other a lifetime instead of merely a few weeks. "You chose the perfect time for a visit. I have so much to tell you."

While Havelock stood guard outside, LaLa ushered Evangeline into the flat with steps that bordered on bubbly, though her living quarters felt quite the opposite. As soon as she crossed the threshold, Evangeline saw that it was not the same warm, welcoming space it had been before. The fireplace was vacant. The bright furniture remained, but the walls were naked and the tables were bare. Even LaLa's little birdcage lanterns were gone, save for one that rested atop a stack of packed trunks waiting beside the door.

"You're leaving?" Evangeline felt a great jab of disappointment. She hoped her assumption was wrong, but even LaLa's clothes seemed to confirm it. Usually, LaLa wore sequins or feathers or shimmering mermaid skirts, but today, her dress was the sedate color of fresh cream, with long sleeves that concealed the dragon flames tattooed on her brown arms. The gown was floor-length, as was the fashion in the Magnificent North, but when she stepped toward the sofa, Evangeline glimpsed a pair of heeled travel boots peeking out from the hem.

"I've been bursting to tell you—I'm engaged!" LaLa thrust out her arm, showing off a thick engagement cuff—gold and gleaming, and as pretty as the ecstatic smile now curling LaLa's lips. "His name is Lord Robin Slaughterwood. It's a rather ghastly surname, I know. But it's not as if I'll actually be adopting it. Since you know . . ." LaLa trailed off with a laugh that Evangeline would not have expected.

LaLa had once confessed to Evangeline that Fates were always fighting the urge to be that which they were made to be. LaLa was the Unwed Bride, therefore her primary desire was to find someone to love her, even though she was always destined to be left at the altar, crying tears so powerful that if a human drank them, they would die of heartbreak. And yet here LaLa was with a fresh engagement cuff and hope filling her pretty eyes.

"I'm so happy for you!" Evangeline said. And she was a little surprised to find that she meant it. If Evangeline had been in this same place months ago, she might have asked LaLa if she really thought this brief happiness was worth the inevitable heartbreak. People called it heartbreak, but Evangeline thought that losing someone you loved broke more than just a heart. When she had lost her first love, it had shattered her entire world. And yet, despite all of that pain, here she was, hoping not just to save Apollo's life but to have another chance at love with him.

"I hope Slaughterwood Castle is near," Evangeline said. "I would love to be able to visit."

"I would adore that." LaLa glowed. "Slaughterwood Castle is only one day's journey away, and I've requested a long engagement, so hopefully, I'll be able to throw lots of parties."

LaLa's boots clacked across the wood floor as she went to one of her trunks and pulled out a beehive cake—because of course she had cake packed away—along with cutlery and golden plates shaped like hearts.

Evangeline knew she needed to ask about a cure for Apollo. As Havelock had reminded her, she didn't have much time. But celebrating another person's joy was important, and LaLa was her only friend in the North.

Evangeline gave herself a few minutes to enjoy the cake along with her friend's happiness as LaLa told the tale of how she and Robin had met and become engaged in just a matter of days. "If you ever want to get married again, pretending to be a damsel in distress always seems to work for me in the North."

Evangeline laughed, but it must not have been very convincing.

LaLa's face immediately fell. Her eyes flickered over Evangeline's gown. She'd taken off her cloak, revealing a Northern mourning gown—pure white silk covered in an elaborate design of black velvet webbing. "Oh, my friend. I'm so sorry—I forgot you're still in mourning for Apollo. This has all been quite insensitive of me, hasn't it?"

As a Fate, LaLa did not experience the same range of human emotions, but this was actually one of the things that Evangeline liked about her friend. While Jacks's lack of humanity made him cold-blooded and remorseless and the bane of her existence, LaLa's seemed to make her more authentic and forthright.

"Please don't feel bad. I'm not truly in mourning," Evangeline confessed, and the rest of the words all seemed to rush out. "Apollo is alive. The stories you heard about his brother poisoning him weren't entirely true. It was actually Jacks who did it—he put Apollo in a state of suspended sleep to manipulate me." Evangeline wasn't sure how much LaLa knew about the Valory Arch. Apollo had once told her that the Northerners believed the story to be more fairytale than fact, and very few people knew what the prophecy was. So Evangeline explained almost everything. "Jacks believes I'm prophesied to be the one key capable of unlocking the arch, and he said that he'll only cure Apollo if I find the stones and open the arch for him."

"Oh my." LaLa paled, skin going gray as her eyes took on a doe-like fright.

It was the first time Evangeline had ever seen her close to scared.

"Don't worry," Evangeline said quickly. "I'm not planning on opening the arch for Jacks. I came here to see if you could cure Apollo."

"I'm so sorry, my friend. Although I do know a bit about potions and spells, the ones I've used were not generally for good, and I've never put anyone in a suspended state. It's very old magic. I believe Honora Valor would use it during wars when there were too many people to mend at once. She'd suspend those that she and her other healers couldn't get to right away."

Evangeline tried not to be disappointed. This was more or less what other healers had told her. "Are you sure you don't know anything else? I'll take any information you have. The new heir arrives tomorrow and—"

"You should open the arch for Jacks," LaLa interrupted.

"What?" Evangeline thought perhaps she'd misunderstood. Moments ago, Evangeline would have sworn that LaLa had looked haunted. But now her gaze was clear.

Had Evangeline misread her before, or was she misreading her now?

"Don't you want to save Apollo?" LaLa asked.

Evangeline felt a shiver of guilt. There were moments when she asked herself this question as well. She wanted to save him, but sometimes she feared she didn't want it enough. She couldn't say that she and Apollo were in love. But she did feel a tie to him. They were connected. She wasn't sure if it was a remnant of Jacks's love spell, if it was their marriage vows, or if Fate had simply entwined their paths, but she knew her future was linked to his.

She thought of the letter she'd tucked away in her pocket, the one she'd memorized because she'd read it so much.

Dear Evangeline,

I wish you could have met my parents. I think they would have loved you, and I imagine they would have said that I don't deserve you.

You and I do not know each other well. I know this. But I want to know you—I want to make you happy.

This week, perhaps, I have tried a little too hard. But I've never done this before, and I don't want to muck it up. I'm sure I will at some point in our future. But I promise you this, Evangeline Fox: whatever happens, I will always try. I only ask that you do the same.

My mother used to say, "The secret to staying in love is having someone who will catch you when you start to fall out of it." and I promise to always catch you.

Faithfully and
forever yours,
Apollo

Evangeline had found the note in Apollo's chamber after she'd been cleared of his murder. At first, the words had made her cry. Then the words had made her hope.

Apollo had been under a love spell the entire time they'd been engaged, but she swore there were moments of affection that had felt real between them. This letter felt like confirmation of that. It felt *real* and made her believe even more that Apollo had truly experienced times when he wasn't under a spell. This letter didn't feel like the writing of a bewitched young man, it felt like a genuine glimpse of the prince—a prince who felt the same way she did.

"I'm willing to do whatever it takes to save Apollo, except for opening the arch for Jacks. You can't really think I should do that?"

LaLa pursed her lips, looking briefly torn. But when she spoke again, her voice was resolute and clear and perfectly disturbing. "The Valory does not hold what you think. If I were you, I would open the arch."

"You know what's inside it?" Evangeline asked.

"The Valory is either a treasure chest, which protects the Valors' greatest magical gifts, or it's a door to an enchanted prison that locks away all manner of magic beings, including an abomination that the Valors created—" LaLa broke off with a scowl. "I hate this story curse."

She set her half-finished cake on the table with a loud *clack*, took Evangeline's hands, and then appeared to concentrate very hard. But this time, when she tried to tell Evangeline what she believed was in the arch, the only words that came out were gibberish.

4

Evangeline's mother, Liana, used to wake up every morning before sunrise. She'd put on a pretty flowered robe that Evangeline always thought of as romantic. Then she'd tiptoe delicately down the stairs and quietly slip into the study, where she would sit beside the crackling fireplace and read.

Liana Fox believed in starting the day with a story.

When Evangeline had been little, she would often wake up early as well. Not wanting to miss out on any of the magic with which her mother always seemed to be surrounded, Evangeline would follow her to the study, then curl up in her lap and promptly fall back to sleep.

Eventually, Evangeline grew too old for laps, but she also became better at staying awake. And so her mother began to read her stories out loud. Some tales were brief, while others took days or weeks to get through. One book—a great tome etched in gold foil that came all the way from the Southern Isles—took an entire six months to read. And when Liana reached the last page of every story, she never said, *The end.* Instead, she always turned to Evangeline and asked, *What do you suppose happens next?*

They live happily ever after, Evangeline usually proclaimed. Most characters, she believed, deserved it after all they'd been through.

Her mother, however, felt differently. She believed most characters would stay happy for now, but not forever. Then she'd point out things that would certainly work to wreak havoc in their future—the apprentice to the villain who was still alive, the evil stepsister who'd been forgiven but was still out there somewhere waiting to attack once more, the wish that had come true but wasn't quite paid for, the seed that had been planted but had yet to grow.

So, you think they're all doomed? Evangeline would ask.

Then her mother would smile, sweet and warm as fresh sugar pie. *Not at all, my precious girl. I think there's a happy ending for everyone. But I don't think these endings always follow the last page of a book, or that everyone is guaranteed to find their happily ever after. Happy endings can be caught, but they are difficult to hold on to. They are dreams that want to escape the night. They are treasure with wings. They are wild, feral, reckless things that need to be constantly chased, or they will certainly run away.*

Evangeline had not wanted to believe her mother then, but she believed her now.

Evangeline swore she could hear the pitter-patter of her happy ending running further away from her as she exited LaLa's flat.

She wanted to chase after it, but for a moment, she just stood there breathing in the cold Northern air and wishing she could curl up on her mother's lap once more. She still missed her fiercely. She wondered what her mother would have said she should do.

Evangeline had vowed to never open the Valory Arch for Jacks, but LaLa's words were making her question herself. *The Valory does not hold what you think. If I were you, I would open the arch.*

It seemed clear to Evangeline that her friend must have believed the version of the story that said the Valory was a magical treasure chest. But even treasures could be dangerous.

And what if LaLa was wrong? There were others, like Apollo's brother, Tiberius, who had been so determined to keep the Valory Arch locked they'd tried to kill Evangeline— Tiberius had actually tried twice! But did Tiberius even know what hid on the other side of the arch, or did he just fear it because he chose to believe the version of the story that said it contained an abomination?

Evangeline should have probably been afraid as well, but if she was being honest with herself, it was no longer the unknown contents of the Valory that most frightened her. It was the idea of partnering with Jacks to save Apollo.

Evangeline couldn't and wouldn't do that again.

She had never kissed the Prince of Hearts, but she had learned that his bargains were much like his fatal kiss—magical and utterly destructive. She'd make a deal with almost anyone else before entering into another partnership with him.

"Any luck?" Havelock asked when they were safely in the carriage.

Evangeline shook her head. "Maybe we should reconsider telling the new heir about Apollo's condition to buy us more time to search for a cure. If half the stories about Lucien are true, he may wait to take Apollo's place as prince."

Havelock snorted. "No one is as good as they make this Lucien sound. If we tell him the truth, at best he'll lock Apollo away for his *safety* and you'll never see him again. At worst—and far more likely—the new heir will have Apollo killed quietly, and then he'll do the same to you."

Evangeline wanted to argue. But she feared Havelock was right. The only certain way to save Apollo was to find a way to wake him up before tomorrow.

Tick. Tock. Tick. Tock. There was no clock in the carriage, but Evangeline could hear time slipping away. Or maybe Time was friends with Jacks and it was taunting her, too.

Wolf Hall, famed royal castle of the Magnificent North, looked part fairytale, part fortress, as if the first king and queen of the North had not agreed on what it should be.

There was a great deal of heavy protective stone, but there

were also decorative paints that brightened the doorways, and some of the stones on the ground had intricate carvings of plants and flowers along with reminders of what they were for:

Pegasus Clover—for forgetting
Angelweed—for a good night's sleep
Gray Silkweed—for sorrow
Spirit Hibiscus—for mourning
Unicorn Holly—for celebrating
Winterberries—for welcoming

When Evangeline had left the castle that morning, boughs of gray silkweed and bouquets of spirit hibiscus had been everywhere, but now they'd been replaced with bright red wreaths of unicorn holly.

Evangeline's stomach dropped at the sight of it. In the Magnificent North, mourning ended as soon as a new heir was officially named, which was supposed to happen the following day. Although from the altered state of Wolf Hall, it almost felt as if the new heir had already taken Apollo's place.

Evangeline heard minstrels singing of *Lucien the Great,* and the servants had done away with their black mourning outfits, replacing them with crisp white aprons. A few maids around Evangeline's age had festive winterberry sprigs in their braids and color on their cheeks and lips. And all of them seemed to be whispering:

"I've heard he's young. . . ."

"I've heard he's tall. . . ."

"I've heard he's handsomer than Prince Apollo!"

Evangeline's stomach cramped into tighter knots with every word. She knew she couldn't fault these young men and women—people needed reasons to celebrate. Mourning was important, but it couldn't go on forever.

She just wished she had more time. At least there was still one day left before Lucien actually arrived, even if that didn't feel like nearly enough.

Evangeline took a shuddering breath as the hallway she and Havelock traveled grew dimmer and cooler. Moments later, they reached the splintered trapdoor that would lead them to Apollo.

It always unnerved Evangeline that the door wasn't directly watched by a guard, but leaving a lone soldier in the middle of an empty hall seemed too suspicious. Instead, a trusted member of the royal guard waited in the room at the bottom of the stairs.

The small, hidden chamber was nicer than the first time she'd visited. Evangeline didn't know if Apollo was aware of his surroundings. But just in case he was, she'd asked his guards to bring some life into the little room. The cold floors were covered with thick burgundy carpets, paintings of vibrant forest scenes hung from the stone walls, and a raised four-poster bed with velvet drapes had been brought in.

She would have liked for Apollo to be in his own bedchamber, where a fire could chase away the cold and windows could be cracked when the air grew stale. But as Havelock had reminded her, it was too risky.

At the bottom of the stairs, the waiting guard greeted Evangeline with a bow and then spoke quietly to Havelock, giving her privacy as she approached her prince.

Butterflies moved in her chest. She hoped things would be different today, but thus far her prince appeared exactly the same.

Apollo lay motionless, looking like the ending of a tragic Northern ballad. His heart beat so slowly, and his olive skin was cool to the touch. His brown eyes were open, but his once smoldering gaze was entirely lifeless, flat and vacant as pieces of sea glass.

She leaned closer and smoothed the waves of dark hair from his brow, wishing with her whole heart that he would stir or blink or breathe. She just wanted a small sign that he would return to life. "In your letter, you promised you would always try. Please try to come back to me," she whispered, tilting her face toward his.

She didn't enjoy touching him when he was so lifeless. But Evangeline remembered that when she'd been stone, she'd desperately longed for another person's touch. Which was one thing she could give Apollo.

She cupped his waxy cheek and pressed a kiss to his unmoving lips. His mouth was soft, but it tasted wrong, like unhappy endings and hexes, and, as always, he didn't stir.

"I don't understand why you do this every day." Jacks's indolent voice carried through the chamber.

Evangeline felt it rush over her skin, a slow fire that made the broken heart scar on her wrist burn like a brand. She tried to ignore both the scar and Jacks. She tried not to turn, not to look or acknowledge his appearance, but it probably would seem more suspect if she continued to kiss Apollo's unmoving lips.

Slowly, she straightened, pretending that every inch of her skin wasn't prickling like her scar as Jacks swaggered forward.

He was dressed with more care than usual. A series of silver links secured the midnight-blue cape at his shoulders. His velvet doublet was the same deep blue, save for the smoke-gray embroidery that matched his fitted trousers, which were tucked neatly into polished leather boots.

She shot a look past him, toward Havelock and the other guard at the foot of the stairs, but they were doing nothing. Jacks must have magicked them. Most people believed that the Prince of Hearts' only power was his deadly kiss, but Jacks also possessed the ability to turn humans into puppets at his will. His Fately power was more limited in the North, but he could still control the emotions and hearts of several humans at a time.

Thankfully, these powers didn't allow him to control Evangeline. He'd tried before, but she had simply heard his thoughts. He could also hear her thoughts if she projected them. But sharing her thoughts with Jacks was not something Evangeline desired to do right now.

"Do you kiss the prince because you actually enjoy it?" Jacks asked. "Or is it because you honestly think it will magically revive him?"

"Maybe I do it because I know it will annoy you," Evangeline answered archly.

Jacks flashed a smile that was far more wicked than welcoming. "Glad to know you're thinking about me when you kiss your husband."

Heat flushed her cheeks. "I'm not thinking *nice* things."

"Even better." His eyes sparked, gem-sharp blue with threads of silver, and far too pretty to belong to such a monster. Monsters were supposed to look like . . . monsters, not like Jacks.

"Did you come here just to irritate me?"

Jacks sighed, slow and dramatic. "I'm not your enemy, Little Fox. I know you're still angry with me, but you've always known what I am. I never tried to pretend otherwise, you just let yourself believe I was something I'm not." His eyes turned metallic and utterly unfeeling. "I'm not your friend. I'm not some human boy who will tell you pretty lies or bring you flowers or gift you jewels."

"I never thought you were," she said. But perhaps a small part of her had. She hadn't imagined that he'd bring her flowers or presents, but she had started to think of him as a friend. A mistake she would never make again.

"Why are you here?" Evangeline asked.

"To remind you that you can easily save him." Jacks casually shoved his hands in his pockets, as if making another deal with him would be as simple as giving a baker some coins for a bit of bread.

Perhaps, at first, it would seem that way. If she told Jacks she'd open the Valory Arch, Apollo would wake tonight. There would be no more worries about this new heir. But Jacks would still be there—he'd be there until he found the missing arch stones. And Evangeline needed Jacks gone, perhaps as much as she needed to wake her prince. As long as Jacks was in her life, he would continue to ruin it.

She'd been trying to find a cure for Apollo, but maybe what she *really* needed was to find a way to get rid of Jacks.

"The answer is no, and it will always be no."

Jacks crossed his arms and leaned against the bedpost. "If you really think that, then you lack imagination."

Evangeline bristled. "I do not lack imagination. I merely possess determination."

"So do I." Jacks's eyes flickered with something malevolent. "This is your last chance to change your mind."

"Or what?" Evangeline asked.

"You'll really start to hate me."

"Perhaps I look forward to hating you."

The corner of Jacks's poisonous mouth twitched as if the idea vaguely entertained him. Then a clock chimed somewhere above. Seven loud strikes.

"Tick-tock, Little Fox. I was trying to be kind by giving you time to consider the offer I made in the library, but I'm tired of waiting. You have until tonight to change your mind."

She tried to ignore the twist in her gut. If putting Apollo in a state of suspended sleep was Jacks's kind way of trying to persuade her, she dreaded what else he might do after tonight. And yet she still couldn't imagine that partnering with him again would leave her better off.

She turned to leave.

A hand gripped her wrist.

"Jacks—"

But the hand holding her didn't belong to Jacks.

His skin was cool and marble smooth. The hand that had grabbed her burned.

Apollo?

Evangeline turned back to her prince, excitement surging through her. He was—

Wrong.

Moments ago, his eyes had been dull as sea glass, but now they glowed red, like burning rubies and curses.

Evangeline whirled on Jacks—or she tried to. It was difficult to move with Apollo's hand iron tight around her wrist.

She glowered at Jacks. "I thought you were giving me the rest of the night?"

"I didn't do this." His gaze shot from the prince's glowing red eyes to Evangeline's captured wrist.

She tried to pull free, but Apollo's fingers dug in with more force.

She tugged harder.

He squeezed tighter, painfully tight, making her yelp as she yanked against him.

His eyes still glowed that awful red, but he didn't appear awake—he seemed possessed, or perhaps desperately fighting to wake up.

Her chest tightened with panic. "Apollo—"

"He can't hear you." Jacks pulled out a dagger with a shining black blade.

"What—"

"He's going to break your bones!" Jacks slashed Apollo's hand with the knife.

Blood spattered her skirts as the prince dropped her wrist and the red disappeared from his eyes.

Evangeline cradled her injury—Apollo had left a bracelet of blue and purple bruises.

Drip.

Drip.

Drip.

She was bleeding, too. But the blood wasn't coming from the hand that the prince had taken. It was her other hand. Red welled in a diagonal cut across the back of it, mirroring the wound that Jacks had just given Apollo, as if she, too, had been sliced. She tried to swipe it away, hoping it was just spatter from Apollo. But her hand continued to bleed.

Jacks's eyes were storm-dark as he watched blood well from

the wound. Swearing, he tore a handkerchief from his pocket and hastily wrapped it around her cut. "Stay away from here, and do not kiss him again."

"Why—what's happening?" she asked.

Jacks spoke between clenched teeth. "Someone has just put another curse on you and your prince."

5

Another curse.

"It looks like a mirror curse," Jacks said.

Evangeline tried not to panic again, but her nerves were fraying at the edges. If she were a book, she would have felt as if her pages were slowly being torn free of the spine. She was bruised, she was bleeding, her husband was cursed, now she seemed to be cursed. And Jacks was still holding her hand.

She pulled free of Jacks's icy grip, but she didn't feel any better. If anything, a fresh chill coated her skin.

Jacks spoke, his voice eerily calm and deliberate. "As long as this mirror curse is in play, Apollo will share any injuries you receive, and you'll share any injuries he receives. But it's his death you need to worry about. If he dies, you die." Jacks's eyes cut back to the handkerchief he'd wrapped around her hand. For a second, he looked entirely inhuman. The calm fled his expression, turning his face vengeful and unholy.

Another day and it might have pleased Evangeline to see the Prince of Hearts so affected. But she wasn't sure she really believed his reaction. Not after he'd just warned her that she had one night left to make a deal with him or else.

"Did you do this?" she asked.

Jacks glared at her.

"Don't pretend you'd never hurt me in order to manipulate me. You just said that if I didn't agree to open your Valory Arch, I'd really start to hate you."

"I hurt everyone, Little Fox. But you have to be alive to hate me." His eyes iced over. "I do not want you dead, and I'll kill anyone who tries."

He stalked from the room.

The guards at the foot of the stairs unfroze, instantly released from the Prince of Hearts' control. A rush of words and movement followed as both took in the altered scene.

"What's going on—is that—blood?"

The soldiers rapidly converged on Evangeline, restored to their wits and duties just in time to block her from rushing up the stairs after Jacks to demand more answers.

She held up her hand, showing both guards her bandaged wound as she quickly came up with a lie. "I was attempting something new to wake Apollo, but it didn't work. I'll explain more later, but I have to go now."

She needed to follow Jacks. The way he rushed from the room made her suspect that he knew who'd placed this new curse on her and Apollo, or that he thought he knew. "Both of you, please stay with the prince—and attend to his wounded hand. He needs more protection than I do."

Havelock looked as if he wanted to argue, but Evangeline didn't give him the chance. She darted up the stairs, rabbit quick.

She was halfway up the stairs when: *Dah-dah-dah-daaaaaah!*

Trumpets, an entire host of them, loud and celebratory, filled the castle with music.

Evangeline's steps faltered. Why were trumpets sounding? She should have brushed it aside; she didn't have much time if she wanted to trail Jacks. But then she heard the giggling. A few feet down the hall, a pair of young maids were huddled together. "Do either of you know what that music was all about?"

The taller of the girls looked at Evangeline askance, but the shorter one was politer. She answered with an apologetic smile, "I think it's part of the welcome ceremony for Prince Lucien. He surprised everyone by arriving early."

The hallway started to spin. Why had no one told her he'd arrived early? She'd been busy, but someone should have found her.

"I'm sure someone would have informed you," the petite maid blurted as if guessing her thoughts. "But I heard Prince Lucien was worried it would be insensitive to make you watch the event where he replaced your beloved as heir. That's why he rushed up the ceremony."

"So thoughtful," the taller maid said dreamily.

"I like him already," the short maid agreed.

I want to punch him, Evangeline thought.

It wasn't just that the new heir had arrived early, it was the underhanded nature of it. She should have been invited to the ceremony.

Why had Lucien left her out? She didn't believe for a second that it was to spare her feelings. Of course, she didn't have time to worry about that now. She needed to follow Jacks.

"Princess Evangeline," intoned a voice from behind her.

It was tempting not to turn, but then two soldiers appeared by her side. Both were dressed in the Acadian royal colors—bronze, gold, and maroon—but she did not recognize either one.

"You've been summoned to the receiving solarium," said the one on her right. "Prince Lucien has requested your immediate presence."

Evangeline tried to muster her optimism as she followed these unknown guards. But all she felt was a growing pit inside her. It was unnerving that she had not been invited to Lucien's coronation, yet she was practically being dragged to meet him now.

As she neared her destination, the air warmed and sweetened with the scent of mulled wine and poorly timed celebrations. The solarium was rarely used for evening meetings. With stretching walls of windows that invited in the light, it was meant for daylight hours or the occasional sunset soirée. But the new heir must not have known that. Tonight, the waiting hall outside it was full of life and light, candles dripping from chandeliers, chatting guests with painted cheeks, and loud laughs that edged on drunken.

It seemed she was not the only one who'd been invited to meet Lucien. But apparently, she was meant to be seen first. The soldiers directed her past all the others, to another pair of guards who immediately parted the arched solarium doors.

Evangeline painted on a smile, hid her bandaged hand behind her skirts, and stepped forward gamely. She did not expect to find the saint the papers had described, but she was ready to feign the required pleasure at meeting the young man who was taking Apollo's place on the throne.

Lucien kept the solarium darker than the lively outer hall. The moon spied through the towering windows, a waning crescent that added atmosphere but no illumination. Candles burned in sconces, but they brought more smoke than light, varnishing the room in haze that might have intrigued others but made Evangeline slow her steps. All was dim, save for the area directly in front of the blazing fire, where the heir sat sprawled in a wingback chair, twirling a golden crown.

"Good evening," she forced out cheerfully, taking another step closer to the amber firelight. But as soon as she reached it, her limbs refused to move.

This young man was not the heir—or even truly a young

man anymore. He was too unnaturally handsome, his eyes were too luminous, his jaw could slice a diamond, and his golden-brown skin actually glowed.

He was a vampire.

And the first boy she had ever loved.

6

Luc gave her a crooked smile, still twirling the golden crown around his fingers as if it were a child's toy. "Hello, Eva."

Evangeline clenched her hands into fists.

Once, she might have run to him. Once, she might have wept for him. Now, she wanted to throw things at him. Sharp, hurtful things.

Luc had once been the boy she'd thought that she would marry, but the last time she'd seen him, he'd been locked in a cage as part of a ceremony to become a vampire. Jacks had warned her against saving him—but she had listened to her heart instead. She'd helped free Luc, and he'd thanked her by trying to rip out her throat with his teeth.

"What are you doing here?" she demanded.

Luc pouted. "Are you still angry about the other night?"

"You mean when you tried to eat me?"

"It wasn't like that. Well, maybe it was a little like that." He grinned, flashing his fangs as if they were the equivalent of a shiny new pocket watch, an accessory to match his doublet, which was black velvet with deep bloodred embroidery.

"This isn't funny, Luc. What are you doing here?"

"Aw, come on. You're clever, or you were. I'd have thought you'd have figured it out." He twirled the crown again, round and round his fingers. It was just a simple circlet, but it was made of gold and it shone through the miasma, making it rather obvious what should have been apparent since the moment she'd walked in: *Luc* was *Luc*ien.

"*You* started the ridiculous rumors about Lucien Acadian?" Evangeline had thought this Lucien was too good to be true, but she'd never actually imagined the young man who taught children to read and found homes for stray puppies could be Luc. Luc was a lot of things, but he wasn't cunning enough to rule a kingdom, let alone steal one.

How had Luc pulled this off? She knew vampires possessed *allure,* an ability that allowed them to dazzle humans if a human looked them in the eye. But Luc would have needed more than that to turn himself into the heir. He wasn't even *from* the Magnificent North.

If only she'd found a way to wake up Apollo, this would have never happened.

"I thought you'd be more impressed. I'm a prince now!" Luc jauntily tossed his crown into the air and caught it with the top of his head.

She cringed.

Luc scowled, the expression marring his handsome features.

"I don't understand how or why you're doing this, Luc, but it isn't going to work. You can't just make up a name and claim a throne."

"Don't worry so much, Eva. Only the name is a lie." He started playing with his crown again, letting it slip from his head onto his fingers. "Chaos said altering my name would make it easier for people to accept the truth—turns out, I really am a long-lost distant relation of the dead prince."

Evangeline winced at the words *dead prince* and resisted the urge to shake her head. She didn't believe for a second that Luc was Apollo's long-lost relation. But of course, Luc would believe it. He had always been a little entitled. It was a minor flaw she'd ignored in the past, but suddenly, it didn't seem so harmless. As a human, Luc had thought he deserved every nice thing, and now that he was a vampire, he clearly thought himself worthy of much more.

The question was, why would Chaos give the throne to him? Evangeline had met Chaos on several occasions. The first two times they'd crossed paths, he'd pretended to be a royal guard, but it turned out he was the Vampire Lord of Spies and Assassins.

Perhaps he'd placed Luc on the throne because Chaos supposed that, as a new vampire, Luc would be easy to control. Although that was difficult for Evangeline to believe as well. Luc was too impulsive. Even if he did what Chaos desired in terms of laws and policies, Evangeline imagined Luc losing control of his vampire urges. If he'd attacked her—someone he'd supposedly cared about—she couldn't picture him holding back with others.

Evangeline had a sudden terrifying flash of Wolf Hall full of courtiers and servants who were bleeding or dead or turned into vampires.

This would be a disaster. Evangeline wanted to say as much, but she doubted Luc would take it well. Instead, she wondered why Luc had called her here, alone. She would have never feared him as a human—she'd loved him—but that boy had disappeared as soon as Luc had been infected with vampire venom.

"Why don't you come a little closer?" He cocked his head toward Evangeline, and she felt heat nip her earlobe and then sensed his burning gaze on her throat.

"Stop that, Luc."

"Stop what?" Another smile, but it didn't touch his eyes—they were dark and brown and *hungry.*

She needed to go—she needed to find that cure for Apollo more than ever, to get Luc off his throne—but if she left Luc alone, she feared what else he might do. *Who else he might bite.*

"Luc, please—" Evangeline paused at the sound of footsteps.

They were just outside the doors and as soft as the muffled feminine voice that followed. "I was summoned by Prince Lucien to join him for dinner."

Evangeline tensed at the last word. "Tell me she means actual food."

"I'm sure that's what *she* means," Luc said.

Evangeline's stomach started to roil.

"If you're jealous, I'll happily have *you* for dinner instead." Luc flashed Evangeline a smile that was probably meant to be playful but was made of too much teeth.

Her blood rushed, uncomfortably hot. "That's not funny."

"It wasn't meant to be." His nostrils flared.

The solarium door opened.

Evangeline braced to see the girl who'd come for *dinner*. But it wasn't a girl. It was Havelock.

"Who are you?" Luc's lips curved into a snarl.

Havelock ignored him, looking only at Evangeline. "Princess, there's something you need to see straightaway."

"I'm not sure that this is the best time." Evangeline shot a worried look toward Luc. She couldn't leave him alone to feed on some poor girl. But of course, Havelock didn't know what Luc really was. She didn't even know if Havelock was aware vampires existed, and in this moment, he might not care.

Havelock's face was a series of strained lines, and when he spoke again, his voice was a rough thing that bordered on frightened. "This is urgent."

Evangeline felt it then, damp on the back of her hand. One drop of blood leaked through the bandaged wound she shared with Apollo.

Luc inhaled from across the dark room. A sound like a growl came from his throat. And then in a flash, Luc was in motion.

She'd forgotten how fast a vampire could move. He was a

powerful blur as he crossed the dim room and took hold of her with two brutal hands. Before she could run, one hand clamped around her waist, digging in, as the other fisted her hair and wrenched her neck toward his parted mouth.

Evangeline screamed.

But Luc's lips never touched her skin. One instant he was there, all sharp teeth and primal hunger. Then he was being torn away, and she was being held. Gentle hands instead of harsh ones wrapped protectively around her, pulling her toward a cold, hard chest. He smelled of apples and cruelty, but Evangeline was shaking too hard to push Jacks away as he led her out of the dark solarium.

"I'm going to kill that boy," he fumed.

Around them, the hallway lights were blinding, dizzying to Evangeline, who already felt a little faint. Luc had not managed to bite her, but the wound on her hand was dripping again and her mind was spinning.

"Havelock—"

"Is fine," Jacks said.

Then the guard was there, a few feet to the side, looking dazed—possibly under Jacks's control—but, thankfully, not appearing to be bleeding or injured.

"But Luc—"

"Is being subdued." Jacks's arm tightened around her, pulling her farther down the too-bright hall away from the solarium.

"Wait—" Evangeline dug her heels in and wrenched herself free. "Who is subduing Luc?"

"Someone who won't hold him back forever." Jacks's mouth formed a flat line. He tried to tug her away again, but Evangeline darted back.

She was thankful Jacks had stopped her from becoming Luc's next snack, but saving her once didn't make Jacks a savior. He was still her villain, not her hero. "I'm not going anywhere with you."

"It's not safe for you here," Jacks said calmly, as if she were a stray kitten he was trying to herd. And yet she noticed his knuckles were clenched and a muscle throbbed angrily in his neck.

"Excuse me." The diminutive voice carried up the hall from the solarium doors. "Is Prince Lucien ready to see me for dinner yet?"

Evangeline turned, alarmed once again as her gaze snagged on the petite girl just a few feet away. Her face was delicate, her dress petal pink, and the sight of her filled Evangeline with fresh dread. It was Marisol. Her stepsister.

Evangeline had not seen her since the morning after Marisol had gotten Evangeline arrested for Apollo's murder. Marisol had known Evangeline was innocent, but underneath her sugar-sweet exterior lived a heart corroded by jealousy, which had prompted Marisol to turn Evangeline in for a crime she hadn't committed.

Seeing her now, looking princess-pretty, was like a knife to Evangeline's memories, reopening all the wounds that Marisol had inflicted with her betrayal.

Marisol's misdeeds initially hurt so much that Evangeline

had considered using her royal position to ban her stepsister from Wolf Hall—possibly the Magnificent North entirely. But no matter how much Evangeline had wanted Marisol gone, she hadn't been able to send her away. Evangeline's feelings for her stepsister were complicated. She wanted to forgive Marisol. She wanted to be better than Marisol had been to her. But maybe Evangeline wasn't better. Because as much as she was loath to admit it, she was prepared to let Marisol walk through the solarium doors, come face-to-face with Luc, and reap the pain that she had sown.

7

It would have been easy for Evangeline to simply stand there. To let Marisol enter the solarium without warning her. Marisol's history with Luc was her own fault. She'd put Luc under a love spell to steal him from Evangeline. Then, when Luc had been disfigured by a wolf attack, Marisol had rejected and shunned him. Luc deserved the chance to confront her.

But Evangeline knew that wasn't what he wanted from Marisol.

Evangeline felt a twist in her gut.

"I know what you're thinking," Jacks said, "but some people get things because they deserve them."

Evangeline knew he was right. Marisol was no innocent. She'd done terrible things. But that didn't mean that Evangeline could just let Luc kill her.

Before she lost her resolve, Evangeline started down the royal hall. Marisol blanched as she neared. Then the girl's eyes went wide as Jacks came up beside her. She slowly took in every inch of him, from his polished boots to his rakish half cape, to the cruel line of his mouth.

Marisol had met Jacks at Nocte Neverending and been instantly enthralled. He'd had dark blue hair then, nothing like the brilliant gold that crowned him now, but she clearly recognized him. Her breath went shallow, excited. Then her eyes hardened and she glared at Evangeline, probably remembering the way she'd warned Marisol away from him. "You are such a little hypocrite."

Told you she deserves it, Jacks thought at Evangeline.

She ignored him, pushing aside his words, along with the bite in her stepsister's voice. All she had to do was warn her. Then hopefully she'd be done with her for good.

"You need to get out of here," Evangeline said. "Leave Wolf Hall and the North."

Marisol snorted. "You can't make me go anywhere. You're just a ruined girl with a dead husband. The servants might call you *Princess,* but most of them still think you murdered your prince."

Evangeline flinched.

Jacks ground his jaw. "You're a nasty piece of work."

"I'm just telling the truth."

"So am I," Jacks said.

Marisol's cheeks grew bright red, but she lifted her chin with a haughty sniff. "I'm going to meet Prince Lucien now."

"If you go through those doors, you will never come back out again," Evangeline said.

Marisol rolled her eyes. "Is that really the best you can do?"

"It's the truth." *Prince Lucien is really Luc, and he's a vampire!* Evangeline wanted to scream, but she feared saying the word *vampire* would only work against her. Jacks had once told her that all the stories about vampires were cursed, but instead of warping the truth, like the other cursed tales of the North, stories about vampires manipulated the way people felt. No matter what a person was told about vampires, they would always be intrigued instead of horrified.

Marisol spun on her heel and strode toward the solarium doors.

Evangeline felt a brief flicker of indecision as she turned toward Jacks.

Before, she'd thought her feelings for Marisol were complicated, but they were actually very simple. All that Evangeline really wanted from her stepsister was an apology. She wanted her to feel some regret or remorse for the selfish things she'd done. She didn't want her dead.

And yet the only way to save her now would be to ask Jacks for help.

Evangeline swallowed. Something metallic coated her tongue. It tasted like a price she didn't want to pay. She reminded herself that she could not trust Jacks. She could not be tricked into believing he was her friend or make a habit of turning to him for help. She would just do it this one time.

"Please," Evangeline whispered to Jacks, "use your powers to stop her."

He raised one imperious brow. "You're asking me for a favor?"

"I'm asking you to show some humanity." Which actually felt almost as dangerous. If Jacks did this for free, it would be easier to once again think he was something he was not. But, from the unfeeling look on his face, that clearly wouldn't be an issue.

"You're asking for the wrong thing," he said.

The guards reached for the solarium handles.

Evangeline's insides tightened. If Jacks wasn't going to stop Marisol, then she was going to have to try again. She didn't know what she was going to do, but she started toward the solarium after her stepsister.

"Don't." Jacks grabbed her hand, his grip firm and cold.

Evangeline started to pull away.

But then she saw Marisol. One moment her stepsister was at the doors, and then she was backing away, flitting like a frightened bird with thin brown hair whipping around her face. She tripped on the hem of her skirts, stumbling a bit against the stone floors before breaking into a run down the opposite side of the castle hall.

Jacks had used his power to save her, after all.

Evangeline's shoulders felt lighter, but her chest felt tighter. She waited for Jacks to say that she owed him now. He'd already dropped her hand, but he was eyeing the last remaining broken heart scar on her wrist. The reminder of the other debt that she hadn't finished paying—the final kiss she owed.

Jacks hadn't mentioned the debt in a while, but she felt a rush of fresh nerves as she wondered if he would collect soon—if this final kiss was what he'd referred to when he'd promised earlier that she would really start to hate him.

Havelock cleared his throat. "Pardon me, Your Highness."

Startled, Evangeline leaped farther away from Jacks. She wasn't sure when the guard had crept up. But one look at Havelock's woebegone face and she knew that she didn't want to hear what he had to tell her.

Not now.

Evangeline didn't think she could handle much more. She wasn't even sure she was doing a very good job of handling what she'd just been dealt. If not for Jacks, Marisol would be dead right now. Evangeline didn't regret asking him to save her, but she couldn't ask him for more. She needed to get away from him and from everything else. She'd been trying so hard to do the right thing, to make the noble choice, to be the hero, and she was exhausted.

Jacks often told Evangeline that heroes didn't get happy endings, but in that moment, Evangeline wasn't looking for happiness. She just wanted a break. A moment of peace before being confronted with another catastrophe. Was that too much to ask?

She looked at her bandaged hand now. The wound she shared with Apollo had stopped bleeding, and the rest of her—aside from her battered heart—was sound. Therefore, Apollo wasn't in any immediate danger. Whatever Havelock had wanted from her could wait.

"I'm leaving," she announced. "And I don't want anyone to follow me." She didn't know exactly where she was going yet, but she could figure that out later. Maybe she'd go visit LaLa and her new fiancé and eat cake until the world turned sweet again, or perhaps she'd just hop onto a horse until she rode herself into a new story. All she knew was that she had to get out of Wolf Hall.

Evangeline had always thought the great Northern castle was magical, and it was—but it was full of the wrong sort of magic. Nearly every single memory she had inside these stone walls was tainted with some sort of curse or betrayal.

Her black-and-white skirts swished around her ankles as she turned away from both Havelock and Jacks.

"Your Highness." Havelock marched after her. "You can't simply leave—"

"I'm sorry," she cut in. "I appreciate you, Havelock, but I can't handle more bad news at this particular minute. So unless you're going to tell me wish-granting unicorns have arrived, I need a moment, possibly quite a few moments, to myself."

She quickened her steps to almost a run. Her skirts were heavy, but her boots were blessedly sturdy, making it easy to take a flight of stairs and then hurry down a hall to a door that led outside. The air was cold as she burst into the Northern night, canopied by a sky of foreign constellations that she had yet to learn.

Maybe she could just return to the south and to her home in the Meridian Empire. She could leave the North and all its curses. But even as she thought it, Evangeline knew that wasn't what she wanted. She didn't want another story; she wanted to fix this story. She wanted to save Apollo. She wanted a chance to know him when he wasn't under a spell. She wanted to believe that their story wasn't over. She wanted the happy ending that she'd come here for.

Evangeline ventured deeper into the garden, frozen flower petals crackling under her shoes. Then she heard another pair of footsteps—lighter than hers, but growing closer.

The broken heart scar on her wrist started burning. Sometimes she was able to ignore the sensation, but right now, it was stronger than usual, as if Jacks wanted her to know that he was inescapable.

Evangeline hastened her pace, hoping to lose him in the shadows of the darkened garden. But Jacks didn't stop following her, and she had a feeling he never would.

She almost laughed at the idea that she'd thought she could run away from him. That he would simply let her go.

Evangeline forced herself to stop beneath the amber glow of a garden lamp shaped like a bowing flower. Cold bit her cheeks and licked her hands, but Jacks didn't so much as shiver as he strode toward her, indifferent to the bitter air that froze the tips of his hair and lashes. He slid through the icy night like a slow-falling star, all unearthly eyes and graceful moves.

She folded her arms across her chest, which probably didn't look as forceful as she wanted with Jacks's handkerchief still wrapped around her hand; one more reminder of how he'd *helped* her, even if it was with another problem he'd possibly created. "Jacks, leave me alone."

He took another slow step. "You're a little scary right now, did you know that?"

She glared at him.

"That was a compliment, Little Fox." He reached toward her and brushed a lock of hair behind her ear with one featherlight touch.

Butterflies moved inside her. Different from the ones that she felt whenever she saw Apollo. *Because Apollo didn't frighten her.*

"What are you doing?" she squeaked.

Jacks chuckled. "If I knew all it took to scare you was a little touch, I would have tried this sooner." His fingertips played with her earlobe.

Evangeline pulled away, almost stumbling on the frozen ground. She hated that her legs were so unsteady. That one small touch could affect her so.

Even seconds later the ground was still shuddering. It didn't feel quite like a true tremor, more like a shiver moving across the garden, and suddenly, Evangeline feared it wasn't just from her wobbly limbs.

Outside the circle of garden lights above them, the world was darker. Curling mist instead of shrubs and trees. As Evangeline looked out, she had the same prickly sense she'd gotten nearly a week ago when Jacks had followed her into the library.

Someone was watching.

"I think someone else is here," she whispered. Her eyes strained until she saw a figure appear in the distance. It was far enough away that it could have just been a trick of the shadows, but it looked to Evangeline like a rider astride a horse.

Jacks frowned. "It's probably that gossipmonger from the scandal sheets."

But Evangeline didn't think so. This horseman looked broader and stronger, and *familiar*.

She took a step forward into the shadows.

"What are you doing?" Jacks asked.

"Don't worry," Evangeline replied. "I'm sure whoever it is couldn't be more dangerous than you."

But the truth was, something about this rider called to her. The only other one who had made her feel anything like this was Jacks. The broken heart scar on her wrist tied her to him, tingling and burning and reminding her that he was inescapable. With the rider, it was different. There was no tingle. It was more like a tether, pulling her toward him with an invisible cord. Snow fluttered around her shoulders as she continued down the moonlit path.

Leaves rustled, the horse whinnied, and a shaft of moonlight lit the horseman, enough for Evangeline to see clearly the familiar edges of his handsome face. *Apollo.*

8

Time stopped, or maybe it was just Evangeline's heart. Apollo was awake. Fully awake. This must have been what Havelock was trying to tell her.

Evangeline felt an impossible burst of hope.

When she looked in the prince's eyes, they were no longer red. Unlike the last time she'd seen him, Apollo appeared fully in control of himself.

Beside her, Jacks went nightmare stiff, and she couldn't help but smile. With Apollo awake, all of Jacks's leverage over her was gone. She didn't need to open the Valory Arch. The horror was over. At least Evangeline wanted to believe it was.

Apollo's stillness as he sat atop his horse was entirely un-readable. He wasn't riding away from her, but he wasn't mov-ing toward her. And suddenly, Evangeline thought of another memory—one she'd have loved to bury forever. Right after Jacks's love spell had been lifted, before Jacks's poison had taken effect, Apollo had been furious and devastated, and he likely hadn't forgiven her yet.

Little Fox, Jacks thought. *I think we should leave.*

Not yet, she thought back. *But you can go.*

Jacks gritted his teeth. Then she heard his voice in her head again, softer this time, as if he were trying to use his powers to coerce her. *This is a terrible idea. A dangerous idea. You need to leave the garden now.*

Evangeline shut him out. She was determined to hope for the best—maybe Apollo hadn't forgiven her for the love spell, but the fact that he was here made her think that perhaps he wanted to. "I'm so glad you're awake."

Apollo took a deep breath, exhaling a small cloud of white. "Gods, you're beautiful."

Three words had never felt so powerful. She took a tentative step closer.

"Don't!" he said harshly.

Evangeline's heart fell.

Apollo raked a hand through his dark hair. "I'm sorry. I—I really don't want to hurt you. I just—" He paused, and through a shaft of moonlight, she could see pain distort his expression. It was raw and wounded and like nothing she'd ever seen on his face before.

This was not the same prince she had married. That prince had a charmed existence. He'd been protected by guards, sought after by subjects, and more than a little in love with himself. When they'd first met, she would have described him as gallant, and picture-perfect. But now Apollo had a past: a love spell had upended his world, another curse had almost taken his life. He'd somehow fought against the second curse and triumphed, but from the look on his face, it still haunted him.

Apollo took a deep breath, looking torn as he said, "I don't know how much time I have, but I want you to know, I heard you. Every day that you came into my chamber—I heard your voice through all the fog asking me to *try*."

His horse trotted one step closer.

Evangeline felt another flicker of hope. It was then she realized that Apollo looked the same as he had on the night he'd proposed. He'd also been on a horse at first, and he'd been dressed much as he was now, a little rugged, save for the elegant golden arrows strapped to his back. He'd been the Archer that night, she'd been his Fox—from *The Ballad of the Archer and the Fox*, her favorite childhood tale—and she dared to wonder if that was the case again. If he was making another grand gesture, an attempt at starting over.

"Does this mean you've forgiven me?" she asked.

"I want to," Apollo said, but his words were oddly tight.

Little Fox, Jacks growled in her head, but she didn't hear what followed over the sound of Apollo's voice cutting him off.

"I wish we could try again—but I think you should go."

"What?"

"Leave, Evangeline." A flash of pain crossed Apollo's face, hollowing his cheeks and scoring lines across his forehead. "I don't want to hurt you."

"What's wrong?" She took a step closer.

"Stop!" he roared. "You need to go." The prince pulled a golden arrow from the quiver at his back. Moonlight glanced off the tip as he held it in his fist.

Evangeline stilled. "What are you doing?"

"Little Fox—get inside!" Jacks roughly shoved her behind him.

Apollo's eyes turned red, the same lurid shade as when he'd grabbed her wrist.

And then Jacks was yelling, "Run!"

Evangeline still didn't understand what was happening, but she picked up her skirts and started to sprint, only she wasn't quick enough.

An arrow whooshed through the air and struck her thigh. She screamed and stumbled as the bolt tore through her flesh. It hurt like a demon, turning everything else dull except for the pain as she tried to make it back to the safety of the castle.

Blood quickly soaked her skirts as she staggered forward.

Another arrow flew by, this one going wide, missing her arm and piercing a flower bush instead. Yet she felt a terrible burn in her shoulder as if she had been shot.

Evangeline didn't know how she reached the door back to Wolf Hall. Blood dripped from a deep gash in her shoulder, down her arm to her palm. It was wet and sticky, and it left a smear of red as she turned the handle and staggered into the warmth of the hall.

Spots of light danced before her eyes. Her vision blurred as she looked down at the golden arrow protruding from a bloody tear in her skirts.

She didn't see another arrow in her shoulder, but the wound hurt just as badly. And there was so much blood, soaking through the white bodice of her dress.

Her thoughts started to splinter, jumping between panic and pain and confusion as she fell onto a wooden bench and bled all over its carefully embroidered cushion. It was cream with dots of little red flowers, only now her blood was turning them into bigger, darker blooms.

She needed to get help.

She tried to shove up from the bench.

The leg that had been struck by the arrow buckled, and she collapsed back down as more and more blood poured forth.

Help. The word came out so softly she wasn't sure she said it out loud. Perhaps it was only in her head. Around her, the castle was turning hazy. Her eyelids were heavy, and now she was seeing more blinking bits of light around the murky edges of her vision.

She closed her eyes, just for a moment. Just to rest for a second.

"Evangeline—"

It sounded like Jacks's voice. But he'd said her name, not *Little Fox.* Jacks never said her name. Then he was murmuring something else. Two more words she'd never heard.

"I'm sorry," he said, just before it all truly went dark.

9

Evangeline fought to open her eyes, but her lids were impossibly heavy. She wasn't sure if she was awake or asleep. She'd thought Jacks had been there before it all went black. But the arms that held her now were scorching hot—or maybe she was the one burning up.

She could hear conversation, but it was barely there. Mostly low words and growls of two arguing voices, with a few scattered words.

"She . . . venom."

". . . human . . . risk . . ."

". . . want . . . die . . ."

"No—"

Her captor tightened his grip, pressing her against a chest clad in leather that smelled of metal and smoke. Definitely not Jacks.

Evangeline felt a sudden rush of alarm. "Let . . . go," she managed.

"Relax," said a voice she didn't recognize. "I'm not going to hurt you."

"No." She tried to claw at her kidnapper, but she couldn't move her fingers. Her body was failing. She was made of useless limbs and broken eyelids. Her skin was drying blood, and her thoughts were turning gray.

But there was one thought brighter and more frightening than all the others. If she was injured, then so was Apollo. He was bleeding somewhere else, probably outside, in the dark garden.

"Apollo," she finally managed. "Prince Apollo . . . needs . . . help."

Her captor tensed. Then she heard another voice, so quiet she knew it was in her head. *I'm sorry, Little Fox. Apollo isn't who you need to worry about. He's—*

Evangeline started to lose consciousness once more before she caught the rest of Jacks's thoughts. Although she knew what he was going to say. Prince Apollo was the cause of her injuries.

Seconds passed as if they were hours. Evangeline could not stay awake for long, but when she did, the pain extended every moment into a century, a lifetime of hurt in exchange for one moment of consciousness.

She was just aware enough to feel cool arms cradling her now. *Jacks's arms.* Everything was fuzzy and distant, but she knew, somehow, that these arms held her closer than the hot arms ever had.

And yet . . .

Evangeline found herself drifting away from the arms and into a dream that felt like the pages of a story yellowed with age: *The Ballad of the Archer and the Fox.*

Evangeline had always loved this story, though as she returned to it now, it was tainted with a sadness she could not recall feeling before.

The tale began the same as it always did, with the most gifted archer in the Magnificent North. He was young and handsome and admired, and he'd been hired to hunt a fox.

It was the craftiest fox he'd ever met, and he hunted it for weeks. The Fox would catch him sleeping—it bit his ears and chewed his shoes and made his life misery—but the Archer never managed to capture it.

The only joy the Archer had while hunting the Fox was on the days he saw the girl. He didn't know her name at first—she was just a pretty peasant who lived in the forest—but he found himself wanting to chase after her instead of the Fox.

She talked to him in riddles, and when he got them right, she'd bring him little treats.

He slowed his hunt for the Fox, wanting a reason to stay in the forest with this peasant girl. She was clever and sweet, and she made him laugh.

But the peasant girl had a secret. She could change into a fox—the very fox he was hired to hunt.

After learning this, the Archer believed those who had hired him had made a mistake. He returned the coins he'd been given and told them the Fox was really a girl.

But his employers already knew this, and they were not happy that he refused to hunt her. So they put a curse on him, one that compelled him to hunt the girl that he now loved.

Evangeline's heart began to race at this part. Whenever her mother had told her this tale, she always forgot what she was saying right before she finished the story. And now, Evangeline was starting to reach the end.

She could feel the Archer's confidence, mingling with his fear, as he sat in the forest outside his beloved's cottage.

The Archer had always been so very sure of himself and what he could do. He'd never been given a task he could not complete. There was no beast he could not track, no target he could not hit. He could shoot an apple from the hand of a friend at a thousand paces away—while it was being tossed in the air! He was a legend, he was the Archer, and he would have sacrificed it all to save her.

Yet, even as he thought the words, the Archer looked down to see he was already notching an arrow, getting ready to shoot the girl he loved as soon as she stepped out of her cottage.

The Archer threw down the bow and cracked the arrow on his knee, wishing it was as easy to break this spiteful curse. He'd been told it would only lift when he killed the girl. The one way to save her would be to stay away. But he couldn't believe they were never meant to be. There had to be an . . . o . . . ther . . .

The dream dissolved, like raindrops washing away peddler chalk on a sidewalk. Evangeline fought to hold on to it. She wanted to know how it ended. But the harder she tried to remain in the dream, the more it began to fade, until she couldn't remember what she'd been dreaming at all.

Everything hurt when she woke. She was no longer being held by hot arms or cold arms or any arms at all. She was on her back, every inch of her burning, aching, despite the softness of the bed she'd been placed in. Her eyes fluttered open slowly, adjusting to the light. There was just enough for Evangeline to see a set of heavy cagelike iron bars crisscrossing above her.

She jolted upright.

Her wounded shoulder screamed in pain, and she fell gracelessly back on the mattress.

"Welcome back, Princess." The voice was velvet smooth, and it did not take long for Evangeline to identify the source.

Chaos, the Vampire Lord of Spies and Assassins, leaned casually against one dark bedpost with the ease of a being that had nothing to fear.

Evangeline tried to muster a bit of bravado, but she felt instantly immobilized. She now knew why there were cagelike bars over her bed. She was in Chaos's underground castle.

Evangeline had only visited once before, but she vividly remembered all the human-size cages hanging amid the old-world elegance of the halls. She shuddered to think why she might be here.

Frantically, she sifted back through her memories. The last several hours were blurry, until she reached the moment right before she passed out. She'd been inside Wolf Hall, bleeding everywhere, and Jacks had said her name, *Evangeline*, not *Little Fox*. Then he'd said he was sorry. Was this why? Because he'd given her over to Chaos?

"Am I a prisoner?" she asked.

"You can leave anytime," Chaos said. "But I doubt you'll get far on that injured leg." He nodded toward her wounded thigh.

The vampire's face was impossible to read due to the cursed bronze helm he wore. It wrapped around his forehead and jaw, covering his mouth so that he could not bite her. Yet she still felt far from safe in his castle.

Evangeline gritted her teeth and looked about the room for an escape. It was around the size of her suite at Wolf Hall, with a fireplace full of candles, dark velvet lounges for sitting, and a dresser for clothes and jewels. It also had a great rounded door, but it was on the opposite end, a distance that seemed insurmountable with her wounded leg. But she could not stay in this bed. She needed to get out of here. She needed to figure out why Apollo had attacked her.

She didn't believe that Apollo had wanted to hurt her. That was clearer to her now. He'd looked pained, anguished. He'd told her to run. He'd tried to save her before he'd tried to kill her. She needed to figure out why.

Evangeline started to push down her sheets, but stopped as she realized that her clothing had been removed. She was practically naked. Instinctively, she clutched the sheets tighter. She didn't even want to contemplate who had undressed her. She wore nothing, save for a short, thin silk slip and the cloth bandages that wrapped around her wounded shoulder and thigh.

She couldn't get out of bed like this. Chaos might not be able to bite her, but if they were in his lair, then other vampires could—and they probably would. Walking around in a scrap of silk felt like an open invitation.

"If I really can leave, then I'd like some clothes and shoes," she said.

Chaos laughed softly, the sound deceptively young. He appeared just a few years older than she was, but Jacks had once told her that Chaos was as old as the North. "I may have exaggerated when I said you could leave at any time."

The rounded door opened with a groan that betrayed its age. Then, silently, Jacks stepped inside.

Their eyes collided across the room. His gaze slowly lowered to the sheets that she held over her barely there slip. But then, before she even had time to blush, he looked away.

Evangeline felt a strange stab of disappointment as Jacks went back to tossing the shimmering black apple that he held in his hand.

The cloak he'd been wearing earlier was gone. She remembered that he'd carried her, but there was no blood on his soft gray doublet.

"Have you told her the good news?" he asked cheerfully.

"Not yet," Chaos replied.

Evangeline divided a look between them. *Confused* did not begin to describe how she felt. Jacks loathed vampires—or at least that's what she'd thought. The last time she'd been here with him, he'd seemed to hate every moment. Now Jacks appeared completely at ease, and the comfortable way that he and Chaos spoke made it seem as if they were almost friends.

"What's going on?" Evangeline asked.

But even as she asked it, the pieces fell into place. Jacks had told her that if she didn't agree to open the arch within a day, she would really hate him.

This must have been why. Jacks was working with Chaos.

Evangeline flashed back to her conversation with Luc, how he'd revealed that Chaos was the one who'd helped him steal the throne. It was bizarre to imagine that Jacks would be involved with this ruse as well. But after learning Luc was the heir, Evangeline's first thought had been that she needed to wake up Apollo more than ever. Perhaps, if she'd had more time, she would have turned to Jacks.

It still seemed extreme, but Jacks was willing to go to impossible lengths to get what he wanted.

"She looks confused," Chaos said.

Jacks stopped tossing his apple and turned to Evangeline. "Your husband almost killed you. Because of him, you have a ruined shoulder and deeply wounded leg. Left to human methods, it will take your shoulder weeks to heal. Your leg will take longer and will probably never be the same. There's also the risk of death from infection. But Chaos has kindly offered to help the healing process along."

A female vampire with dark hair and red lips entered the chamber and approached the bed where Evangeline lay.

"No!" She clutched her sheets tighter, understanding dawning as the female bared her fangs.

There were two types of vampire bites: ones that allowed vampires to merely feed, and ones that infected their prey with vampire venom. Vampire venom had tremendous healing properties, but it also had the potential to change the infected person into a vampire. Being bitten didn't mean a person would have to change—any human infected with venom had to drink human blood by dawn to transform into a vampire.

But Evangeline had seen what the vampire venom did to humans, how it turned them desperate enough to break cages and locks just for one bite. Evangeline had no desire to be a vampire now, but what if that changed once she was infected?

"We should get started," Chaos said. "This won't be easy, but we have shackles to restrain you." He motioned toward a wall. In between a pair of velvet drapes, Evangeline saw two sets of chains with manacles. "Or, if you prefer, we could put you in a cage?"

"No." Evangeline vehemently shook her head. "I don't want to do this at all. Let me heal on my own." She looked pleadingly at Jacks.

He bit down carelessly on his apple and turned to Chaos. "I think you should use a cage."

As soon as Jacks said the word, Chaos reached for a lever embedded in the wall. Bars instantly crashed down around her bed, trapping her inside.

"No!" It all happened so fast, Evangeline didn't even know she'd screamed until she heard her voice echo through the room.

She tried to grip the steel, but that was a mistake. Chaos grabbed her wrist through the bars. "I'm doing you a favor."

Holding her tight, he offered her arm to the female vampire.

Evangeline struggled and cried out again.

Teeth flashed, and then she felt them sink painfully into her wrist.

10

Everything burned for one sharp moment. Evangeline fell back against the bed.

Then . . . the pain dissolved. Not just from the bite but from her wounds, which healed almost instantly.

She blinked, and it was as if a veil had been lifted from her eyes.

When she'd first woken up, the room had been dim—a suite of smoke and shadows. But now it sparkled with glittering candlelight. It was the prettiest shimmer she'd ever seen. Everything in the room seemed to glow—the gilded portrait frames, the polished legs of the table, even the awful manacles on the wall.

Then there was the bed, which felt even more luxurious. Her pillow, the mattress, the sheets wrapped around her body were so much softer than before. They were silk and white, and Evangeline swore she could smell the color—crisp and clean and bright, like sunshine streaming through an open window after a mist of rain.

Crunch.

Jacks took a bite of his apple, drawing her attention to the foot of the bed, where he stood, looking like eternal heartbreak. His fair skin faintly glowed, his eyes shone like stolen stars, his hair was spun gold, and the cruel plains of his face filled her with a longing so deep it felt like an ache.

She wondered if Jacks always looked like this and her human eyes weren't capable of taking him in, or if he somehow dampened his appearance, but now that she had the venom surging through her, she could see what he really was, despite any of his efforts to try to hide it. Just one look set her blood on fire, and she liked the way it burned.

She tried to take a deep breath, but when she inhaled, all she could smell was the dark sweetness of him, and she wondered how he'd taste. Would he be cool on her tongue? Would brushing her lips over his neck stop her blood from burning and her heart from racing?

Jacks took another bite of his apple.

Her incisors immediately lengthened. She pushed her tongue against them, trying to shove the sharp points back in and stop the sudden throb in her mouth. She really didn't want to bite him—his blood was human enough, and if she bit Jacks, she would change. But just thinking the words *bite* and *Jacks* sent a shudder through her that wasn't entirely unpleasant.

"Careful," Jacks drawled. "You're not looking at me as if you hate me right now."

"I do," she said. But it came out all wrong, hoarse and breathless—and *hungry*.

Her fangs sank into her lip, hard enough to draw blood.

Jacks's eyes latched onto the drop.

Something unreadable flashed across his perfect face. And then his voice was in her head. *Do not forget what happens if tonight goes badly. You do not want to become one of* them.

Jacks's thoughts were full of disdain. He might have been friends with Chaos, but it seemed the Prince of Hearts still didn't like vampires.

He dropped his black apple on the floor and stalked toward the rounded door.

"Don't leave!" Evangeline growled, the words coming out before she could stop them. She knew it was better if he went—without blood, she couldn't turn into a vampire. But she couldn't believe that he was simply walking out the door.

When he'd been infected with vampire venom, she'd stayed an entire night with him to make sure he didn't bite a human and change. But tonight he'd only spared her a few moments.

She gripped the bars of her cage tight enough to dent them. Then, horrified, she pulled away. She hadn't even realized that she'd moved. Even now that she'd released the cage, her hands were clenched into white-knuckled fists as if her body still wanted to break free.

In a flash, Chaos was right in front of her, leaning against the bars that her hands still wanted to grab.

"For vampires, control requires time," Chaos said. "Part of why we move so fast is because our physical forms are guided by instincts that humans do not have."

Like Jacks, the vampire appeared more dangerously immortal. She hadn't noticed his clothes before, but now she saw that, for once, Chaos wasn't dressed like a soldier. He wore tailored black pants, a fine black shirt, and his cursed bronze helm, which had more detailed carvings than she'd ever noticed. The spikes that jutted out over his cheekbones were covered in tiny thorns as they pointed toward his hypnotic eyes.

She usually tried to avoid his eyes—vampires took direct eye contact as an invitation to bite or a means to control. But right now, Evangeline didn't have full control of herself. It was just as Chaos said—any thought she had turned into movement. She thought about his eyes, and suddenly, their gazes locked.

But Chaos's eyes were not the same eyes she remembered. She would have sworn they were emerald green, but now they were pure shadow. They were dark and endless, and devouring. This didn't feel like looking into a pair of immortal eyes; it felt like locking eyes with Death itself.

Chaos is a murderer, LaLa had once said. And Evangeline now saw it in his gaze. His helm might prevent him from biting, but it didn't prevent him from killing.

Evangeline tried to back away and instantly felt her spine slam against the other end of the cage.

Chaos laughed, low and silkier than she remembered. "You're not in danger from me, Princess. In fact, I'm here to make sure nothing happens to you tonight."

She caught a whiff of apples then, sweet and briskly cool. It was the fruit Jacks had dropped onto the floor. He'd left the room, but just the thought of him brought a new, exquisite ache to her mouth, a burn that she knew in her soul only one thing could stop—

"You're growling," Chaos warned.

Evangeline wrapped her hands around the bars of her cage, the ones right in front of Chaos. Again, she didn't even remember moving across the bed. But this time, she didn't let go of the bars. Pressing her hands against the metal—feeling it dent under her strength—helped take her mind off the throbbing in her mouth and the pain in her gums as her fangs lengthened again.

"Careful there." Chaos's hands clamped down on Evangeline's. He might have broken her fingers with his powerful grip if not for the venom surging through her. But that didn't mean his hold didn't hurt.

"Let me go." She yanked against him, fighting to pull free until her breathing turned ragged.

Meanwhile, Chaos wasn't even winded. If anything, his shadowy gaze was ablaze with something like excitement as he squeezed her fingers even harder. "I could stay like this all night, Princess."

Evangeline's instincts took over then. Chaos might be stronger, but that didn't mean he possessed all the power.

Her lip had stopped bleeding, but after another quick nip from her teeth, there was fresh blood. Leaning forward, she pressed her mouth to the cage and said, "Please open."

The bars lifted immediately.

A flash of surprise lit Chaos's dead eyes.

Evangeline felt a rush of victory, right before he flattened her to the bed with the full force of his body.

The air squeezed from her lungs as she fought in vain against him. He was so heavy and hot atop her. And she swore he burned even hotter the more she struggled. Yet she couldn't bring herself to stop the fight. She wasn't sure if it was the venom or just her human instincts reacting to the fact that she was pinned to a bed by death incarnate.

She tried to claw at his helm, but Chaos effortlessly grabbed her wrists and pinned her arms above her head. "Why are you doing this?" she wheezed.

"Jacks asked me to keep you human."

"I don't need you to keep me human! I have no desire to change."

"But you're not in control of your body."

"Because you're on top of it."

Chaos lifted some of his weight, though his hands continued to trap her wrists, and his legs still pressed firmly against hers.

Dimly, she knew this was for the best. He was right, she wasn't in complete control, but she'd never felt more trapped in her life. She thought she had been uncomfortable inside the cage, but now it was even worse. With Chaos pressed against her, it wasn't just her mouth that burned, her entire body was on fire. Her skin was flushed, her heart was racing, and the heat pouring off Chaos only made it worse.

She thought of Jacks and the way his cool skin would instantly soothe hers. She remembered how he'd touched her that night in the crypt—his mouth on her neck, his chest pressed to hers. He hadn't bitten her, he'd just touched her. That was all she wanted.

"Jacks won't care if you let me go," she insisted. "As long as I'm still a key capable of opening things, he isn't concerned about anything else."

"You're wrong about that, Princess. Jacks doesn't want this life for you." Chaos met her eyes again, flames mingling with the shadows of his deathlike gaze.

Evangeline paused her struggling. For a moment, she wanted to believe the vampire. She liked the idea that Jacks cared what happened to her. But it was far more likely that Jacks just wanted her to think that he worried as another way to manipulate her.

"Did Jacks tell you to say that?"

"Jacks doesn't tell me what to say."

"But he told you to keep me human." She attempted another kick.

Chaos pressed the full force of his weight against her once more. "I'm doing this for Jacks out of loyalty. But that is not the only reason I'm here."

"Then what's your other reason?" she needled.

"I'm disappointed you have to ask." Chaos angled his head. The bronze jaw of his helm brushed her cheek, briefly searing her skin.

Sweat beaded against her brow as the words she'd noticed earlier, the ones inscribed upon the helm, began to glow. The tongue was an ancient script she'd seen before, one she recognized but couldn't decipher—*the language of the Valors.*

"What does it say?" she asked.

"It's the curse that prevents me from removing the helm."

And Chaos wanted the helm removed. No wonder he was so hot against her—so hungry. She didn't know how long the helm had prevented him from feeding, but Evangeline imagined it had to be agony for a vampire to live without blood. She had only been infected with the venom for a short period of time and she already felt a little mad.

"Let me guess—you want me to unlock your helm with my blood."

He made a sound too damaged to be called a laugh. "Your blood unfortunately isn't capable of breaking this curse. But . . . every curse has . . . a back door." Chaos said the last set of words haltingly, as if he'd intended to say something else but the words had magically twisted.

It made Evangeline think of when LaLa had tried to tell her what she believed the Valory Arch contained, but the story curse had prevented her.

Suddenly, Evangeline knew what Chaos wanted. He wanted

the same thing as Jacks. That was why the two of them were working together. "You want me to open the arch. You think that the Valory holds the key to unlocking your cursed helm?"

"I don't think. I know it does," Chaos said, something like pain seeping into his voice. He took a deep breath, and his chest moved against hers, turning her skin violently hot again.

"What the hell are you doing?" Jacks growled.

Evangeline turned toward his voice, sweat trickling down her cheek, as she found him standing in the doorway. A vein throbbed furiously along the line of his smooth, marble neck. His skin looked so cool, and she was so hot. All she wanted was to press her mouth to his throat and maybe lick it just once. Her blood rushed faster at the thought, and her fangs started to lengthen.

"Jacks, get out of here!" Chaos ordered. "Unless you've changed your mind about her becoming a vampire."

Chaos gripped Evangeline's wrists tighter, pressing them—along with her—more firmly to the bed. She writhed against his grip; he was crushing her again with the full weight of his body.

Something loud cracked in the doorway.

Her eyes shot back to Jacks, who was fisting the now splintered edge of the door. *Had he done that with his hands?*

He certainly looked livid enough. His silver-blue eyes turned midnight dark as he watched her struggling under Chaos.

Evangeline dimly knew that she should stop her thrashing. If she broke free from Chaos and managed to bite Jacks, the life she had—the life she wanted to keep—would be over. But she also wanted this. She wanted Jacks to stop her struggling. She wanted him to rip Chaos off her chest so that he could pin her to the bed instead.

Evangeline took a rasping breath, and her gaze collided with Jacks's once more.

He scrubbed a hand over his jaw. With Evangeline's heightened senses, she could hear it clench under his palm. Then she heard the scrape of Jacks's boots as he sharply turned and disappeared down the hall.

11

Evangeline felt the instant dawn arrived. All her limbs, which had been too strong before, were suddenly too weak to move. She'd become a girl again, with ordinary senses and normal incisors, and a deep sense of discomfort as she lay there under Chaos, excruciatingly aware that her slip had ridden up past her thighs, all the way to her hips.

A wave of mortification washed over her at the thought she had been like this all night—and that Jacks had seen her like this as well.

She'd been so hot before that she hadn't noticed how exposed she was, but now she could feel the cool air sliding over her skin as Chaos finally released her wrists and pushed up from the bed.

Evangeline kept her eyes tightly closed and tried to slow her breathing. It was childish to pretend she was sleeping, but she didn't want to face him—or anyone, really. Last night she had not been herself.

She sensed Chaos standing over her, watching her for a reason she wasn't sure she wanted to know. Then she felt his hand smoothing down her slip until it fell back to her knees.

Gooseflesh covered her skin. She remained very still until finally she sensed that Chaos had left. She tried to open her eyes, but she couldn't find the strength to do more than flutter her lashes. With the venom gone, she wasn't just human, she was entirely drained.

She recalled that Jacks had been the same way after he'd been infected with vampire venom. She'd thought he was being dramatic as he'd curled up against tombstones and collapsed in various doorways. But now she was impressed that he'd possessed the resolve to move at all.

Evangeline did not know how long she'd slept. But as she rubbed the sleep from her eyes and dared to climb out of bed on her shaking legs, she imagined it could have been an entire day.

Her stomach rumbled, and her throat felt dry. She was grateful to find someone had left a few things for her: a tray piled with food, a dress, and a copper tub for washing. The water was cool, but she was glad for the chance to scrub the blood and grime from her body and her hair.

Once she was clean, she ate as much as she could manage. There was hearty bread, rich cheese, cold slices of meat, and her favorite fig jam. But with so many thoughts swirling through her head, the meal was difficult to enjoy.

As soon as she'd been infected with the venom, all thoughts of Apollo had fled. But now she wondered if he had been healed from his injuries when she had or if he was still wounded. She hoped he was healed and somewhere safe. She still didn't think this was truly his fault. Someone had to have been coercing him.

She needed to figure out who and why. She would start by returning to Wolf Hall and questioning Havelock. The last time she'd seen him, he'd had news. She imagined it was that Apollo was awake, but Havelock had seemed alarmed instead of relieved. Perhaps it was because he knew something.

Evangeline felt a little nervous to return to Wolf Hall on her own. But there was no way she'd willingly stay here with Jacks and Chaos.

She wondered again if it was Jacks who'd somehow forced Apollo to shoot her. But Jacks needed her alive. He wouldn't have done this . . . at least she didn't think so. It was difficult to be entirely certain of anything with Jacks. Except for the fact that he was untrustworthy, which was another reason why she needed to get out of here as soon as possible.

Evangeline picked up the dress that had been set out for her. The frothy flowered confection was as pretty as a sunrise, but it was more akin to a dressing gown than a proper garment, slender and light with billowing off-the-shoulder sleeves and a neckline so low it felt as if she'd be practically begging any nearby vampires to bite her.

She was unsurprised to find a vampire standing guard on the other side of her chamber door—the red-lipped vampire who'd bitten her last night.

"Could you tell me where the exit is?" she asked politely.

The female regarded Evangeline as if she were a child and she wasn't particularly fond of such creatures. "You're not allowed—"

"Don't say it," Evangeline cut in. She knew this vampire could probably break her neck with merely her fingers, but she also knew that Chaos didn't just need her alive, he needed her *willing* blood to open the Valory Arch, so she doubted any guard would be allowed to break any part of her. "If you tell me I can't leave, I'm going to be very cross with Chaos, and then he'll be very cross with you. So, let's avoid all the crossness. Just let me go, and please tell me where the exit is."

The female stepped aside with a smirk, making it clear she'd let Evangeline go, but she wouldn't tell her how to get out.

Which was fine. Evangeline had been here before. She was sure she could find the exit on her own. The last time she had visited with Jacks, they'd escaped by following steps that led up toward the graveyard above.

Gamely, Evangeline took every upward staircase she found. There were lots of empty cages and shackles, and more than once, she had to quicken her pace when she caught the sound of footsteps. She was breathless and a little jumpy by the time she reached what she hoped was the topmost hall.

There were no shackles or cages here, just deceptively fancy decorations—gold candelabras, velvet settees, wispy drapes. Then, finally, there was a door—heavy and metal and locked.

She reached for her dagger, but of course it wasn't there. It hadn't been with the dress. She must have lost it that night in the garden, which was a good thing. She would have hated if Jacks had found it on her and realized that she'd been carrying around his old knife.

Thankfully, Chaos believed in decorating with weapons, so it was easy enough to find another knife to prick her finger with.

Quickly, before any vampires could catch the scent of her blood, she offered the door a few drops. She still didn't want to be a key or part of a prophecy, but she couldn't deny she was enjoying the one perk that came with the position. She felt powerful as she said, "Please open," and the door immediately complied.

Freedom tasted cold.

The world was as dark as kept secrets, and she wished she'd tried to pilfer a cloak before leaving. Upon waking up in her windowless room, she'd assumed it was day, but it was actually night. And it was not the sort of evening meant for whisper-soft dresses and delicate silk slippers. The snow must have melted during the time she'd been underground, for there were only sticks and dirt beneath her feet as she ventured out into the cemetery that rested above Chaos's underground kingdom.

The graveyard had more trees than she'd remembered, their barren canopies stifling the moonlight and making everything murkier as she tried to remember which way led out toward Valorfell.

For a second, she hesitated. Now that she was out and feeling a little lost in the night, it was easier to fear that perhaps this was a mistake. Maybe it wasn't the wisest thing to return to Wolf Hall. But her other option was returning to Jacks and Chaos.

With a breath so cold it burned her lungs, Evangeline continued forward. She thought she saw the mausoleum where she'd spent the night with Jacks. For a second, she felt a fresh shiver roll across her shoulders at the memory. When the prickling sensation continued all the way down to her wrist and her broken heart scar, she feared perhaps it meant that Jacks was there. But when she darted a look around, the forest was empty save for the trees. So many trees.

Evangeline didn't remember the forest being this dense. The trees were as close as matchsticks in a box. She turned around, but she must have gone in the wrong direction again, for she found herself at a cliff's edge, overlooking the foaming ocean.

Hugging her arms to her chest, she turned back the way she'd come. The air was growing chillier, and she tried to warm herself by quickening her steps. They were louder than she liked. So noisy that it took her a minute to notice there was another sound in the forest.

Clomp. Clomp. Clomp.

The plodding noise was more animal than human. It sounded like a horse lost among the graves.

Evangeline froze, remembering the last time she'd heard hoofbeats.

Carefully, she took a step back into the shadow of the trees. Then she took another step. She swore she didn't make a sound, but just a second later, the horse came into view, along with its rider. His shoulders were broad, his back was straight, and although she couldn't clearly see his face, she knew this was Apollo.

He appeared to be completely healed, too. He looked strong and healthy, and she felt a strange and impossible pull toward him, one she had to fight, as she watched him from the shadows.

The way his horse was moving, slowly plodding, made it clear he wasn't passing through. He was searching for something.

For her.

She knew it in her soul. But how had he known she was there?

"Evangeline." He called her name like a plea, one that tempted her to answer, but she forced herself to stay in place. "If you're out there, you need to run," he said, more ragged than before. "If you go this minute, I won't chase you—I have control of myself right now. But I don't know how long it will last." Apollo took a shuddering breath. "I don't want to injure you, but something has come over me. Finding you—" he choked out. "Hunting you is all I can think about."

Clouds parted from the moon, and Evangeline caught another glimpse of Apollo's face through the trees. His entire expression was etched with something like heartache, something so raw she felt it like an actual wound. She wanted to be optimistic and tell herself it would all be fine—if he'd woken from Jacks's spell, then Apollo could fight whatever was overtaking him now, but she didn't know what was happening. And the two of them were starting to feel doomed.

She tried to hold her breath, but she could see it sneaking out in thin puffs of white that she hoped didn't give her away.

"I don't know for certain if you're out there. If that's the pull I'm feeling right now. But if you're listening, *help me,* Evangeline." His voice softened at her name, before it sounded torn again. "Find a way to break this spell that compels me to hunt you, and I promise, I'll do nothing but protect you."

He reached toward the quiver at his back and pulled out a golden arrow. It glowed under the moonlight, flickering as the prince's hand shook. Evangeline tried to hold very still. Apollo was clearly fighting whatever was trying to control him.

Or whoever it was.

Earlier, she'd been quick to shove aside the idea that Jacks had done this. But Evangeline hadn't completely dismissed it, and now, as she shuddered in the darkened forest, she wondered again if Jacks orchestrated this to make sure she had no one to depend on but—

A hand clamped over her mouth, and a powerful arm wrapped around her arms and chest.

Don't make a sound, Little Fox.

12

Jacks tugged her back into the forest, lifting her feet off the ground as he pulled her farther from Apollo.

Let me go! she thought angrily. Just because she was in danger from Apollo didn't mean she was safe with Jacks. Her slippers fell to the dirt as she squirmed in his grip.

Not interested in biting me anymore? Jacks taunted in her head.

Evangeline's cheeks went suddenly hot, but she didn't let that distract her from slamming the back of her skull into Jacks's face.

His hold briefly slipped, but then it tightened again, securing her more firmly against his chest.

Stop fighting me, or he's going to kill you, Jacks projected into her thoughts. He used the hand on her mouth to turn her head as Apollo rode through a patch of distant moonlight. He looked like a fairytale come to life, a dashing silhouette—until she glimpsed the light from his eyes, now glowing red. The same awful color they'd turned the last time he'd attacked.

Evangeline ceased her struggle. She knew she wasn't safe in Jacks's arms, but in that moment, he seemed to be the lesser of two terrifying evils. *What did you do to him?*

You think I did this? Jacks thought. She could feel his rushing heartbeat against her back, a livid symphony to his angry words.

Don't sound so outraged, she thought back. *You've repeatedly told me that you're a monster and warned me that if I didn't do what you wanted, I would come to hate you.*

Jacks crushed her harder to his chest, and this time, his words weren't just in her thoughts. "I've told you, you have to be alive to hate me. I did not curse your husband to hunt you down and kill you. I admit," he said tightly, "one of your early wounds was partly my fault. I threw a knife at Apollo's shoulder to stop him from shooting you. I could lie and say I wasn't thinking of the mirror curse, but I knew full well that any injury inflicted on him would also hurt you. I just thought being stabbed would be preferable to being dead."

Jacks released her roughly.

Evangeline staggered forward. He caught her arm, steadying her, but then he quickly dropped it.

"This curse isn't my fault, but I know what the curse is," Jacks growled. "And I think you might know it, too."

Her gaze flashed back to Apollo, and this time, she didn't

just see his red eyes, she saw the entire picture of him—astride a horse, bow in one hand, quiver at his back, determination setting his jaw. He was dressed once again like the Archer from her favorite childhood story.

Evangeline had always adored *The Ballad of the Archer and the Fox* because she, too, was a fox, albeit a very different sort from the girl in the tale. But she was still a fox, and suddenly, she knew why Apollo was hunting her.

"Apollo is the Archer," she breathed.

"No," Jacks said sharply. "Apollo is not the Archer. But it seems someone has resurrected the Archer's curse and placed it on him. That's why he is trying to kill you, and he will continue to try until he succeeds. Someone wants you dead. I swear, Little Fox, that someone is not me. But if you don't believe me, by all means, continue tromping through the forest."

Evangeline felt a rush of blood to her ears, yet she could still hear a tiny voice telling her she was about to make a mistake. But what was the mistake—trusting Jacks or running from him?

You know I'm right, Little Fox.

But did she?

It was so tempting to believe Jacks. She knew he didn't want her dead. But she reminded herself that Jacks had tricked her before. And even if Jacks had not arranged this, she had vowed to never trust him after all he'd done.

She took a step deeper into the trees, away from both Apollo and Jacks.

Jacks's eyes flashed. He looked as if he wanted to stop her. But he just stood there with his hands clenched into fists.

It was painful walking without her slippers. But Evangeline pressed forward, farther away from both young men. She continued through the densely forested part of the cemetery, where there were only sleeping dragons and twigs, and—

Crunch.

Something louder than a twig broke under her foot.

Then everything happened at once. Evangeline didn't see Apollo turn her way; she just heard the sound of his horse fiercely galloping toward her.

Run, Little Fox!

But she was already running, as fast as her poor battered feet would take her, which wasn't fast enough. She could hear Apollo approaching.

"Evangeline!" His voice was resonant and deep, more like a plea than a threat.

She wondered if Apollo knew that killing her would kill him, too.

She paused for a fraction of a second, glancing over her shoulder just long enough to see him give her a broken look and aim an arrow right at her heart.

Evangeline ran faster.

The arrow whooshed past her, but she felt it scrape her cheek.

And she was headed in the worst direction, toward the impending cliff face, with the furious waves crashing beneath.

"Jump!" Jacks yelled. Out of nowhere, he was suddenly right beside her.

"I can't swim," she cried.

"Then hold on." He wrapped a strong arm around her waist, and together they fell.

13

Evangeline couldn't breathe.

The icy water hit hard as earth. She thrashed on instinct, but Jacks held her tightly. His arms were unyielding, dragging her up through the crushing waves. Salt water snaked up her nose, and the cold filled her veins. She was coughing and sputtering, barely able to suck down air as Jacks swam to shore with her in tow. He held her close and carried her from the ocean as if his life depended on it instead of hers.

"I will *not* let you die." A single bead of water dripped from Jacks's lashes onto her lips. It was raindrop soft, but the look in his eyes held the force of a storm.

It should have been too dark to see his expression, but the crescent moon burned brighter with each second, lining the edges of Jacks's cheekbones as he looked at her with too much intensity.

The crashing ocean felt suddenly quiet in contrast to her pounding heart, or maybe it was his heart.

Jacks's chest was heaving, his clothes were soaked, his hair was a mess across his face—yet in that moment, Evangeline knew he would carry her through more than just freezing waters. He would pull her through fire if he had to, haul her from the clutches of war, from falling cities and breaking worlds. And for one brittle heartbeat, Evangeline understood why so many girls had died from his lips. If Jacks hadn't betrayed her, if he hadn't set her up for murder, she might have been a little bewitched by him.

"Let me go." She wriggled against the arms that held her, refusing to fall under his spell.

"I'm not kidnapping you," Jacks grumbled. "The rocks on the shore will cut your feet, and I don't think you want to be bleeding when we return to the vampires."

"I don't want to go back there," she wheezed, still breathless from the water.

"No one ever wants to go back there. But Apollo will keep hunting you until you're dead."

She took another struggling breath. "If you really didn't do this, can't you use your powers to stop him?"

"No." Jacks's damp chest pressed against her as he trudged farther along the beach. "The curse only breaks when the Archer kills his prey. But . . ." Water dripped down from his golden hair as he hesitated. "Every curse has . . . a back door. If you open the Valory Arch, the spell on Apollo can be undone."

Evangeline's eyes narrowed. Jacks's words were similar to what Chaos had told her, and yet . . . "This seems rather convenient."

"Then you clearly misunderstand the situation." Jacks's voice turned heated. "The Valory Arch has remained locked for thousands of years because it is nearly impossible to unlock. If there was another way to break this curse on Apollo and ensure you didn't die, I would do it. Because even if you agree to open the arch, it's far more likely that Apollo will kill you first. The Archer's curse won't let him rest until you're dead."

Evangeline wanted to keep arguing. She hated to concede anything to Jacks. But it was also getting harder to believe that Jacks would put her in *this* much danger, especially when she could still feel his heart beating just as furiously as hers.

Although if Jacks was telling the truth, if he hadn't cursed Apollo this time, then someone else had.

The thought was sobering.

Evangeline remembered the last person who'd tried to kill her, before Apollo: Tiberius. As far as she knew, he was locked away in the Tower, and he had no idea his brother was alive. So she doubted he had done this. But perhaps someone else from the Protectorate had.

Evangeline didn't know too much about the Protectorate—they were a secret society that most considered a myth. She was only aware they existed because their primary goal was to ensure the Valory Arch never opened, which was why Tiberius had tried to kill her.

She didn't know how many remaining members the Protectorate had. It was possible there were more out there who knew she was the key. Although if they really wanted her dead, all they would have had to do was kill Apollo after placing the mirror curse on him. It didn't entirely make sense that they would do this. Unless someone else had placed the mirror curse, which also seemed unlikely.

"We need to question the guards who were watching Apollo."

"Already done, while you were asleep," Jacks replied. "They said there were no visitors other than you and me."

"Could someone have erased their memories?" Evangeline's first thought was Marisol, whom she knew was a witch. But Marisol didn't know that Apollo was alive.

"I doubt any memories were erased," said Jacks. "For all we know, this curse could have been cast before he was poisoned. There were a lot of jealous girls and thwarted parental hopes after that ball."

"Is that what you think happened?" Evangeline looked up at him.

Water dripped from Jacks's golden hair, catching the moonlight as it fell. Even after jumping from a cliff and falling into an ocean, he still looked like a ruthless fairytale—a fallen prince who refused to break.

"I don't think it matters. Finding whoever did this is a waste of time because it won't undo the curse. There is no cure that anyone knows of. The only way to save yourself and Apollo is to open the Valory Arch."

Evangeline studied Jacks's implacable face for another beat. As reluctant as she was to trust him, she could not believe that Jacks had done this.

"Did Chaos cast this curse?"

"No," Jacks said. "Chaos wouldn't do anything to put you in real danger. He wouldn't risk losing another key."

"Did you just say *another* key?"

Jacks's perfect mouth turned darkly taunting. "Did you believe you were the only one?"

Evangeline didn't answer. She had, in fact, believed that.

"According to Chaos, the last key lived the longest," Jacks said. "She managed to retrieve one of the arch's four missing stones before the Protectorate chopped off her head."

Evangeline already felt cold and shaky from their midnight swim, but suddenly, she felt very mortal, as if she'd been transmuted from iron into a thin sheet of glass.

14

That night, Luc appeared in Evangeline's bed. The young man lay propped on his side, brown hair flopping over one eye as he smiled like a naughty boy who'd just snuck into his first bedroom. "Hello, Eva."

She tried to move away, but her limbs were far too tired.

He flashed his fangs, white and sharp. And then they pierced her throat, tearing her flesh as he drank her blood. He drank and drank and drank, moaning in pleasure as she cried in pain ... until she blinked herself into another dream.

She was back in the forest, leaves crunching beneath her naked toes and fog cloaking her bare shoulders. Her neck no longer bled, but her blood pumped faster at the sight of Apollo atop a white mare.

"I wish I didn't have to do this." His deep voice broke as he drew his arrow and shot it through her chest.

She felt the bolt pierce her heart, rip it into two, as her body went limp in arms that had not been there before.

Jacks's arms. They were cool as he held her on his lap.

"I've got you," he said. The way he spoke was so gentle, so very unlike Jacks, she was reminded it was just a dream again. What surprised her was how pleasant it suddenly was. How safe it felt to be so close to him.

She'd come to the Magnificent North in search of love. But maybe she just didn't want to be alone, didn't want to be untethered. She didn't want to be a person who could disappear without anyone knowing she was gone. She wanted to be important to someone. If her heart stopped, she wanted someone else to feel it—the way she could feel Jacks's heart now, as she let herself rest her head on his chest.

He gave her a smile both beautiful and depraved. "I'm disappointed you could forget what I am so easily."

Then he dropped her from his arms.

She woke with a start.

Her eyes flashed open.

Jacks looked down on her from the dark nightstand where he'd perched himself. His long legs draped negligently over the edge of the furniture as his hands played with an apple and a knife.

"You talk in your sleep," he drawled. "You said my name— a lot."

Evangeline felt a rush of heat crawl up her neck. "Obviously, I was having a nightmare."

"It didn't look that way to me, Little Fox, and I was here all night."

Her heart pitter-pattered at the thought that he'd watched as she'd slept. *Was that why she'd dreamed about him?*

"Don't fret, I won't tell your husband that you're obsessed with me." Jacks tossed his white apple and caught the fruit with the tip of his dagger. A dagger she recognized with another flash of mortification. It was the blade with the blue and purple jewels, the one she'd stolen from him and then lost.

"Hope you don't mind that I took this back." Jacks twisted the knife until the jewels caught the candlelight. "And don't worry, I won't tell Apollo that I caught you carrying around my knife, either. He and I are friends, after all, and I'd hate for him to get jealous."

Evangeline snorted. "How can you say you're still friends after everything you've done?"

"What have I done that's so bad?" Jacks challenged.

"Oh, I don't know—cursing him, multiple times."

"Every prince gets cursed. A prince without a curse will be forgotten by history, and trust me when I say that Apollo wants to be remembered. Now—" Jacks nodded toward a gown laid out at the end of the bed—the same bed she'd been caged in the night before. "You should get dressed."

Evangeline frowned at the garment, although the dress was actually dreamy. It had the type of long slit sleeves she'd always thought of as romantic, sheer and a very soft shade of pink. The bodice was a little deeper in color and covered in an intricate series of braided rose-gold cords that went all the way down to the hips, where layers of impossibly thin fabric, dusted with hints of sparkle, flowed out to form the skirt.

But just because Jacks had helped her out of another sticky spot last night didn't make them allies. Her dream about his arms being safe was clearly a delusion.

She crossed her arms over her chest. "You need to stop ordering me around."

Jacks ignored her comment. "Once you get dressed, we can start our search for the missing arch stones." He hopped off the nightstand, crossed over to the gown, and tossed the dress at her face.

"Jacks!" She caught the gown with her hands. It was wonderfully soft against her fingers and far cleaner than she felt. But she wasn't about to let him bully her. She dropped it on the bed. "I still haven't agreed to help you open the arch."

He gave her a look that said he didn't think her joke was funny.

But she wasn't kidding. "I want to know why you want to open it so badly."

Jacks flashed a dazzling smile, curving and perfect and utterly cruel. "I'm flattered you've taken such an interest in my wants. But you really should start thinking about your husband more than me." His eyes turned dagger-sharp. "In case you've forgotten, Little Fox, Apollo is under the Archer's curse. If you don't agree to open the Valory Arch to break it, he will kill you. Just like the Archer murdered his fox."

Jacks pulled the apple from his knife and gave it a perversely cheery toss.

Evangeline gritted her teeth; she knew it was pointless to argue with him. But he'd ruined so many other things, she wasn't going to let him destroy her favorite fairytale as well.

"You don't know that," Evangeline said. "No one knows for sure if the Archer killed the Fox."

"Oh—" Jacks laughed, hard and nasty as his smile. "The Archer definitely killed the Fox."

"That's not what I believe. He could have fought the curse! Or the Fox could have found a way to break the curse. No one knows how the story ends, so anything could have happened."

"But it didn't," Jacks snapped back. "Ballads never end happily, everyone knows that. No one has to actually read the whole story to know the Archer has blood on his hands. Open the arch, Evangeline, or die just like the Fox."

Jacks stopped tossing the apple and stabbed it with the dagger.

Evangeline frowned as the dark juice from the fruit dripped onto the floor.

She really didn't want to give in to him. But her refusal to open the arch was starting to feel like stubbornness instead of wisdom. After what LaLa had said, Evangeline wasn't quite as fearful that the Valory contained something horrible, but she still didn't want to give whatever it contained to Jacks. She didn't want to partner with him or have anything to do with him. But she did want to break the Archer's curse—she needed to break it, or she would spend the rest of her life running from Apollo, and he would spend the rest of his life hunting her.

She supposed in a way it was a sort of ever after. The curses linked the two of them inextricably, promising their lives would forever be intertwined, but this wasn't the way she wanted them to be together.

"Fine," Evangeline said.

"Does this mean you're going to open the arch?" Jacks quirked a brow. A tiny thing, and yet she could tell he was genuinely pleased.

She was briefly tempted to keep fighting him. But now that she had made up her mind, she was ready to get on with it. The sooner they found the stones to open the arch, the sooner she'd be rid of him.

"Yes, I'll help you open the arch," she said. "But I'm not getting dressed while you're in here."

"That's too bad," Jacks murmured.

Then he was gone.

And Evangeline was grateful he could not see her sudden blush.

15

Jacks whistled merrily as he and Evangeline walked down the low-lit hall together on their way to meet with Chaos. She had never heard Jacks whistle before. She supposed he did it now because she'd finally agreed to open the Valory Arch. But for some reason, she hadn't expected it to make him this kind of unabashedly happy.

Jacks was all dimples and whistles, and it was unsettling how curious this happiness made Evangeline. *What could Jacks possibly want inside the arch?*

He'd found another apple as she'd gotten dressed—it was unbitten and blue, and he tossed it in time with his merry song.

"You're staring."

"I was just wondering why you always carry apples."

Jacks chuckled under his breath. "Trust me, Little Fox, you're better off not knowing."

He took a slow bite of the fruit, eyes darkening as they

slowly slid from her lips to her neck, following the exposed line of it down to her clavicle and then to her breasts. Her breathing felt heavy as Jacks's gaze lingered on the intricate cords that wrapped around her chest, tracing the golden lines with his eyes in a way that made the braided ropes feel as if they were being tightened, as if his cool fingers were pulling them more tautly around her, until it was a little difficult to breathe.

"You started it with your stare," he murmured.

This was more like the Jacks she knew, taunting and a little cruel.

"Do you have any news of Apollo?" she asked coolly.

"No," Jacks said. "Chaos sent out vampires to search for him last night, along with a few humans who could stay out until after sunrise, but no one has seen him and the scandal sheets haven't mentioned him. If he's smart, he's trying to get some distance from you, to make it easier to fight the curse. But," Jacks added darkly, "that can only last so long."

"What about Havelock?" Evangeline asked.

"What about him?"

"Has anyone questioned him to see if he knows who put the Archer's curse on Apollo?"

Jacks side-eyed her. "I already told you, finding out who cast this curse won't help us."

"But I'd still like to know. Maybe you're used to people trying to kill you, but I'm not."

"That's unfortunate, because Havelock is gone, too. We tried to find him after questioning the guards who were watching

Apollo, but no one in Wolf Hall knows where he is. My guess would be wherever Apollo is."

Jacks stopped at the ancient wooden door to Chaos's study. He twisted the iron handle, but the door did not budge.

He knocked. But the vampire didn't answer. It seemed he wasn't there just yet.

"Unlock it," Jacks ordered.

Evangeline bristled. "You could at least say *please.*"

"I could, but then you might think I'm being nice, and I would hate to confuse you."

Lightning quick, Jacks pulled out his dagger, stabbed her finger, and grinned as he watched her bleed. "Better hurry before the vampires come."

Evangeline gave him a dirty look. But she quickly unlocked the door. Although she doubted any vampires would attack her—not as long as Chaos needed her to open the Valory Arch so that he could take off his helm. Chaos might have been a vampire and Jacks a Fate, but they both needed her rather desperately, it seemed.

The thought emboldened Evangeline to do a little exploring as she and Jacks entered the unoccupied study. If not for the chains and fetters attached to the chairs, it might have been easy to imagine they were at Wolf Hall. The floors were ancient polished stone, the chairs were fine leather, and the marble chessboard atop Chaos's desk was a work of art. The pieces were larger than normal, making it easier to see they weren't ordinary kings and queens, knights and rooks and pawns. They were carved to look like the Valors, and just like the great statues in the harbor outside of Valorfell, all the heads of the pieces had been removed.

Jacks took another bite of his apple, filling the dim room with sweetness as he watched Evangeline near the desk.

"Not sure you should be snooping," he said.

"Not sure I care," she retorted. "The vampire needs me too much to hurt me."

Evangeline rounded the desk with a little more sway in her step.

She wasn't exactly certain what she was looking for, she just knew that this was her one opportunity to look without consequence. Since arriving in the North, Evangeline had always been the person in the room with the least amount of power, but that was no longer the case. She was the girl from the prophecy. She was the key—a magical thing capable of magical things! She didn't need to linger in a doorway like a scared little kitten or sit politely in a chair and wait.

She started to open the desk drawer when she saw it on the corner of the desk—a gem sparkling underneath a glass cloche.

Evangeline lifted the cloche, and the jewel inside shone brighter, throwing glimmers of pink and gold across the room. It looked like a wish that she could wear around her neck. Or perhaps some enchantress had taken a handful of wonder and somehow placed it in this necklace, though *necklace* felt like far too common a word for whatever this treasure was.

Her fingers tingled as she touched the chain. "Do you think Chaos acquired this gem for me?"

"No." The vampire appeared in a shadowy flash and snatched the necklace from her hand.

"Give it back!" Evangeline grabbed for the gem on instinct, but Chaos held her wrist.

"This isn't for you," he said.

He was wrong. She knew he was wrong. The gem didn't sparkle so brightly in his gloved hand. It needed to be hers.

She swung at him with her free arm. It didn't matter that he was stronger or bigger or that it probably hurt her far more than it hurt him when she managed to strike at his chest. She had to have that necklace.

"That doesn't belong with you!" She lunged for him.

"Not a good idea, Little Fox." Jacks's hands banded around her, roughly dragging her from the vampire and her precious gem.

"Let me go, you monster—" She tried to butt him with her head.

Jacks took a hand from her waist and wrapped it around her neck, holding her immobile as Chaos went to the desk and locked the gem inside an iron box.

Immediately, Evangeline felt like she'd been plunged in cold water. As soon as the lid closed over the stone, her boldness, her extreme confidence, her desire to claw out Chaos's eyes with her fingernails vanished in a flash.

She sagged against Jacks's grip. "What just happened?" Her

skin felt flushed, her breath was uneven, and Jacks's hands were still on her.

"Can you control yourself if I release you?" Jacks asked. "Or do we need to shackle you to one of the chairs?" He sounded as if he was laughing again—because of course Jacks would be entertained while she was mortified.

"I'm fine." Evangeline wriggled against Jacks. Slowly, he uncurled his fingers from her, but not before she felt his knuckles softly brush against the underside of her breast.

Her stomach dipped. But Jacks's face was so impassive, she imagined the touch must have been a slip.

She shook her head as she staggered farther from him and the necklace Chaos had locked away.

"What was that thing?" she asked.

"That *thing* is the luck stone," Chaos said. "It is one of the four magical missing arch stones."

Evangeline remembered then what Jacks had said about the previous key, that she'd died after finding one of the missing stones. The gem on the necklace must have been that stone.

Chaos strode away from the desk, but his movements appeared to be tighter than usual. He clenched and then unclenched his hands as if he'd just finished with something challenging.

"Did the stone affect you as well?" she asked.

"The stone affects everyone," he said.

"It didn't do anything to me," chimed Jacks.

"Only because the luck stone makes people reckless, and you're always reckless," Chaos replied.

Jacks shrugged. "What's the point of being an immortal if you live like a human?"

"But I thought you could die?" Evangeline asked.

"Why? Planning on murdering me?" Jacks's eyes glittered.

Chaos speared him with a glare. "Don't tempt her."

"Relax." Jacks toyed with one of the shackles dangling from the arm of a chair. "I gave her the chance to stab me once, but even then she wouldn't do it."

"And I'll forever regret that," Evangeline said. But to her horror, the words didn't taste as true as they should have. She reminded herself that Jacks couldn't be trusted. He was the reason she was in this mess. Except, once again, those words didn't feel true. Jacks was not the one who'd cursed Apollo this time.

She remembered the feel of Jacks's heartbeat, furious against hers, as he'd dragged her out of the ocean after they had escaped Apollo. For once, Jacks hadn't felt in control. He'd felt like a feral fairytale warrior, determined to do whatever it took to save her. She knew his reasons for wanting to keep her alive were less than noble. But sometimes reason was no match for feeling. She reasoned that it would be far better to hate him, but she could no longer muster the feeling.

Chaos cleared his throat.

Evangeline looked up to see the vampire standing before his desk, arms crossed over his broad chest as he watched her with something like concern. It was difficult to tell for certain with the helm concealing his face, but he didn't need to worry.

Evangeline might not have hated Jacks, but she still knew better than to trust him.

"There are three stones left to find," Chaos explained. "Each stone has a different power. Evangeline, because you're the key, you will feel each stone's magic the most, making it easiest for you to identify them. However, as you could probably tell from the luck stone, the power of the stones makes them dangerous."

"What are the powers of the other stones?" She remembered the disappearing librarian had mentioned their names, but she couldn't recall what they were.

Jacks perched on the arm of a chair and counted mockingly with his fingers. "One for luck. One for truth. One for mirth. One for youth."

"Those don't sound too bad," she said.

Jacks gave her a dirty look. "Mirth has the potential to make you lose your mind even more than the luck stone did. People will kill to hold on to their youth. It could also bring about jealousy or immaturity, so that one will be tricky to steal. And truth—" Jacks smirked. "The truth is never what you want it to be, Little Fox."

16

Evangeline should have been paying attention to the secret passage.

Chaos was guiding her and Jacks to a place where the vampire said that she'd be able to start her search for the missing stones. But instead of watching her steps or reading the words marked on the shadowy walls, all she could do was replay Jacks's taunt: *The truth is never what you want it to be.*

He'd said it like a warning, as if his truth were as destructive as his kisses. Yet his words only made her wonder: What was Jacks's truth? What did he want from the Valory, and why didn't he want her to know?

Of course, Jacks seemed to enjoy tormenting her, so perhaps that was why he kept it a secret. Evangeline wasn't sure she was convinced by this explanation, but at least she had the new hope that she could find out everything from Jacks once she collected the truth stone.

"Here we are." Chaos halted at a door with an emblazoned image of a wolf's head that had been slashed across the center by either a beast or a hand with a great set of claws. Then he handed her an iron key attached to a velvet ribbon. "I know you can unlock any door, Evangeline, but you should probably avoid spilling blood while you're here."

Evangeline knew she should have felt some sort of fear. But either the story curse's effect on vampire tales was impeding it, or she was just feeling stubborn. In a world of immortals, she had one power, and she didn't want to be told not to use it.

Of course, she didn't say that as she turned the key Chaos had given her.

On the other side of the door, bookshelves, thick and sturdy and packed with ancient tomes, lined the rounded walls, all the way up to a ceiling so high one would need several ladders to reach it. Thankfully, there were indeed multiple ladders of aged rosewood, as well as a number of small balconies that dotted the upper shelves like iron stars.

The air shifted as Evangeline entered, redolent of old paper pages that called to her like a siren's song. Like all admirers of fairytales, she'd always loved the scent of books. She loved the paper dust in the air, the way it swirled in the light like little sprinkles of magic. And most of all, she loved the way that fairytales always made her think of her mother and endless possibilities.

The floor underneath her slippers was covered in a tapestry carpet embroidered with the image of an arch flanked by two knights in armor, one of whom had no head. Atop the rug sat a rounded table with a lamp and some journals, all courted by two dusky velvet chairs that, thankfully, did not have any shackles attached.

"As lovely as all of this is, how is this supposed to help me find the remaining stones?" she asked. "I thought all books were unreliable because of the story curse?"

Of course, this hadn't stopped her from looking in libraries for answers before, though they had never led her anywhere useful. When she'd searched the royal library, she'd been hunting for information on the Valors, but there had been no books on the Valors. She had supposed it was because of the story curse. But it seemed the curse hadn't done away with the books—it was Chaos. He appeared to have every book on the Valors hidden away in this library.

The spines said things like:

How the North Became Magnificent: A Glorious History
The Wolf King
The Valors' Court of Wonder
Wolfric and Honora: The First Epic Love Story of the North

There were also titles pertaining to the Great Houses, but the majority of books were related to the mysterious Valors. "Have you collected all these, just to find the stones for the arch?"

"I thought placing them in my library would be the best way to keep them safe. Because of the story curse, the words in most of these volumes change a little every time they are read." Chaos's gloved fingers traced an old leather spine, and Evangeline watched as the title shifted from *Castor Valor: A Prince Among Princes* to *Castor Valor: A Plague Among Princes*. "However, since I rarely allow them to be read, most of the stories inside have been preserved."

Evangeline shook her head as she stared up at all the countless leather spines, some of the words flickering before her eyes just for daring to glance at them.

She didn't even know where to begin. "Perhaps we could pull the luck stone back out just—"

"No," Chaos and Jacks both replied at once.

"What if we just use it to find the right book?"

Jacks seemed to consider it, but Chaos shook his head. "The last key wore the luck stone after she found it. She believed it would give her good fortune, and it did. But it also made her far too reckless and ultimately led to her death."

"What if Jacks were to use the stone?" She turned to him. "You said it didn't affect you."

"It didn't. But it's also not going to help me. Only the prophesied key can find and reunite all four missing stones."

Evangeline wanted to think Jacks was exaggerating—or that perhaps he just wanted to get out of spending time in a library. But then she remembered their trip to the Fortuna Vault, how he'd watched her as they'd walked through all that treasure, observing her reactions. She also supposed, given Chaos's rather compelling reason for wanting to open the arch, he must have spent time searching for the missing stones—and given how long he'd been alive, he had a lot of time. Yet he only possessed one, which had been found by the previous key.

Now, Evangeline needed to locate the other three. She wondered if they really thought she could do it . . . or if they were just willing to see how many she could collect before she died as well.

The following day, when Evangeline woke up inside her borrowed room, she half expected to find Jacks at the edge of her bed, ready to toss a gown at her face as he told her it was time to get to work and find the stones.

Instead, there was just a note tucked next to the teapot on her breakfast tray.

Little Fox,
Had to leave. Things to do.
Try not to die while I'm gone.

—J

"Try not to die," she muttered. She didn't know why she was surprised, either by Jacks's callous words or the fact that he'd disappeared almost as soon as she'd agreed to do the one thing he wanted. But she *was* surprised—and maybe just a little hurt.

What could he have to do that was so important? She knew he couldn't help her find the missing stones, but she also knew how desperately he wanted them. And how badly he'd wanted her alive, yet he'd just left her, alone, in a castle of vampires.

Maybe she'd been right yesterday: Jacks and Chaos just wanted her to get as many of the stones as she could before the quest took her life.

After dressing in one of the many gowns that had been delivered to her room from Wolf Hall, Evangeline made her way through the hidden tunnels back to Chaos's secret library. Despite Jacks's note, she kept expecting him to softly walk up beside her or to saunter through a secret door in the wall. But Jacks did not appear.

The library was quiet without his teasing, or his laughter, or his tossing of apples. The only sounds were the occasional flickers of the glowing lanterns that filled the hidden library with warm, syrupy light.

She tried to take comfort in the books. Stories had always felt as if they were her friends. But all these stories felt like distant relations to the tales that she knew.

Chaos had been right about the way the stories inside the books would change. In almost every book she read, words shifted before her eyes. Usually, they were minor things. She saw accounts of Honora Valor alter the color of her eyes from hazel to brown. Stories of Wolfric shifted his hair from golden to red.

But a few things never seemed to change, such as the names of the Valor children and a few of their defining characteristics. Aurora was sweet and was always described as the most beautiful girl who'd ever lived, followed by her twin, Castor, who was said to be quite noble. Vesper could see the future. Tempest and Romulus—another set of twins—were great inventors, responsible for the magical arches. Dane was some sort of shifter, and Lysander had a gift that involved memories. Every story said they were handsome and kind and generous. The family was close, protective of one another, and beloved until . . .

Something horrible happened.

But Evangeline couldn't seem to uncover what this tragic event was. She knew the outcome—the Valors built the Valory, sealed something inside of it, and then their heads were all chopped off, ending the Age of the Valors and ushering in the Age of Great Houses.

It was in between these ages that the stones had been created and hidden away. Unfortunately, Evangeline could find little about that mysterious time in between.

All she could find were tales that skirted the edge of what happened.

She found stories of *before*—of the Age of the Valors, when knights always won, good always beat out evil, honor was always rewarded, and fairytales always ended happily.

Then there were the tales of *after*—the Age of Great Houses, which often flickered and changed to the Age of Great *Curses* as she read.

One volume, *A History of Famous Beheadings,* had an entire chapter on the Valors' deaths, but it made no mention of the Valory Arch.

An excerpt read:

> Mist fell like tears in Valorfell, coating the streets with shadows and cold while people wept silently in their homes. Most mourned the great Valor family, but few let it show, for fear the Great Houses would slay them as well.

The author went on to curse the names of all the original Great Houses: Fortuna, Slaughterwood, Merrywood, Redthorne, Hawkleaf, Casstel, Bloodgrave, Verita, Ravencross, Darling, Havok, Bellflower, and Acadian.

Acadian was Apollo's surname, and reading it made her picture him, sitting atop his hunting horse, battling against the curse, and she wondered where he was at this moment. She was uninjured; therefore, she could assume he was unharmed, at least physically. Emotionally, what was this all doing to him? The first night he'd been awake, when she'd seen him in the garden, he'd already seemed like a different prince from the one she'd married. He'd been wounded and haunted. A little of that wouldn't destroy him. But what if this curse went on too long? Who would Apollo be then?

The following day, Evangeline decided to read more about the Great Houses. There were thirteen original Great Houses, and they had gained the most after the fall of the Valors, which made her wonder if they had been involved in sealing the arch and hiding the stones. Especially as the stones were magic and possibly provided some measure of fortune to whoever possessed them.

She decided to look into House Slaughterwood first, since LaLa was marrying Lord Robin Slaughterwood. Unfortunately, it seemed there were no book spines mentioning House Slaughterwood, or if there were, the story curse had altered them. It did that a lot.

The next House she researched—House Merrywood—turned into *Bitterwood* as she read. Although nothing about this Great House or its namesake village seemed bitter.

Merrywood the village was said to be a charming township built in a forest, home to enchanted square fairs, magical foxes, and a trio of semi-infamous scoundrels who were all said to be charming and handsome and nothing but trouble. The trio was composed of Prince Castor Valor, Lyric Merrywood—son to Lord Merrywood—and a cocky archer.

The archer was given no name, but Evangeline immediately

wondered if this was the Archer from *The Ballad of the Archer and the Fox*.

"Find anything interesting?"

She startled at the velvet voice and dropped the volume in her hand. It fell to the floor with a heavy thud.

"Sorry I frightened you." Chaos leaned easily against the opposite chair, clad in leather armor that perfectly outlined all his sculpted vampire perfection, and she knew he wasn't sorry at all. He was entertained that she had jumped. There was a soft, unexpected crinkle around his eyes, giving just a hint of something human.

But Evangeline still remembered when his eyes had not appeared human at all, when she'd looked in them and seen death.

The vampire angled his head, his gaze leaving her to study the pile of books on her table. "You're reading about the Great Houses?"

"Yes, but there's one House I haven't been able to find any books on. Do you have any volumes on House Slaughterwood?"

"There's nothing worth reading about House Slaughterwood. They're just a bunch of spineless brutes." Chaos strode to the shelf and retrieved a book with a dusky lavender cover.

"Perhaps try this one." He handed her the volume he'd just taken from the shelf.

It was a slender thing, wrapped in a thick black ribbon and embossed with gold foil.

The Rise and Fall of the Valors: Beloved First Royal Family of the Magnificent North

The title twisted as she read it, some of the letters turning into branches, others transforming into weapons and making Evangeline a little dizzy.

The first page of the book did the same. The letters and words kept flickering into other things, as if the tome were so excited someone had finally picked it up that it didn't know what to say.

"This one seems a touch overeager—" Evangeline broke off as she looked up to find Chaos had already left. And it seemed he wasn't the only thing that had disappeared from the library. After setting the book he'd handed her aside—because the words simply refused to settle—she reached down to find the volume she'd dropped when Chaos had first entered.

Only, like the vampire, the book was gone.

All that remained was a fluttering piece of paper.

17

Had Chaos taken the book, or had it simply disappeared? Evangeline didn't remember vanishing books being part of the story curse. But it made more sense than Chaos stealing one of her books.

She gingerly picked up the paper on the ground, wondering if it had fallen from the vanished volume.

The page was old and yellowed. The handwriting looked unfamiliar, but the words were ones she'd memorized.

Evangeline studied the page. A little dragon was pictured under the words *One for Luck,* which had been crossed out—possibly because the luck stone had been found. *One for Truth* had a picture of a skull and crossbones. *One for Mirth* had a garden of spring flowers dusted with little stars. *One for Youth* had a shield with flames licking the bottom.

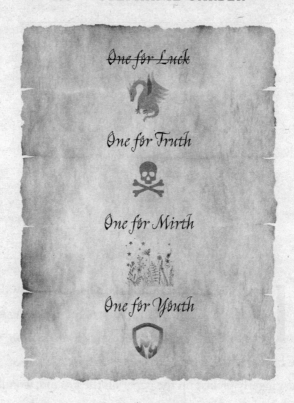

One for Luck

One for Truth

One for Mirth

One for Youth

Evangeline wondered if the last key had written this. The symbols must have been clues to where she thought the stones were.

But what did the symbols mean?

The following week dripped by slowly, like melting candle wax. Evangeline spent every day in the library, trying to make sense of the symbols she'd found on the last key's list. Both the crossbones and the flowers were too common, and while the shield with the flames was more singular, she couldn't find a single reference to it in any books. Chaos didn't recognize the image, either. He checked on her progress every day, but he was always quick to leave. And Jacks . . .

She tried not to think about Jacks. Evangeline didn't like the way it hurt when she thought about how he'd just left her here.

The highlight of her day was the daily scandal sheet, which was delivered with her breakfast. At first, she'd started reading it to see if it mentioned anything about Apollo, and maybe she was curious to see if it mentioned Jacks as well. But now she enjoyed the sheets because they were the one thing that made her feel connected to the world outside of Chaos's underground castle.

Today, the title was a little smudged. Evangeline couldn't make out the first word of it, but the other two were all the article really seemed to need.

The Daily Rumor

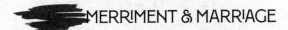 MERRIMENT & MARRIAGE

By Kristof Knightlinger

Everyone loves a theme party, but not as much as soon-to-be Lady LaLa Slaughterwood and her fiancé, young Lord Robin Slaughterwood. To celebrate their recent, and very sudden, engagement, the pair is hosting a party of historic proportions. Rumor has it, members of all the Great Houses will be in attendance.

> I think my invitation must have been lost in the post, for I have yet to receive it, but I have learned that the party will last a full week and that costumes are required.

Evangeline imagined there was an invitation waiting for her at Wolf Hall, and she felt a longing to accept it, to go to this party and celebrate with everyone. It was a smallish feeling, but her heart was already so splintered with loneliness that for a second she thought this sharp little pang might shatter her apart.

She immediately felt frivolous for being sad about missing a party. But she would have wished to see LaLa even if she weren't having a party. If her friend were mourning instead, Evangeline would have wanted to be there. She just wanted to be anywhere. With anyone.

Even Jacks would have been welcome company.

She felt another hurtful wrench at the thought that he still hadn't returned. But she pushed the feeling away as her eyes wandered to the next article.

FORMER PRINCE TIBERIUS ACADIAN APPREHENDED AFTER DARING ESCAPE ATTEMPT

By Kristof Knightlinger

This article was thin, more speculation about the escape than actual information. Yet the hairs on Evangeline's arms rose as she read about Tiberius.

It wasn't fear. It should have been. Tiberius had tried to kill her, *twice*. As a member of the Protectorate, Tiberius had believed she needed to die because she was capable of opening the Valory Arch, and like the rest of the Protectorate, he was committed to making sure the arch would never open.

But suddenly, Evangeline wondered if perhaps being a part of the Protectorate didn't just mean killing girls with pink hair. Maybe the Protectorate was also hiding the missing stones.

Of course, it was reckless to even think of visiting Tiberius in prison to ask what he knew about the stones. If Jacks were there, he'd undoubtedly say the idea was too dangerous. But Jacks was gone, and Evangeline's hope had always burned brighter than her fear.

18

Evangeline listened carefully for the sound of horse hooves or footsteps or anything else that might have indicated Apollo was back to hunting her.

The leaf-strewn path of the old Northern forest was as quiet as the fog that licked her ankles, yet Evangeline quickened her pace, boots crunching too loudly against the frosty ground. She would have probably been safer if she'd asked Chaos to accompany her, but she'd feared he might not like the idea of her paying a visit to the young man who'd tried to kill her. So she hadn't said a word of her plans, sneaking out as the vampires slept away the day.

There was an old path to the Tower, where Tiberius was being held. But she didn't really need a road. The structure was tall enough that Evangeline could easily see it from the cemetery above Chaos's castle.

The Tower rose out of an old forest that was just past the

cemetery. According to the stories, the Tower wasn't built until after the Age of the Valors. Their reign was supposedly so
wonderful they didn't need to worry about locking people up,
for dangerous crimes did not happen while they were in power.

It was difficult to believe that was all true, especially looking
at the Tower now. Its stones were so old and worn it was impossible to tell what color they had once been. There were no
windows. No doors. No way to look out at the forest that surrounded it.

Evangeline felt a measure of pity for Tiberius. She told
herself it was silly to feel bad for the person who'd tried to
kill her, but the last time she'd seen Tiberius, he hadn't been
murderous, he'd been in despair.

He'd sobbed when he'd confessed to accidentally killing his
brother, which was part of why she hoped he'd be willing to
help her today.

And although she truly did feel bad about the dreary con-
ditions of the prison, she imagined they might also aid her in
gaining information. She just needed to find a way inside. In
addition to possessing no clear door, there also appeared to
be no guards who might give her entry.

Fortunately, Evangeline had ways to work around the lack
of a visible doorway.

She dug into the basket of bread she'd brought for Tiberius
and pulled out a dagger. Vampires were surprisingly careless
with their weapons, so it had been easy enough to find a re-
placement for the knife Jacks had taken back. The dagger she'd

chosen was gold, with pretty pink gems on the hilt and a tip that sparkled.

One touch and blood spilled freely from her finger.

After a silent apology to Apollo, who was now bleeding as well, she quickly started marking the stones as she repeated the words:

Please open.

Please open.

Please open.

She didn't know how many stones she asked. It felt as if she'd tried to talk to the entire base of the Tower before one helpful stone finally cracked and a hidden door swung wide.

She took a deep breath and immediately coughed. The air on the other side of the door tasted like bones.

Two guards, who appeared to have been playing cards, immediately stood. One looked so startled, he knocked over his wooden stool, which thunked loudly against the damp stone floor.

"You shouldn't be here," he said as the other guard gaped, clearly recognizing her rose-gold hair.

"I'll tell you what," Evangeline said brightly. "I won't tell anyone that the door to this place was so poorly guarded that I was able to simply saunter in if you just let me have a little chat with Tiberius." She finished with a shake of her pink hair for the guard who didn't seem to know who she was.

He still looked as if he wanted to argue, or possibly put her in a cell, until the second guard kicked him in the leg and said, "We're sorry, Your Highness, but Tiberius isn't allowed any visitors."

"Then just don't tell anyone I've stopped by," Evangeline said. And before either guard could argue, she started up the cold stone stairs.

As soon as her boots touched the first step, she could hear Jacks's voice. *This is your worst idea yet, Little Fox.*

The voice was so clear, she paused to look behind her, but there were only the guards closing the door she'd just entered through.

She waited another second in case Jacks knocked or slipped through the crack before the door shut. But Jacks didn't appear, and she didn't hear his voice again.

Evangeline shook her head and started back up the steps, determined not to think about Jacks. As long as Tiberius was still locked in a cell, he could not hurt her. She'd offer him some bread. They'd chat. She'd tell him he could help save his brother. He'd tell her where the three missing stones were hidden. And all would be right in the Magnificent North.

She climbed another set of stairs. She was on the third level now, and there was still no sign of Tiberius. There was no sign of anyone. Every cell she passed was empty, save for the occasional gust of wind slipping through the cracks.

A spider crawled over her boots. She jumped, nearly stumbling back a step.

"She put an end to a royal family, and yet she's afraid of a spider." The voice was followed by a droll snicker.

Evangeline's shoulders tensed as she regained her footing and peered down the hall to where she finally found Tiberius Acadian. She flushed as he continued to laugh. Even in prison, he hadn't lost his princely bearing. He held a crude cup of water as if it were a goblet of wine.

"I'd offer you some," he said, "but I don't have any poison to add to it."

"I'd have thought you'd have learned your lesson about trying to kill people with poison."

"Ah, but you're not a person. You're a key." Tiberius curled his lip as he stalked toward the bars. "What do you want?"

Evangeline held out a loaf of bread from her basket.

Tiberius eyed the food suspiciously. Yet Evangeline could see there was hunger in his gaze. As he was a prince, she'd thought he would have been taken better care of. But luckily for her, that didn't appear to be the case. His title didn't matter here, and the Protectorate had clearly abandoned him. His cell was drafty and dark, lit only by a few foul-smelling tallow candles.

Evangeline ripped off a piece of bread and slowly started to chew. "See, it's perfectly safe. I'm not your enemy, Tiberius. In fact, I came here to tell you some good news. Your brother, Apollo, is alive."

Tiberius stilled. Then he sneered. "You're lying."

"You tried to kill me, twice," Evangeline reminded him. "Do you really think I'd come here just to tell you a lie? Apollo is truly alive." She paused, letting the words hang in the air until the derisive mask Tiberius wore slipped just enough to reveal he believed her—he didn't look as if he wanted to, but in Evangeline's experience, what people wanted to feel and what they actually felt were rarely the same thing.

"I know if given the chance you would probably still try to kill me, but I also believe that you care about your brother, and that is why I am here. The poison Apollo ingested put him into a state of suspended sleep that looked like death. About two weeks ago, he woke from it, but he's still not himself. He's been infected with another curse."

"What kind of curse?"

"A very old one. It's the same curse that was placed on the Archer in *The Ballad of the Archer and the Fox*."

"And let me guess: you're my brother's fox." Tiberius grinned. "This is too perfect. Apollo is alive, and soon you'll be dead."

Tiberius finally grabbed the offered loaf of bread and smugly began to chew.

"There's one thing I left out," Evangeline said. "If your brother succeeds in killing me, then he'll die, too. Apollo and I are linked. Any injury that befalls me harms him as well."

"Not my problem," Tiberius said.

But Evangeline could not believe he was as callous as he seemed. She knew he cared for Apollo. She'd watched him weep and fall to pieces over his brother.

Evangeline set down her basket and retrieved her golden knife. Pushing aside her cloak, she shoved the long sleeve of her dress up her arm.

"What are you doing?" Tiberius asked, eyes going wide as

Evangeline placed the blade to her arm and scored four words into her skin.

WHERE ARE YOU APOLLO?

The marks were light, just enough to scratch the words without drawing any blood. If it hurt, she couldn't feel it over the tightness of her chest as she waited, hoping that Apollo would reply and Tiberius would believe everything she'd just told him.

"Are you mad?" Tiberius asked.

"Watch." Evangeline sucked in a gasp as the first letter appeared. Apollo did more than scratch her skin: he carved back words until she bled.

DON'T LOOK FOR ME

Each word smarted. Then her other arm started to sting as more words appeared.

I DON'T WANT TO KILL YOU

Tiberius ran a hand over his face, paler than before.

Evangeline felt an unsettling chill at the words Apollo had written, but she also felt a whisper of victory. Tiberius looked as if he believed her now, and he seemed terrified.

"If Apollo succeeds in hunting me down, then he will die—in truth this time—and you will lose your brother forever. But if you help me break his curse, you'll have your brother back, and I'll ensure you're freed." She added the last bit hastily, and a part of her regretted it, but she needed to be as convincing as possible.

Tiberius pulled at his neck, still watching the last drops of blood from her arm drip onto the grimy prison floor. "Say I did believe you—what would you need me to do?"

"Tell me where the Valory Arch stones are hidden. I know you're afraid of what the Valory holds, but I believe it contains a back door that will allow me to break the curse on Apollo and save his life. I just need to find the missing arch stones. Please, tell me where they are. Help me save your brother."

Tiberius took a slow, beleaguered breath. "No."

"What do you mean, no?"

"I'm refusing your request. Denying your plea. All of this changes nothing, Evangeline. I'd rather see you die than help you find the stones."

She couldn't believe what she was hearing. "How can you say that? This is your brother's life."

Tiberius's eyes were glassy, but his voice was resolute. "I've already mourned his death, and better his one death than the deaths of countless others and the end of the Magnificent North as we know it, which is what will happen if you open that arch, Evangeline Fox."

"You don't know that."

"I know more than you. Do you even know anything about these stones you're searching for? They aren't just bits of rock. And they haven't been hidden just to keep the arch closed. These stones have powers that call to one another. They long to be reunited, and the last time all four stones were put together, one of the Great Houses was destroyed. I saw the ruins—I felt the horrible hollowing magic. Just bringing the stones together is potentially cataclysmic." Tiberius met her eyes through the bars, his gaze still glassy and somber. "I do love my brother, but saving his life isn't worth this risk. If you have a heart, let him shoot it with an arrow. Turn yourselves into another tragic Northern ballad and keep the rest of us safe from the power locked inside the Valory."

19

Evangeline decided this forest was magical. She should have noticed before—the scent of the lush green trees was just a little too sweet, as if sugar had been mixed in with the snow that dotted pine needles and leaves.

She rather liked the scent, but she'd have happily traded it for plain, unmagical snow if it meant the forest would stop re-arranging itself.

Evangeline didn't know how long she'd been walking on this path. It was the same path she'd taken to the Tower, only instead of leading her back to Chaos's underground castle, the path just kept weaving through the trees. The sky above was turning purple. Soon it would be full night, and she shuddered to think of how lost she'd feel then.

It made it even worse that the trip had been for nothing. She had been so wrong. Even now it was difficult to believe that Tiberius had chosen fear of an old prophecy over love for his brother.

She could never reveal this to Apollo—if she were ever able to save him.

Her breath came out in pale streaks as she looked down at the words freshly scratched into her arm: *I DON'T WANT TO KILL YOU.*

Leaves behind her rustled, a bird cawed, and Evangeline startled.

Quickly, she retrieved the gold dagger from her basket and held it out as she turned.

"Hello, Eva." Luc walked out from between a pair of snow-dusted trees, flashing a grin that might have been boyish if not for the hint of fangs.

"What are you doing here?" Evangeline asked. She was relieved it wasn't Apollo, but she didn't lower her knife. Luc might not have been cursed to hunt and kill her, but he had tried to bite her the last two times she'd seen him.

"You don't need to hold out that knife." Luc's pretty mouth fell into a pout. "I came to say I'm sorry for the other day. I really didn't want to bite you. Well . . . I did want to bite you, but I didn't want to hurt you. I've missed you." He looked at her through his lashes, gold flecks in his eyes glimmering in the darkness.

Her pulse fluttered, and she hated that it still fluttered for him. Although she had a feeling it was vampire allure and not actually Luc affecting her this way.

She wasn't sure exactly when she'd fallen out of love with Luc. In fact, she wasn't entirely certain that she had. It felt more like she'd left behind her love for Luc with the version of herself that she'd been *before*. Back when she believed that first love and true love and forever love were all the same.

She used to think love was like a house. Once it was built, a person got to live in it forever. But now she wondered if love was more like a war with new foes constantly appearing and battles creeping up. Winning at love was less about succeeding in a battle and more about continuing to fight, to choose the person you loved as the one you were willing to die for, over and over.

For so long, Luc had been that person. Even though he wasn't now, as she looked up at him, it was easy to imagine that he could be again.

He took a step closer, his pout turning into a crooked smile so familiar it made her ache. Nothing had been familiar lately. She'd spent so much time alone in Chaos's library, being close to Luc now, even in the dark forest, made her feel surprisingly warm.

"You know," he said softly, "biting is really like kissing but better, if you do it right." Luc angled his head and leaned in toward her neck.

"No!" Evangeline placed both her hands firmly against his chest and tore her gaze away from him, focusing on the night and the stars and the tops of the trees as she attempted to shake off his allure. "You still can't bite me, Luc. I'm not a snack."

"What about just a nibble?"

Evangeline glared.

He sighed. "Are you completely over us, Eva?"

For a second, Evangeline didn't know how to respond. She'd thought this was just about the biting. But looking at Luc now, she found something like loneliness in his immortal face. Being a vampire was undoubtedly not what he'd expected.

He looked up at the darkened night. The only sky he'd ever see now that he was a vampire. There were a handful of stars, scattered like gems from a broken necklace, but it was mostly just the waxing crescent moon, taunting with a bladed smile that would never give sun-warm light. Evangeline couldn't imagine being banished from the sunshine, never being allowed to venture into the bright light of day. She wondered if that's what he was *really* looking for. Not her but a piece of sunlight. A piece of something from his past to cling to.

She would have thought becoming a prince would have made him happy—at least for a while. But it was probably too much work and not enough play. Although she couldn't imagine Luc's council actually trusting him to do anything important.

"What are you doing out here, Luc?"

"I heard some guards say they saw you around the Tower, so I slipped away as soon as it was dusk. I wanted to find you, to see if you wanted to go to a party with me."

"I can't."

"You don't even know what kind of party it is." Luc reached into his back pocket and pulled out a gold invitation with gleaming white ink, so bright she could read it in the moonlight.

The words *Mirth, Merriment, and Marriage* were printed at the top.

"It's a costume party." Luc waggled his brows. "All the Great Houses are going to be there, if you're into that sort of thing—"

Luc kept speaking, but Evangeline's attention was on the invitation, which was for LaLa's engagement party.

This morning, when she had found the article about the party, the first word in the title had been smudged, but now as she reread the invite, she realized that word had been *mirth*.

The word alone wouldn't have convinced her that the mirth stone might be there, but then she replayed what Luc had said about all the Great Houses attending, and a wild idea bubbled up.

Given how much the Great Houses had gained after the fall of the Valors, she'd suspected that they'd hidden the missing Valory Arch stones, and now she wondered if they would be bringing them to this party. She remembered Tiberius's words: *These stones have powers that call to one another. They long to be reunited.*

Perhaps at LaLa's party, the remaining stones would come together again. Something light and sparkling rose inside her at the thought. And Evangeline knew she needed to go to this party.

"Thank you!" She kissed him on the cheek.

He flashed a crooked grin. "Is that a yes?"

For a second, it was tempting—mostly because if Jacks found out, she was certain he'd be annoyed. But in the end, she told Luc, "No—but thank you for the invitation."

Before he could argue, or ask for another *bite,* Evangeline scurried off, hoping the forest would finally let her escape.

20

Chaos was gone when Evangeline returned to his underground castle. She feared that he was out searching for her, although there was no one around to confirm her suspicions.

She suspected that Chaos had warned his vampires there would be consequences if anything happened to her. After her first day or so there, she never saw any vampires aside from Chaos. Of course, Evangeline didn't make it a habit to tromp about in search of any. She only searched for Chaos now because she would need to ask him for transportation to attend LaLa's party. But she supposed this could wait until tomorrow.

After failing to find Chaos in his study, Evangeline went to bed.

Sometime later, when she was just on the edge of asleep and awake, she thought she heard him enter—she definitely heard *someone*. But when she opened her eyes, no one was there.

The suite was empty and cold, and yet she couldn't shake the feeling that seconds ago it had been different.

The following day, as soon as it was dusk, Evangeline started toward Chaos's study. She had an extra bounce in her step at the thought that she'd be leaving this place soon, and if all went well, she'd find the stones she needed to break the curse on Apollo.

At the thought of Apollo, she rubbed her wrist where his carved words snuck out from her sleeve. The shallow wound didn't hurt anymore, but there was an ache in her chest as she turned the corner into the gaming court and—

Jacks.

She fumbled to a halt, slippers skidding against the stone floor.

He was a few feet away, sitting in the gaming court at a polished wooden table with a checkered board half-covered in red and black pieces. Above him hung a cage full of dripping wax candles that tossed ocher light on both the checkers and the pretty girl that Jacks was playing with.

The girl tapped her nails against the table, biting her lip fetchingly as her eyes flickered from the simple game to Jacks.

He looked like the picture of a naughty prince as he lounged in his black velvet chair. His golden hair gleamed under the light, the locks artlessly askew as if the girl had just run her fingers through it.

Evangeline felt a flash of—she wasn't quite sure what it was. It certainly wasn't jealousy. Jacks looked rather bored as he moved a red checker. And yet, if Jacks was so bored, why hadn't he come to find her? Was he planning on letting Evangeline know he'd returned?

Evangeline didn't want to be bothered by this. It really was a good thing that Jacks hadn't come back to find her. And yet, seeing him here now made her feel small, insignificant.

She'd thought he wanted the Valory Arch open more than anything, but first he'd run off and left her, and now he was sitting around playing checkers.

Jacks barely flicked his gaze in her direction. "I also play chess."

Evangeline's cheeks burned with embarrassment. She hadn't meant to project that thought about the checkers. "I was just surprised. I didn't know you played games that didn't involve hurting people."

"Oh, there's that other game," the girl chimed in. "The one—"

"You can leave now," Jacks interrupted.

The girl's mouth was stuck mid-word. "You—I—you—" She struggled, briefly making little pouting huffs before her round face glazed over.

An instant later, she rose and quietly left the court.

"You shouldn't have done that," Evangeline said.

"Why?" Jacks leaned back in his seat and looked lazily up at her. His clothes were as relaxed as his posture, a dark blue velvet doublet half-undone, low-slung belt, storm-gray trousers, and weathered leather boots with buckles on the side. "You want me to bring her back?"

"No," Evangeline replied. But it was too quick.

A smile tugged at the corner of Jacks's mouth. "Jealous, Little Fox?"

"Absolutely not—I don't like it when you use your powers to control people."

"You've asked me to do it in the past."

"I had a good reason."

"I actually believe you would have done the North a tremendous favor by ridding it of your stepsister, but we can always fix that mistake later." Jacks rolled a black apple back and forth across the edge of the table with his palm. "Now, did you want something? Or just my attention?"

He flashed one of his dimples as his mouth formed a mocking smirk.

Evangeline hadn't missed this at all. "You're asking the wrong girl, Jacks. Unlike *her*, I know you're not a god."

"Yet you're the one who prayed at my church." He kicked his boots up on the table. "What was it you said? *I know you understand my heartbreak.*" His laugh was soft.

She felt her cheeks go splotchy, which of course only made him laugh harder.

"Clearly, I was mistaken," she said.

She'd also been terribly naive to believe that Jacks could understand human feelings or care about ones that weren't his. Evangeline didn't say that bit aloud. She merely turned to go. Perhaps she'd missed him a little while he was gone, but clearly, those thoughts had been mad.

"Wait." Jacks jumped up from his seat and grabbed her arm. "What's this?"

She tried to pull away, but Jacks's nimble fingers were quick. He shoved up the edge of her sleeve to reveal one arm of Apollo's crudely carved words. *I DON'T WANT TO KILL YOU.*

Jacks's nostrils flared. "Looks as if your husband has gotten worse at his love letters."

"It's nothing." Evangeline yanked back her arm. But Jacks was far stronger.

He pulled her to him with one quick tug. So close, suddenly she could see details she hadn't noticed before. The shirt under his doublet was incredibly wrinkled, and there were tired circles under his eyes that made her wonder what he'd been off doing over the last ten days.

"Where were you?" she asked.

"I was killing innocent maidens and kicking puppies."

"Jacks, that's not funny."

"Neither is what's carved into your arm." He glared at the words. "When did this happen?"

Evangeline pursed her lips.

If Jacks was upset by the sight of the wound, she didn't want to think about how he would react if she told him she'd received it during a visit with Tiberius. Jacks would probably shackle her to one of the walls to keep her from leaving again.

What she needed to do was distract him with something else.

Evangeline finally wrenched her hand away, took out the scandal sheet that mentioned LaLa's engagement celebration, and thrust it into his hands.

Jacks took one look at the paper, and his expression turned hard. "No. You're not attending a party at House Slaughterwood."

"That's not your decision to make." Evangeline stabbed her finger at the page. "I know the first word is blurry, but it says *mirth*, as in the mirth stone!"

"That doesn't mean the stones will be there."

"But I think they will be. See the part where it mentions that members from all the Great Houses will be in attendance? I suspect that the arch stones have been hidden among the Great Houses and that they will have the remaining stones with them at the party."

Jacks looked down on her imperiously. "Even if your theory is right about the Houses having the stones, why would they bring them?"

"While you were away, I learned that the stones call to one another—they long to be reunited. When Chaos showed me the luck stone, I felt its power, and I wanted it more than I have ever wanted anything in my life. So I think whoever has the stones will be wearing them at this party because they won't let them out of their sight."

Jacks worked his jaw. He no longer looked entirely opposed to the idea, but he didn't seem very happy about it, either. "Chaos can't know we're going to House Slaughterwood."

"Why?"

"Because if he knows, he won't let us go." Jacks crumpled the sheet of newsprint in his hand. And Evangeline couldn't be sure, but it looked as if his fingers were shaking.

"What's wrong with House Slaughterwood?"

"House Slaughterwood is the reason we're all in this mess, Little Fox."

21

Evangeline did not know what lie Jacks had told Chaos about their plans. But the following evening, she found that Chaos had filled her bedroom with an exciting assortment of elegant gowns and slippers and hats and cloaks and jewels. So much pink silk and cream satin and hand-stitched flowers sewn onto trains.

The sight of it all made Evangeline feel unexpectedly guilty that they were concealing the truth from Chaos.

When Evangeline had been infected with vampire venom, he had been there to make sure she didn't feed on anyone and complete the transformation into a vampire. She'd never thanked him because she still felt embarrassed about the way they'd been tangled together that night. And she had no idea what to think of the way Chaos had smoothed her slip down before leaving. He was a monster for sure, but it seemed he was also a gentleman. *A gentleman monster.*

What could have made him so opposed to a visit to House Slaughterwood? She had tried again to look it up in his library, but then she'd remembered there were no books on House Slaughterwood, and when she'd first asked Chaos about it, he'd steered her in another direction.

She'd tried to ask Jacks more about what he'd told her: *House Slaughterwood is the reason we're all in this mess.* But he'd refused to say more on the matter, and Evangeline had the surprising impression that it was out of loyalty to Chaos. It was uncomfortable to imagine Jacks as capable of loyalty and friendship. It was much easier to believe he had no honor whatsoever. Although given how driven Jacks was, if he were to be loyal, she could see him being loyal to the death.

A shiver tripped down her spine at the thought, and Evangeline returned to her packing. In the morning, she'd be leaving with Jacks for House Slaughterwood, and she had yet to finish filling her trunks.

She picked up a pink velvet dress lined in white fur, thinking it might be nice for the carriage ride, when she noticed the lavender book on the end of her bed. *The Rise and Fall of the Valors: Beloved First Royal Family of the Magnificent North.*

At least that was what the title was supposed to say. The gilded letters were bursting apart like fireworks. The book had been in motion since Chaos had first handed it to her more than a week ago; every day, she tried to read it, but the letters were too busy. Only now, it wasn't just a few of the letters—the entire title was breaking apart and reforming into the name of a tale she was intimately familiar with.

Evangeline set down the velvet dress and picked up the book. The words *The Ballad of the Archer and the Fox* now shimmered across the front, mingling with an image of an archer and a fox.

She braced, waiting for the title to keep shifting, but for once, the words on the front of the book remained still.

"What game are you playing?" she asked.

The cover stayed the same. Although she thought she saw the Archer wink, as if trying to dazzle her into opening his book. For a minute, she wondered if perhaps more than the cover had changed. *What if the story inside had shifted as well?*

If this magical book had actually turned into *The Ballad of the Archer and the Fox,* then could it contain information about the Archer's curse?

Evangeline couldn't believe she hadn't considered the possibility before. Jacks had been so insistent there was no cure for Apollo outside of opening the Valory Arch that she hadn't even bothered to look. But what if the original fairytale had an easier answer for how to end the Archer's curse?

Evangeline couldn't help but hope as she perched on the end of the bed and opened the volume.

Unfortunately, it seemed the cover had been a deception after all. The book's first page was a portrait of a severe young man and a graceful young woman. Beneath were written the words *Vengeance Slaughterwood and his beautiful bride-to-be.*

Clearly, this book was playing tricks on her, yet Evangeline didn't put the volume down. Minutes ago, she'd been wondering about House Slaughterwood, and now this book seemed to be giving her an answer.

She continued to study the picture. The portrait of Vengeance was quite handsome, but there was something unkind in his expression. His bride-to-be was extraordinarily pretty, but the book didn't say who she was.

Evangeline turned the page and found a second portrait of Vengeance. He looked even meaner and older than he had in the previous picture, and he was with another woman, Glendora Redthorne. She was not nearly as pretty as the last girl, but the caption was the same: *His beautiful bride-to-be.*

Evangeline wondered why he would have two brides-to-be. What could have happened to the first?

She flipped the page again, hoping for more information about Vengeance or the rest of the Slaughterwoods, but there was just another, unrelated portrait: *The dutiful daughters of House Darling.*

The page after that showed a group of young noblemen.

It seemed this book wasn't just about the Slaughterwoods after all. It was just some sort of portrait book.

Disappointed, Evangeline considered returning to her packing. But on the next page, she came across a picture of three young men standing near a tree that had a bullseye board tacked onto it. One young man looked friendly, one looked highborn, and one looked exactly like Jacks.

The hairs on her arms rose up. Jacks's clothes were different, an older style that made her think of days when roads weren't mapped and much of the world was still unexplored, but his handsome face was unmistakable.

Her eyes shot to the bottom of the page.

She found herself holding her breath as she searched for Jacks's name, but the caption just said: *The Merrywood Three.*

The word *Merrywood* flickered to *Bitterwood,* and suddenly, Evangeline remembered that she'd seen another reference to this trio. It had been in the book that had disappeared after she'd dropped it.

The book had described the members of the Merrywood Three as scoundrels. They were Prince Castor Valor, Lyric Merrywood—son of Lord Merrywood—and a nameless archer who she suspected could have been the same Archer from *The Ballad of the Archer and the Fox.*

Evangeline studied the picture again, attempting to figure out which one of these three young men Jacks could have been.

The young man beside Jacks looked the friendliest—with brown skin, the warmest smile she'd ever seen, and an arrow in one hand, which instantly made Evangeline think he must have been the Archer. But then she remembered that the stories here were all cursed. She wasn't sure if that curse applied to pictures, but she decided to keep an open mind.

The other young man was taller than the friendly one, about the same height as Jacks. The tilt of his chin made her think he thought himself slightly superior, and a part of Evangeline could understand why. This young man was almost painfully handsome. The type of handsome that made her wonder if he was entirely human.

Normally, that was how she thought of Jacks, but in this rendering, Jacks looked human, not immortal. Evangeline had never considered the idea that Jacks had been human before, but if he was part of the Merrywood Three, then clearly he'd been human once. And being human looked good on him—or maybe it was just that he looked so happy.

In the picture, Jacks was tossing an ordinary red apple and laughing in a way that lit up his entire face. He never looked this happy now, and she couldn't help but wonder what had changed.

"Little Fox!" Jacks knocked as he called her name through the door.

Evangeline startled and nearly toppled off the bed as he strode into the room. His resemblance to the picture was uncanny, and yet the feeling she got from looking at him now was entirely different. It was as if a sculptor had taken a dagger to who he had once been and carved out all the softness.

"You're staring at me." Jacks's mouth curved up as he spoke.

Her cheeks instantly pinked. "You burst into my room."

"I knocked and said your name and—" He broke off.

His eyes latched onto the book in her hands. They flared, dark silver. There and gone so fast, it could have been a trick of the light. Or maybe he had seen the picture, except the picture was suddenly gone. The pages of the book were blank.

The outside of the book was blank as well, all the golden

script gone, making her uncertain as to what Jacks might have seen.

"Our carriage arrives in half an hour," he said tightly. "Forget the sad stories and finish packing."

Sad stories. If that's what Jacks had seen, then clearly he wasn't looking at the same picture she had seen.

"Wait." Evangeline held up the blank page of her book as if the drawing might reappear. "I saw your portrait in this volume."

Jacks's blue eyes crinkled with laughter. "You're seeing me in fairytales now. Should I be concerned you're starting to form an obsession?"

"No," she said stubbornly, refusing to be embarrassed. "It was you. You were one of the Merrywood Three!"

Jacks sighed, amusement turning to something like concern. "Whatever you saw in that book was a trick. The Merrywood Three died a long time ago, and I was never one of them."

"I know what I saw."

"I'm sure you do. But that doesn't mean you can trust it. These stories, the pictures, they lie."

"So do you," Evangeline countered.

Although, as much as she hated to admit it, Jacks was right. This book in particular had just shifted its cover before her eyes—twice—and then its contents had disappeared entirely, which made what she'd seen more than a little suspect.

But if he was telling the truth, why had his knuckles suddenly gone as white as the apple in his hand?

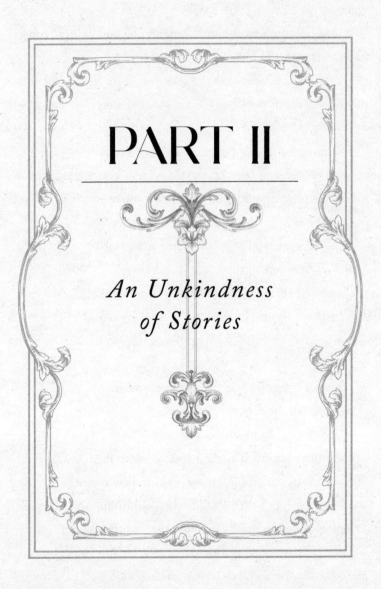

PART II

*An Unkindness
of Stories*

22

Jacks had the travel carriage of a villain. The exterior was smooth matte black, perfect for blending into dark alleys and shadows, yet it had just enough gold trim around the wheels and the windows to be unexpectedly tempting.

This was not the same coach they'd ridden in before, when she'd met with him under the misguided hope that he would remove the love spell he'd placed on Apollo.

Inside this carriage, there was plush black carpet on the floor, thick black velvet cushions on the benches, black lacquered panels for the walls, and more hints of gold edging the icy windows in a decorative pattern of swirling thorns.

Evangeline felt particularly bright, dressed in the pink velvet gown that she'd picked out last night.

Slaughterwood Castle was a full day's journey to the east of Valorfell, and the farther she and Jacks traveled, the colder it became. The world outside the windows was a wonderland of white and ice and pale blue winter birds with wings that turned to frosted lilac when they flew.

She might have asked Jacks about the birds, or which part of the country they were now in, but he was asleep.

His golden head rested against the window, only moving when the coach went over a bump in the road. Trying not to stare—because she wouldn't be surprised if he could sense it, even in his sleep—Evangeline went back to studying the sheet of clues that she'd found in Chaos's library.

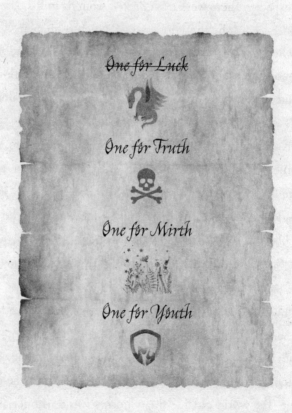

One for Luck

One for Truth

One for Mirth

One for Youth

Across from her, Jacks stirred.

Evangeline slowly lifted her eyes from the page in time to see his shoulders shudder—as if he was having a bad dream.

She wondered, briefly, what sort of things might haunt Jacks. He had once told her the story of the girl who'd made his heart beat again—the one girl who had survived his fatal kiss. She was supposed to be his one true love, but instead she stabbed him in the heart and chose to love another. At the time, Evangeline had believed that was Jacks's greatest tragedy, but now she suspected there were even deeper wounds in his past.

Once again, she thought about the picture she'd seen of the Merrywood Three. She knew Jacks said they had died and that the storybooks lied. Yet she couldn't completely dispel the idea that Jacks was part of this trio.

If only she knew more about them. All she knew was that Lyric Merrywood was the son of a lord.

The archer wasn't named, but she was still drawn to the idea that he was the Archer from *The Ballad of the Archer and the Fox*.

Then there was Castor Valor, the prince.

According to the stories, all the Valors had been beheaded. But if anyone could have escaped death, it would have been Jacks. And if Jacks had been the only Valor to survive, if he'd lived to see his whole family killed, then of course it would have destroyed him. It also explained why he would want to open the Valory Arch—as one of the Valors, he would know better than anyone what the Valory contained.

Jacks rolled his neck and made a sound somewhere between a sigh and a groan. He was waking up.

Evangeline turned her gaze out the window before he opened his eyes and caught her staring.

Outside, the scenery had shifted. She wondered if they'd taken a wrong turn. Gone were the snowdrifts and winter birds. Murky gray replaced the blue of the skies and turned the snow on the ground to sludge.

In her father's curiosity shop, Evangeline had once opened a very fine-looking crate of imported storybooks from the Icehaven Isles. The covers were lovely mint-green leather, with rose-gold embossing and the most beautiful foil designs. She'd felt impossibly eager to open them and see what sort of tales were inside. But all she'd found was ash, as if someone had set a match to the center of the pages and burned away each word.

This place reminded her of those books, but instead of words, it was color and feeling and hope that had been vanquished—it was green needles on trees and red painted doors and blue cobblestones. Even the color of the snow had been leached away, turning it a despairing shade of gray.

In the distance, it looked as if there might have been a village once, but now there were only the bones of dead cottages and abandoned pieces of a township. The road changed as well, turning bumpy and craggy and shaking the carriage as it wended its way through a forest of skeletal trees without any leaves.

Evangeline shivered. She hadn't realized until that moment that the coach had been growing colder and colder. The heated bricks at her feet had lost their warmth, and now they felt like ice. She tried to pull her cloak tighter, but it didn't help. It was as if this chill were a living thing. Fog seeped in through the cracks around the carriage door, smelling faintly of decay. It covered her boots and froze her toes as the coach rocked over a great gash in the road that nearly jostled her out of her seat.

"Don't fret, Little Fox, it's just this place," Jacks said, but his voice lacked its usual swagger.

"Where are we?" Evangeline asked. Her voice sounded brittle—a frightened thing that wanted to close the curtains and look away. Yet she could not take her eyes off the unsettling scene.

As the carriage kept rumbling on, the village disappeared, and for a stretch, there was nothing but the charred remains of trees. She thought she perhaps saw some sort of inn still intact, but the place was too far away, and then they were nearing a sign that took the breath right from her lungs.

WELCOME TO THE GREAT
MERRYWOOD MANOR!

The sign was as desolate as everything else, chipped and faded, and as sad as the feeling that was growing inside her. Her cheeks became wet with tears. She might never have been here before, but the sign reminded her of the way the book described House Merrywood—the Merrywoods were said to be joyful, generous people, and their home was a place of warmth and love. But all that remained of this house was the carcass of a once magnificent staircase that climbed out of a great pile of ash into nothing.

"Here's the answer to your questions about the Merrywood Three," said Jacks darkly.

"They did this?" Evangeline asked.

"No. This is where they all died." He turned away from the window. He didn't meet her gaze, but she could see the light in his eyes was gone. His gaze was now as gray as the world outside of the window.

Evangeline didn't know if Jacks was actually feeling an emotion that resembled something human or if it was just the power of this terrible place.

Then she remembered Tiberius's words about the arch stones: *I saw the ruins—I felt the horrible hollowing magic. Just bringing the stones together is potentially cataclysmic.* She hadn't wanted to believe him then. She'd held one of the stones. It had felt powerful, but not catastrophically so. And yet what else could have caused this sort of desolation? What was powerful enough to destroy not just a place but all hope and joy?

"What exactly happened here?" she asked. "Is this the Great House that was destroyed by the Valory Arch stones?"

Jacks's eyes snapped back to hers. "How did you hear that story?"

"I must have read it in a book."

"You're lying." His lips pressed into a fine line. "That's Protectorate rhetoric. The stones didn't do this. They're powerful, but this was not their destruction."

"How do you know?"

"Because I know what really happened here."

Evangeline swiped the tears from her eyes and did her best to narrow them at Jacks.

He responded with a sliver of a laugh. "As much as I enjoy the theatrics, if you don't believe me, all you have to do is ask what happened."

Suddenly, she felt even more skeptical. Jacks was never forthcoming with information. But she wasn't about to pass up a chance to question him. "What really happened, then?"

He turned back to the window. For a minute, she didn't think he'd respond. Then he said in an unexpectedly muted voice, "Lyric Merrywood, son of Lord Merrywood, had the misfortune of falling in love with Aurora Valor."

Evangeline was familiar with Lyric Merrywood. And of course, she also knew the famed Aurora Valor, the most beautiful girl to ever live.

"Lyric," Jacks went on in that same reticent voice, "was Lord Merrywood's only son, and he was too good-hearted to realize what a mistake it was to love Aurora Valor."

"Why was it a mistake?" Evangeline asked. "I thought Aurora was beautiful and sweet and kind and everything a princess should be." The last words came out a little bitter, and Evangeline realized she felt an inexplicable dislike of the princess, though as far as she knew, Aurora Valor had done nothing wrong aside from sound perfect in every tale.

"You don't like her," Jacks guessed.

"She just sounds too good to be true."

"Lyric certainly didn't think so," said Jacks in a tone that didn't reveal if he agreed or disagreed. "He was so desperately in love with her, he dismissed the dangerous fact that she was engaged to Vengeance Slaughterwood."

"Aurora was his bride-to-be!" Evangeline exclaimed.

Jacks looked at her askance. "That's what I just said."

"I know—I just got a little excited because I saw a picture of Vengeance in a book, but his fiancée wasn't identified."

Jacks appeared briefly surprised by this before continuing. "Lyric said the engagement didn't matter because it wasn't a love match: Aurora and Vengeance had been betrothed since Aurora's birth. Vengeance's father, Bane, had been Wolfric Valor's greatest friend and ally. So, when Wolfric became king, he pledged that one of his daughters would marry Bane's eldest son.

"Aurora tried to break off the wedding to marry Lyric, but her father refused. Wolfric said Aurora was a silly girl who knew nothing of love." Jacks's mouth twisted wryly, and again, she couldn't tell if he felt the same or not. "Aurora knew that no one ever won a fight with Wolfric. So she told her father that she would go through with the marriage to Vengeance. But on the morning of the wedding, she ran away. That was when Vengeance learned of her affair with Lyric Merrywood, and let's just say Vengeance lived up to his name...."

The coach rumbled forward as Jacks trailed off. They'd left the gray and the ruins behind, returning to a world of crisp, white snow. The sun was out again, shining its cheery light and adding flecks of iridescent color to the ice on the trees.

Jacks turned away from the window as if he couldn't stand the sight of it all.

Or perhaps it was the sign up ahead that he didn't wish to see.

YOU ARE ENTERING
THE LANDS OF
HOUSE SLAUGHTERWOOD

Welcome, if you are a guest!
Beware, if you are not . . .

Evangeline doubted she would have felt warmed by this sign under any circumstances. But after Jacks's story, the greeting felt especially unsettling.

She reminded herself that the story curse could have twisted part of Jacks's tale. But his story explained the two different engagement pictures she'd seen of Vengeance, and Jacks hadn't struggled for words. His quiet voice had possessed an understated confidence as if he'd not just heard the story but had been there to experience it.

Jacks had repeatedly told her he didn't care about anyone or anything. But it was hard to believe him right now. Maybe that's why he'd turned his head away from the light—so it wouldn't shine on him and illuminate how he really felt.

The thought made something inside of her ache for him.

Before she could think better of it, Evangeline leaned across the carriage and put her hand atop his.

Jacks sighed as if disappointed. "Don't feel sorry for me, Little Fox. I told you, this place makes everyone sad." He pulled his hand away with a scowl. But it couldn't quite hide the sorrow that was still deep in his eyes.

She couldn't help but feel for him. Again, she considered the idea that Jacks was hurting because he was Castor Valor. The last of the Valors, the only survivor of a royal family whom the people of the North had seemed to love until they'd brutally killed them, and friend to a young man who had also been murdered. But Castor Valor hadn't been in this story, and neither had the third member of the Merrywood Three, the Archer.

Evangeline might not have pressed the matter. But Jacks had made it clear he didn't want to be treated with care. And the more she thought about the story, the more she wondered if Jacks had only told it to her so that she'd feel as if he'd opened up and she wouldn't ask more questions.

"Your story didn't mention Lyric's friends—Castor Valor and the Archer. Did Vengeance Slaughterwood kill them as well?"

"Only Castor," Jacks said flatly. "He was the noble one out of the group. He'd tried to warn Lyric of the attack, but he ended up getting killed as well."

Evangeline watched Jacks's handsome face closely for any sign that he was lying—a flicker of something that would tell her he was really Castor—but Jacks could be so difficult to read sometimes. All she sensed was that he fit somewhere into this story and that it had something to do with why he wanted to open the Valory Arch.

"If you really weren't a member of the Merrywood Three, then how do you know all of this?"

"Everyone who was alive then knew the story. Aurora Valor was a princess, Castor was a prince, and Lyric and Vengeance were sons of lords."

"What about the Archer?"

"He was no one," Jacks said coldly, "except maybe to the Fox. But I've already told you how that story ended." He gave her a smile that was all teeth, as if warning her away.

For a second, she wondered if perhaps she was wrong about him being Castor. Maybe Jacks was actually the Archer, and he wanted to open the Valory Arch to somehow save the Fox.

The thought should have felt romantic, but instead, it struck a false chord with Evangeline.

"Now," Jacks said sharply, "it's my turn to ask questions, and I want to know where you heard that ridiculous story about the arch stones destroying one of the Great Houses."

Evangeline hesitated.

"Come now, Little Fox, you can't expect me to tell you things if you won't tell me things."

"I went to see Tiberius," she confessed.

"You what?" he snarled.

"Oh no—you don't get to be upset. You were gone. You wrote me a note that was practically two words and left me alone in a castle full of vampires."

"And because of that, you just thought you'd go have a chat with the person who tried to kill you twice?"

"I wasn't having any luck in the library. I thought he might know where the stones were hidden."

Jacks's only response was a look that said he wanted to pull over the coach, take her up to an isolated tower, and throw away the key.

"He's locked in a prison," she said. "It was perfectly safe."

"He wants you dead. That's a powerful motive to try to escape."

"But he didn't," Evangeline persisted. "What else was I supposed to do? You said yourself the books all lie."

Jacks raked a violent hand through his hair. "Did Tiberius suggest we go to this party?"

"No, he refused to help, even after I told him that my life was linked to his brother's."

"You told him that?" Jacks's nostrils flared. "If Tiberius shares this with anyone from the Protectorate, they'll find and kill Apollo in order to kill you."

For a flash, Jacks looked like he wanted to kill someone, too.

"Calm down, Jacks. When I visited Tiberius at the Tower, it looked as if the Protectorate had abandoned him. Even if I'm wrong, I truly don't think that Tiberius would put his brother in danger again. He wouldn't help me open the arch, but he looked conflicted about it. I don't believe he really wants to kill his brother."

"You give people too much credit," Jacks grumbled. "And you should have told me this right away."

"Why, so you could kill him?"

"Yes."

"No, Jacks. You can't go around murdering people because they're a problem."

"You can't save everyone and yourself. How do you think you're going to get those stones?" His voice turned hard and a little mean. "Do you believe the owners will just hand them over because you give them a pretty smile? If the stones are here, people are going to die at this party."

"No—I'm not going to kill anyone to get the stones. And neither are you."

"Then why are we even here?" Jacks sneered.

The coach rolled over the mighty drawbridge that led to Slaughterwood Castle, and Evangeline took it as an excuse to look away from Jacks. This was exactly why she was always reminding herself not to trust him. Of course he would think the only way to get what they wanted was to murder someone for it.

Evangeline could not let Jacks ruin this. She knew he was bitter about the past, and she didn't blame him for that. She also wondered if he thought LaLa's engagement didn't matter because as the Unwed Bride she was likely not to get married. But Evangeline still refused to believe that. In a world where there were Fates and magic and curses and prophecies, Evangeline couldn't help but believe there was also the potential for everyone to find a happily ever after.

She squared her shoulders and turned back to Jacks with new determination. "LaLa is my friend, this is her engagement party, and it is going to be magical. No one is going to die at this celebration. You are not going to kill people while we're here."

Jacks leaned back in his seat and picked up his apple, mouth twisting into a sullen frown. "That's a terrible plan, Little Fox." He took a wide bite, sharp teeth tearing at the fruit. "Someone is going to die. It will either be one of them or one of us."

23

The grounds were warmer than Evangeline would have expected—especially for a House with the word *slaughter* in its name. Nearing the castle felt like stepping into a tale that a bard might share in front of a fire as travelers drank ale and ate stew.

This place was old. The kind of old that changed the scent of the air. Evangeline was still sitting in the carriage, but as they neared the looming castle, she swore she could smell the dust of long-ago battles and the smoke from hearth fires that had burned centuries ago. Even the grainy flaxen light pouring from the countless windows looked like a remnant of the past.

After their carriage came to a halt, Evangeline followed Jacks outside. She didn't know if any of the missing arch stones had already arrived around the necks of other guests. But she did not feel any hints of the mirth stone as she and Jacks neared the row of waiting servants. They lined the drive like decorative soldiers, dressed in immaculate silver coats stitched up to mimic armor.

Two servants darted toward the coach to grab their luggage. Several of the other maids and grooms grinned and nodded at Jacks; he was practically scowling, and yet he still managed to dazzle. Evangeline did not have the same effect. She smiled at everyone, but the few servants who looked her way did so with disdain, all narrowed eyes and flattened lips.

She tried not to let it bother her—it could have simply been that the servants were feeling cold or that she was feeling frayed. But then she heard the words, spoken in tones too loud to be called whispers.

"I still think she killed the prince."

"I don't know why everyone raves about her hair."

"She should go back to where she came from."

Jacks dropped a heavy arm around her shoulders, sending a shock straight through her as he pulled her suddenly close. "Want me to kill any of them for you?"

"No, they're just gossiping."

"Then what if I merely give them the urge to cut out their own tongues?" he asked, flashing one of his dimples.

Evangeline stifled a giggle, though she knew she shouldn't be amused. She had no doubt he was serious about the tongues. "Don't you dare—"

"You sure? They deserve it." *The whole House deserves it.*

The thought was so quiet, Evangeline wasn't sure Jacks intended for her to hear it. But before she could remark on it,

LaLa was there, bursting through the manor's double doors in a welcoming shower of golden, dragon-scale-shaped sequins and open arms.

"It's so good to see you, my friend!" She wrapped Evangeline in a hug that made everything feel warm. Until that moment, Evangeline hadn't known how much she needed a hug. *When was the last time someone had hugged her?*

It had probably been LaLa, which made Evangeline squeeze her friend extra tightly. "I'm so glad to be here."

"Not as glad as I am. Most of the guests are Robin's friends, so I was thrilled when you wrote and said you could make it." LaLa's grin was incandescent as she pulled away. "You two are the last ones to arrive. Everyone else is changing for dinner. Except for those who went out to hunt some poor little beastie, Robin included. So you'll have to meet him later."

"I still can't believe you're engaged to him," Jacks muttered.

LaLa's pretty smile hardened. "You do not get to judge my choices, Jacks. Evangeline told me what you did. I know how you framed her for murder and poisoned Apollo."

Jacks shrugged insouciantly. "It was to open the arch. I'd have thought you'd approve. Or—"

"Shhh—" LaLa hissed. "You can't talk about such things in this house."

Jacks groaned. "First, I can't kill anyone or cut out any tongues—"

"Whose tongue did you want to cut out?" LaLa interrupted.

"Just a few of your fiancé's servants'."

"Actually, that might not be a bad idea," LaLa said, and Evangeline had a horrible feeling that her friend was not joking, either.

Fortunately, LaLa was smiling again as she ushered Jacks and Evangeline inside the manor.

It smelled like mulled wine and possessed all the grandness that Evangeline had come to expect from the Great Houses of the North. The arched ceilings were dramatically high, and the floors were covered in a mosaic of tiles that depicted men and women in battle, holding up swords or shields or the occasional bloodied head.

The history of House Slaughterwood seemed to clearly fit its name. Instead of books on shelves, there were more ancient weapons—war hammers, morning stars, maces, crossbows, and battle-axes. Every person who made it into a painting on the wall wore armor, save for one woman. She had a pleasant face and a very warm smile, and she reappeared in portraits quite often as LaLa led Jacks and Evangeline up a grand set of stairs.

It took Evangeline a minute, but eventually, she recognized the woman as someone she'd seen a picture of last night— Glendora. She'd been Vengeance Slaughterwood's second bride-to-be—and unlike Aurora, Glendora had clearly gone on to marry him.

It seemed terribly unfair that Vengeance could destroy a whole House and then have a family of his own. Evangeline might have remarked upon it, but she didn't want to bring any grief to LaLa by mentioning ugliness from the past.

"Here we are," LaLa said shortly after they reached the fourth floor. "This is one of my favorite suites." LaLa's arms swung wide as she opened a door with a cheery *swoosh*.

Snow fell like magic outside the suite's bay windows, adding a little whimsy to the early night and to the room, which was fitted with an enormous roaring fireplace, thick fur carpets, a lovely window seat, and a striking four-poster bed with a voluminous velvet quilt the color of sparkling wine.

"The view is truly spectacular," said LaLa. "In the morning, you'll be able to see Glendora Slaughterwood's famed winter garden.

"And here are just a few party favors," she trilled, motioning toward a large pile of wrapped parcels. "I also included a gown for tonight, in case your things were too wrinkled, and there's a dress for tomorrow as well, in case you forgot to pack a costume."

"That's so very generous," Jacks said, somehow making it sound like an insult as he wandered to an ancient desk and picked up a bookend shaped like a tiny dragon.

LaLa's smile faded. "Put that down, Jacks. Your room is in a different wing."

"No." He plopped into the leather chair and kicked his buckled boots up onto the desk. "I'm staying next door to Evangeline."

"You can't," LaLa protested. "The Darlings are there."

"Then move them to a different room. Every time I leave this girl alone, someone tries to kill her." Jacks's voice stayed friendly, but his eyes turned to two ice blades as he said, "Right now, there's a curse on her husband, and it's a nasty piece of work that forces him to hunt her down like a fox."

LaLa's face turned stricken. "Evangeline—"

"Please don't worry, my friend. I didn't mention it when I wrote because I didn't want to spoil your engagement." Evangeline gave Jacks a pointed look.

He shrugged and tossed the little dragon as if it were an apple. "It's not as if she's really going to marry him."

"Jacks—" Evangeline hissed.

"I'm just speaking the truth. We all know who LaLa really is—or at least I do." He threw the dragon higher.

Mortified was not a strong enough word for how Evangeline felt just then.

"I'm so sorry," Evangeline said to LaLa. "Jacks must have left his manners in the carriage. You don't need to put him next door to me. You could place him in the barn—or the dungeon if there is one."

"No, Jacks is right," said LaLa. "If you're in danger, he should stay close."

She wore her smile again, but it was starting to look rumpled, like a piece of clothing that had been taken off and put back on too many times. Not even the golden sequins of her gown could make it dazzle.

Evangeline felt partly responsible. "LaLa—I'm so sorry for bringing my tragedy here."

"Please don't apologize. Parties aren't any fun without a little drama. I should really be thanking you." LaLa gave Evangeline a smile that was perhaps a little too wide.

Evangeline pretended she believed her. She smiled back as if curses and murderous princes were things that merely lived inside stories. And for an odd moment, the only one in the room who appeared entirely honest was Jacks. He set the dragon on the desk with a thump and stalked out the door. Although he'd actually won his fight about the room, he appeared even unhappier than before.

"I'm really sorry about him," Evangeline said.

LaLa waved a hand as if it were nothing. "I'm used to Jacks's mercurial moods. And he's always disliked House Slaughterwood."

"He told me Chaos was the one who had a problem with the House," Evangeline replied, although after Jacks's story in the coach, it was clear he disliked the Great House as well. But now she was curious as to whether his story could be entirely trusted. She didn't want to repeat it—the murderous tale of Vengeance Slaughterwood hardly seemed appropriate talk for LaLa's engagement party—and yet she wondered if her friend could confirm if the tale was true. "Jacks also told me that House Slaughterwood is the reason we are all in this mess."

LaLa sighed heavily. "House Slaughterwood has done terrible things, but we've all done terrible things for love."

She grinned then, making Evangeline suspect that LaLa's definition of *terrible things* was a bit like Jacks's: they really didn't matter as long as they got a person what they wanted.

She left seconds later, with a kiss on Evangeline's cheek and some words about getting changed into something quickly for dinner.

After a day of riding in a carriage, Evangeline felt like soaking in a bath instead of changing, but she had no idea when Jacks would return, and she didn't want him walking in on her as she dressed.

She started to sort through the clothes that LaLa had left.

Then she heard the whispers.

"Careful . . ."

"Archer's curse . . . hunting . . . almost killed her."

The words came from the room next door, low and hushed. Evangeline shouldn't have been able to hear them, and she definitely shouldn't have tiptoed closer to listen better—but it sounded like Jacks and LaLa, and they were obviously talking about her and Apollo.

Evangeline cupped her hands to the wall and clearly heard Jacks ask, "Can you undo the curse?"

Her breath caught in her throat. He couldn't have meant *that* curse. The Archer's curse was the only reason she'd agreed to open the arch.

She listened closer. LaLa's voice was barely a whisper. "I'm sorry. Nothing has changed since you came here last week. There's still nothing I can do."

"You can try."

"You know there's no cure."

"You can try to find one," Jacks ground out. "She could die."

"You won't let her."

"I—" He growled. An angry sound that shook the wall.

For a second, there was nothing else but the heavy beat of Evangeline's heart. Either Jacks spoke too low, or she didn't hear what he said over all her swirling thoughts. He'd told her not to look for a cure to the Archer's curse. He'd repeatedly said it was pointless. But it seemed as if he was doing just that. Based on what LaLa had said about *last week,* it seemed as if this was what Jacks had been doing while he was away.

Evangeline reminded herself that she still couldn't trust him. She knew she was just a tool to him, and as LaLa had said, humans that became too close to Jacks always died. Even if Jacks was trying to break the Archer's curse, he undoubtedly still had another horrible plan to make sure that she opened the arch.

Evangeline couldn't let herself think that Jacks's search for a cure meant he cared for her. She knew this was true, yet it was getting just a little harder to fully believe it. Because *she* was starting to care for *him.*

"How close are you to finding the stones?" LaLa asked.

"We need three."

For a beat . . . nothing.

Then, very softly, from LaLa: "I hope you brought enough apples."

E vangeline may have been unsure about a number of
things, but she knew for certain that LaLa had given
her the most magnificent dress for dinner.

The gown made Evangeline feel as if she were wearing a
happily ever after. She'd curled her pink hair and piled it loosely
atop her head, pinning it in place with jeweled flower-shaped
clips, so as to better show off the gown's daring neckline. The
cut left her shoulders mostly bare, save for the delicate straps
that plunged down into a flattering V-cut neckline formed of
ethereal fabric that looked as if it had been wept by the stars.
Chips of broken gems, shimmering in shades of pink and blue
and violet, covered the bodice and then gently dispersed over
the hips of a flowing skirt with a slit that went up to her thigh.
It was bold, and it made her feel adventurous as she spun in
front of the wardrobe mirror, twirling until the broken gems
glittered to life.

"What exactly are you doing?" Jacks drawled.

The breath left her lungs, and the broken heart scar on her wrist caught fire. She hadn't even heard him enter. Evangeline stopped mid-twirl, her skirts still swishing as she caught his dashing reflection in the mirror.

Her heart gave a silly jolt. She tried to stop it. But while Jacks was many terrible things, there was no denying that he was also painfully handsome. It was the golden hair. In certain lights, it looked like real gold, shining over eyes that glittered more than human eyes ever could. So maybe it was the eyes as well. And perhaps she could blame a little on his lips. They were perfect, of course, and right now they were smiling with amusement.

"So, this is what you do when I'm not around?"

Evangeline felt the sudden urge to hide inside her wardrobe, but she tamped it down as she turned and met his gaze with a smile of her own. "You think about what I do when you're not around?"

"Careful, Little Fox." He took a step forward. "You sound rather excited by the idea."

"I'm not, I assure you," she said, wishing she didn't sound so breathless. "I merely like the thought that I torment you as much as you torment me."

Jacks flashed one of his dimples, making him look deceptively charming. "So you're the one who thinks about what I do when you're not around?"

"Only because I know you're up to no good."

"No good." He laughed as he said the words. "I would hope you know by now that I'm up to far worse than just 'no good.'" Jacks slid his arm through hers.

Her stomach tumbled. She would have pulled away, but she didn't want to reveal how much he affected her. Although she had a feeling he already knew, or he wouldn't have taken her arm and pulled her so close to his side.

"Remember," she said instead, "no killing anyone here."

Jacks gave her an impressive scowl. "Some of these people deserve to die, you know."

"But it's LaLa's party," she reminded him.

He looked as if he wanted to keep arguing. It was actually impressive the way he held on to his scowl as they went down flight after flight of steps to the great dining hall of Slaughterwood Castle.

"Can you at least try to smile?" she asked.

He flashed his teeth.

"That looks predatory."

"I am predatory. *So is everyone else here,*" he whispered.

At the door, knights in full armor greeted them by uncrossing a pair of lances, and once again, Evangeline felt as if she were entering an old tale.

A small forest must have been killed to build this dining room. The arched ceilings were at least five stories high, and Evangeline immediately saw why.

There was a trebuchet just beyond the entry, massive and rather horrible. The dining hall had clearly been built around the enormous weapon—in fact, the whole manor might have been.

Jacks appeared unimpressed by the structure, barely sparing it a look as they stepped deeper into the hall.

Aside from the trebuchet, everything else was tasteful. The walls were covered in panels of aged stained glass that glittered under sprawling chandeliers shaped like branches of jeweled flowers. Then there were the actual flowers. Garlands of gold and white blooms had been strung from wall to wall, filling the air with their sweet perfume as some of the petals drifted down like snow, covering the shoulders of guests who had started pouring into the seemingly endless room.

LaLa had yet to arrive, but the hall was buzzing with gentlemen wearing embroidered doublets and ladies with tiaras in their hair, baubles in their ears, and sparkling gems at their wrists and throats. So many gems. Any one of them could have been a missing arch stone. But thus far, Evangeline didn't feel any magic pulsing from the people she brushed past. She'd have liked to talk to some of them, but they all made a point of not looking her way.

This party was not going at all how she'd imagined. In her head, she'd pictured an event infused with the magic of the mirth stone, full of joy and smiles. But it seemed the only smiles were for Jacks.

Passing guests nodded at him, remarked on the new brilliant color of his hair, or waved and said, "Good evening, Lord Jacks."

There were no greetings for Evangeline. The servants carrying platters of meats and trays of heavy goblets were treated with more regard than she was.

"It's because you're not from a Great House," Jacks said quietly. "You could be the queen and they still wouldn't like you."

"They all seem to like you," she whispered.

Just then, a pair of girls drifted closer. One wet her lips before smiling at Jacks, and the other was even bolder. Evangeline watched her meet Jacks's eyes before brazenly bringing a goblet of wine to her breasts and tracing the low cut of her dark plum gown with the rim.

"Are you controlling them?" Evangeline asked.

"Don't need to." Jacks winked at the pair.

They giggled in response.

Evangeline decided she didn't like the sound of giggling.

She pulled her arm free of Jacks's. The room was feeling hot and stuffy and far from magical. "Maybe we should visit the veranda to look for the stones," she said.

But Jacks was no longer paying attention to her.

His eyes were on the door where another young woman had just walked in. An extremely beautiful girl dressed in a tight, low-cut raven-black gown and long black gloves that contrasted with the moonlight-colored hair that spilled down her back in a long shimmering curtain.

"Do you know her?" Evangeline asked.

"She looks familiar," Jacks said quietly, eyes still fixed on the young woman as she glided into the hall and took a pewter goblet of wine.

Evangeline had no reason to dislike this girl and her moon-light hair. Yet she felt something twist inside her as she watched Jacks's eyes follow the young woman. She moved through the crowd toward a pair of well-dressed young men, who appeared more than happy to engage her in flirtations.

Thankfully, she wasn't wearing a necklace or a bracelet that Evangeline could see. Though even if she had worn ropes of jewels around her throat, Evangeline would have put off talking to her.

She cast her eyes about the great firelit hall to continue her search. She mostly looked at the women and the rocks around their throats. But there were also quite a few men with gemmed buttons on their doublets and jeweled medallions around their necks. Some of the medallions even had impressions of shields, though unfortunately none of the shields had flames like the one on Evangeline's sheet of clues.

Across the room, a young man smiled when he caught her spying.

He was handsome, and she didn't look away. He wasn't wear-ing a medallion, but he did have jewels on his silver doublet. They sparkled as he took a second goblet from a servant and held it out as an offering. *Hello*, he mouthed.

Evangeline cut a quick look at Jacks.

He was still distracted by the girl with the moonlight hair.

She took this as a chance to step away and cross the room toward the gentleman with the drink.

He wasn't quite so young or attractive up close. But his sapphire buttons were very sparkly, and his voice was kind. "It's a pleasure to finally meet you. I'm Almond Froggly."

He held out the drink.

Jacks intercepted the wine before she could take it. "Go away, Almond. Evangeline isn't going to marry you."

Almond's cheeks flushed red as beets, and without another word, he did as Jacks commanded.

"Jacks," Evangeline hissed. "I was just talking to him to see if he had the stones."

"He didn't," Jacks said. "Someone that boring couldn't have magic. And he's not from one of the Great Houses."

"That doesn't mean you can just control him."

"No controlling, no killing. You're taking all the fun out of this party, Little Fox." Jacks drank from the goblet of wine in his hand. "Since we're looking for magic stones, we need to talk to people who seem magical."

He tipped his drink toward a trio of girls wearing glorious forest-green dresses and tiaras that sparkled like treasure. "They're all from House Darling."

They were beautiful as well. Clearly sisters, from the look of it. They were all graceful moves and serene smiles as they sipped their drinks and waved away servants with trays of meat pies and honeycomb-drenched cheeses.

Evangeline tried to remember what she'd read about House Darling as they approached and all three girls widened their smiles to genuine grins at the sight of Jacks.

"It's so wonderful to see you, Lord Jacks." The tallest of the sisters put her hand on his cheek, and Evangeline felt that horrible twist inside of her again.

Sense any magic? Jacks asked silently.

Evangeline shook her head. She hoped that would mean they would walk away. But although Jacks wasn't usually nice to anyone, he was being polite to these sisters.

"Why have you not come to visit?" said the girl who'd touched his cheek. "And when did you change your hair?"

She reached up again to run her fingers through Jacks's golden locks. Evangeline felt a surge of discomfort and took that moment to step away again. And—

She crashed into the chest of a tall young man with thick black hair, smooth bronze skin, and a smile that made her knees weak.

25

Evangeline was not too proud to admit that she was easily dazzled. She liked pretty stories and pretty things, and this young man was far more than just pretty.

"I'm sorry," she said, and she couldn't even feel embarrassed that she was breathless.

His voice was deep and his handsome face was touched with a smile that widened as he said, "It's entirely my fault. I was hoping to bump into you, and I may have been a little too eager."

He reached for her hand, and Evangeline felt a sudden thrill. He wore a ring! A shining, roughly cut black jewel. A powerful thing that looked as if it could have been enchanted.

She waited to feel a zing of magic from his ring as he took her fingers and brought them to his lips, but there was merely that gentle tingly feeling that came from being appraised by someone who found her attractive.

"I'm Merrick of House Redthorne," he said.

"I'm Evangeline."

"And I'm Jacks," Jacks said, appearing beside Evangeline, no longer wearing the smile he'd shared with the Darling girls. "How's your new wife, Merrick?"

The young man blanched. "She passed last autumn."

"How tragic." Jacks's voice was all false surprise. "Didn't your previous wife pass the autumn just before that one?"

"She did. I've had quite bad luck," Merrick bit out.

"Well, then it's probably best you not pass it on to Evangeline." Jacks grabbed her arm.

She started to object, but before she could finish, Merrick Redthorne was gone.

Evangeline glowered at Jacks.

"You're welcome," he said smugly.

"You didn't have to scare him away. I wasn't going to marry him."

"Good, because if you did, you'd be dead next autumn." He dropped her arm.

Evangeline gritted her teeth. Of course Jacks could flirt with girls, but she couldn't even talk to a man. "I'm already married, Jacks. I was speaking to Merrick because he had a ring with a stone!"

"Everyone in here has a ring."

"You don't."

"In case you've forgotten, I am not everyone, Little Fox." His eyes dropped to her lips, searing her mouth with one sharp look and instantly reminding her of what he could do with a single kiss.

Evangeline bit down on her lip, just to taunt him back.

Something primal flashed behind Jacks's eyes—desire or anger, she couldn't quite tell. All she knew was that her mouth felt swollen from the force of his gaze and the inescapable sense that he wished to be the one biting down on her lip instead.

And for a second, she wondered what that would be like. She imagined him taking her lips right there, in the middle of the party, tangling his fingers through her hair, holding her close while everyone watched.

She tried to shove the idea away, but it seemed she wasn't fast enough.

Jacks's mouth kicked up as if he knew what she'd been thinking, and then his gaze plunged lower, moving from her lips to her neck, until it rested on the swell of her breasts, where her heart was suddenly pounding.

Laughter trilled in the background and glasses clinked together, but it sounded much farther away than it should have. Evangeline could no longer feel the crushing warmth of all the guests; there was only Jacks. He watched her the way you weren't supposed to watch someone when they knew that you were looking—bold and unabashed and utterly inappropriate.

"You're looking a little hot, Little Fox. Perhaps you should step outside while I keep searching for the stones." His eyes left hers and landed once again on the young woman with the moonlight hair, who was now surrounded by half a dozen young men who were practically salivating. "She looks a little magical. I think I'll start with her."

"She doesn't have stones," Evangeline said tightly. "What about—"

She tossed a look in the other direction, right as LaLa arrived on the arm of a young man who must have been Lord Robin Slaughterwood. He had wild red hair, two swords strapped to his waist, and a laugh that carried across the hall like celebratory music.

"We should greet Robin and LaLa."

Jacks's gaze immediately darkened. "We need to keep searching for the stones."

"I know—that's why we should say hello. Look at the way people respond to Robin. He could have the mirth stone."

Evangeline didn't actually see any stones on Robin—even his family ring appeared to be made of metal instead of gems—but his wide grin was infectious. As he and LaLa worked through the crush, they left a trail of laughter. Within seconds, the party seemed more alive. Conversations grew louder, smiles notched wider, goblets practically leaped from serving platters into hands.

"It's also the polite thing to do," said Evangeline.

Jacks sighed reluctantly.

Evangeline imagined that was as close to a yes as she'd receive. A moment later, they were queued to greet the happy couple.

LaLa, of course, embraced Evangeline immediately. "I knew that dress would be a dream on you. You look ravishing, my friend!"

"So do you," Evangeline said.

LaLa was always radiant, and tonight was no exception. She

wore a series of gold and pearled headbands that dripped even more pearls and gold into her long dark hair, making it look like ocean treasure. Her eyes were lined in gold as well. But her dress was oddly plain. LaLa had changed from her dazzling sequined gown into a sedate burgundy dress with long conservative sleeves that covered up the vibrant dragon fire tattooed on her arms.

Evangeline might have thought it had something to do with Robin—perhaps he didn't approve of tattoos. But he didn't seem to have a disapproving disposition, and he had a sword tattooed along his forearm. So that could not be it.

"This is my fiancé." LaLa looked up at Robin adoringly, and he smiled down on her with all the gentle focus of someone very much in love. And it didn't appear to have anything to do with a magical stone. Now that they were closer, she could see for sure that Robin wore no gems.

As he turned to Evangeline, his grin shifted from affectionate to delighted.

"Finally, the infamous Evangeline Fox! LaLa has told me the stories aren't true, but I've loved hearing them." Robin wrapped her in a bear of a hug, briefly robbing Evangeline of breath, before he set her feet back on the ground. "You are very welcome to my home."

"Thank you for inviting me, and congratulations on your engagement. I'm so very happy for both of you."

"As am I," Jacks drawled.

Robin turned to him. "I don't believe we've had the honor of meeting?"

"This is Lord Jacks," LaLa inserted.

"Lord Jacks," Robin repeated, still smiling but looking vaguely perplexed. "Which House are you from?"

"I'm from a very old House." Jacks took a sip from his goblet. "Everyone in my family died a long time ago."

LaLa's smile fell away. For a second, she looked as if she could have strangled Jacks with her small hands, but instead, she slipped an arm through Evangeline's. "Shall we start the procession to the dining table? I don't know about all of you, but I'm famished."

This put a smile back on Robin's face, but Evangeline felt unsettled as she and LaLa started toward a long table laid out with a lavish feast. There were cooked swans, stuffed goats' heads, and what looked like a baked rooster riding atop a cooked pig.

Evangeline lost sight of Jacks in the procession, but she couldn't stop thinking about what he'd said. *I'm from a very old House. Everyone in my family died a long time ago.*

He could easily have been talking about the Valors. All of them were dead, but then so was everyone from House Merrywood.

It was tempting to ask LaLa about the comment, but her friend had looked so unsettled, Evangeline didn't have the heart to bring it up. And it was probably better if, tonight, Evangeline focused on finding the missing stones, not Jacks's past.

Although she couldn't shake the feeling that Jacks's mysterious past was the entire reason he wanted to open the Valory Arch.

During dinner, Evangeline found herself separated from Jacks.

He was at the other end of the table, seated next to the Darling sisters. He seemed to be in good humor again as he tossed an apple and winked at the tallest Darling girl who'd touched his cheek before. She giggled loudly.

Evangeline averted her gaze, determined to return to her search for the stones. But she couldn't seem to focus on anything except the sound of the Darling girl's giggling. It trilled down the table, so light and bright Evangeline swore it made the glassware chime. It also made something terrible twist inside of her. Something a lot like jealousy.

Or maybe it truly was jealousy, as much as Evangeline was loath to admit it.

She didn't want to feel envious for Jacks's attention. She didn't want to wish that he would try to make her laugh, instead of constantly tormenting her. But the feeling was so powerful, so strong, so—

Evangeline suddenly remembered the last time she'd felt emotions this intense. It had been when the luck stone was present. Perhaps this meant another arch stone was near. She recalled then what Jacks had said when he'd warned her about the stones: *People will kill to hold on to their youth. It could also bring about jealousy.*

That was it! The youth stone must be close. Evangeline felt a wave of relief; she wasn't actually jealous, she was just feeling the effects of the youth stone. This was probably what Jacks had been feeling, too, whenever he'd stepped in to prevent her from talking to other young men.

Evangeline's eyes darted around the people sitting near her. On her right sat Almond Froggly, who focused on his mead and didn't so much as twitch her way.

To her left, the seat was still empty. There was just a wooden placard for someone named Petra Youngblood.

"That would be me." The young woman with the moonlight hair glided into the empty chair.

Evangeline stiffened.

She felt instantly guilty about it. She had no reason to dislike this Petra Youngblood. It was jealous and petty—undoubtedly another side effect of the youth stone. Doing her best to shove the feelings aside, Evangeline said, "It's lovely to meet you. I'm Evangeline."

"I think everyone here knows that," Petra said with a conspiratorial wink.

She was friendlier than Evangeline would have imagined. As they chatted, it became easier to shove aside any lingering feelings of jealousy. In fact, after a few minutes, Evangeline was suddenly struck with a peculiarly familiar feeling that she and Petra had met before, or at the very least crossed paths prior to tonight.

"Were you at my wedding?"

"Oh no." Petra laughed softly. "I'm a Youngblood."

"I'm sorry, I'm not familiar with that name."

"Exactly," Petra said wryly. "People like me, who aren't from one of the Great Houses, don't get invited to royal weddings in Valorfell. I'm lucky to have been asked here."

"It didn't really look that way to me, given how all the gentlemen seemed to respond to you." Evangeline regretted the petty words as soon as they were out.

But Petra only widened her pretty smile. "It seems you're not as naive as they say, after all. Although, perhaps you should pay a little more attention to the gentleman *you* came here with." Petra's eyes slowly swept around all the lords and ladies at the table until she eventually paused at the far end where—

Jacks was gone. His seat was vacant; all that remained was an apple core left on his otherwise empty plate. The seat beside his was empty as well—the one where the tall Darling girl had been.

Evangeline felt her stomach drop. She hoped that Jacks hadn't snuck off with this girl to do what Evangeline suddenly feared he might do.

But he wouldn't do that. He couldn't do that. He'd promised not to kill anyone.

Evangeline cast a nervous look about the hall.

Maybe he'd just taken the Darling girl to look at the trebuchet. Or—

"You might want to look toward the portrait door." Petra slowly pointed a gloved finger toward a gilded frame that was slightly cracked away from the wall, revealing an entry behind it.

Evangeline quickly shoved up from the table.

"Wait—" The girl grabbed Evangeline's wrist. For a second, she looked surprisingly concerned. "Just let them go, Princess. All you're going to do is embarrass yourself."

Other people were, indeed, looking her way, judging her over the rims of their goblets. Her pride warred with her to sit back down. There was a chance she was wrong about what Jacks had gone off to do. But she doubted that. If Jacks had covertly left with another girl, she didn't imagine he was simply playing checkers. He was going to kiss her and kill her.

Evangeline left the table. Her stomach churned as she made her way to the edge of the boisterous dining hall and reached the gilded frame that had been pulled away from the wall.

The portrait inside the frame was of Glendora Slaughterwood, wearing an embroidered red gown covered in broken hearts and a smile that looked sad as she watched Evangeline slip through the secret door.

The corridor on the other side was spiderwebbed and dim, and it smelled of secret trysts, musky and more than a little smoky from the torches jutting out of the walls. Between the flames, she caught glimpses of words carved over and over into the stone. *Glory in Death. Glory in Death. Glory in Death.*

Evangeline hugged her arms to her chest. She wasn't sure what this place was, but she didn't like that even the walls seemed to be encouraging Jacks.

Jacks, she cried silently.

There was no response.

Jacks, she tried again. *If you can hear me, I'm asking you to stop whatever you're doing.*

Nothing. Just the brush of her slippers against the aged stones.

And then—her ears caught the thrum of Jacks's seductive voice, saying soft things in the dark. Her chest felt tight. She couldn't determine what he said. But Evangeline knew the low cadence of his voice.

She sped around the corner, nearly ripping the slit of her skirt in her haste.

The torches gleamed brighter, and the smoke grew thicker, swirling around Jacks's golden hair as he dipped his head toward the Darling girl. Her neck was arched and her eyes were closed.

Evangeline's blood rushed to her ears as she watched Jacks trace the girl's lower lip before—

"Stop!" she shouted.

The girl opened her eyes with a gasp.

Jacks was slower to move. He left his fingers on the girl's open mouth as he took his time dragging his hooded eyes to Evangeline. "Your timing is terrible, Little Fox."

I can't believe you were going to kiss her! Evangeline seethed silently.

Jacks lifted a cavalier shoulder and said in a silent voice only Evangeline could hear, *The dinner was getting boring.*

"You really do have terrible luck with boys, don't you?" The Darling girl gave Evangeline an unconvincing frown—the kind that somehow looked like a smile, as if she loved the idea of Evangeline having horrid luck with boys.

For a second, it was tempting to turn away and leave this girl with Jacks to let her see who actually had wretched luck with boys, since she clearly had no idea who the boy she was about to kiss really was.

Evangeline instantly felt ashamed for even having the thought. Yet it still wasn't easy to look the girl in the eye and say, "You need to go right now."

"I think I'm comfortable where I am. You're the one who doesn't belong, *Princess*." She snickered as her hand moved to Jacks's chest and boldly undid one of his buttons.

Evangeline's heart twisted again. She didn't want to feel this. She didn't want to feel anything for Jacks, and she especially didn't want to be jealous of this girl he was about to kill. But jealousy wasn't a reasonable emotion, all it saw was another girl being wanted and touched.

She told herself it was just the youth stone, but they were far from the party now, and this girl wasn't wearing any gems. She'd had a tiara on earlier, but it had been discarded.

You should go, Jacks echoed in Evangeline's thoughts. *I'll clean this up when I'm done.*

His eyes met hers, more black than blue in the torchlight and utterly unmoved as the Darling girl undid another button.

How can you be so unfeeling? Evangeline thought.

Jacks stroked the Darling girl's cheek, his eyes still on Evangeline. *How can you keep mistaking me for someone who cares?*

Go ahead, then. Evangeline crossed her arms over her chest. If he could be terrible, she could be stubborn. *Let's see if your kiss is really worth dying for.*

The torch lamps flickered, and Jacks's gaze darkened.

"What's she still doing here?" the girl moaned. She reached for another one of Jacks's buttons.

He grabbed the girl's hands by the wrists and shoved her away.

"What are you doing?" she screeched.

Jacks sighed. "Go back to dinner, Giselle. Flirt with someone else until you find a nice husband."

"But you said—"

"I lied," he cut her off.

The girl's face fell, cheeks bursting with pink, and Evangeline felt a brief surge of pity as Giselle quickly shuffled past, disappearing down the dim corridor and leaving Evangeline alone with Jacks.

"Happy now?" He took a threatening step toward her.

Evangeline resisted the urge to take a step back. She didn't think she'd moved, but the cold wall was suddenly at her back, and Jacks was so close—and so much taller than she ever realized—she had to tilt her head to meet his heartless eyes. "You told me you wouldn't kill anyone."

"No," he said. "*You* told me I wouldn't kill anyone. I told you that was a terrible plan."

"But you didn't need to kill her," Evangeline argued.

"What do you know about what I need?" Jacks's long fingers grazed the slit of her skirt.

She swallowed a gasp. The touch had to be an accident.

He flashed a dimple as his fingers moved under the fabric, stroking her bare thigh as he gently parted the slit in her skirt.

This definitely wasn't an accident.

The tips of his fingers were soft, deceptively gentle, as they traveled higher and . . . higher. She told herself to pull away—this was Jacks and he was evil—his hand was definitely doing wicked things. But the racing of her heart didn't feel like fear just then. The rush of her blood and the tingling of her skin felt good. He felt good.

His touch was clearly making her delusional.

Evangeline really needed to push him away. But she grabbed his shirt instead, fisting the fabric in her hands.

He smiled, only it wasn't kind. It was like the wicked end of a fairytale, all sharp teeth that glinted under the torchlight. This was a mistake. A dangerous mistake. She reminded herself he'd just been touching another girl. But it was hard to care when he knew exactly how to touch *her*. How to make her feel like she was the one he'd wanted all this time.

His other hand slowly reached for her hip and hitched it up over his.

Her breath caught in her throat.

"Still think you know what I need?" He pressed in closer, lips nearly grazing her jaw and sending a shiver over her skin as he whispered, "I'm not a human, Evangeline. And I'm not your friend, or your husband, or your lover."

"I never said you were," she breathed.

"Then don't try to make me act like it. It doesn't end well." The fingers under her skirt turned rough and something vicious flashed in his eyes. Enough to make her finally feel a spike of fear. "*This* doesn't end well." His fingers pressed harder.

Evangeline gasped, and at last she pushed him away. "There is no *this*—I'm married."

Jacks ran his finger over the smirk playing on his lips. "You keep saying that, Little Fox, as if it's something I should care about."

A heartbeat later, he was gone.

26

Evangeline's head began to clear as soon as Jacks left her alone in the shadowy hall. She remembered the letter she'd written, warning herself not to trust him. She remembered all the things he'd done. Then she remembered Apollo.

Evangeline closed her eyes. Her legs were still shaking from Jacks's hands, and now her stomach was twisting with guilt as well. What happened in the hallway couldn't happen again.

The Archer's curse had upended everything with Apollo. It was difficult to keep hoping for a future with someone who was trying to kill her. But even if there was no Apollo, Jacks would have never been an option.

Jacks wasn't what she wanted. Evangeline wanted to give love and be loved and feel love at just the sight of someone. She wanted butterflies and kisses. She wanted it so much that sometimes she thought her heart would burst from it. And sometimes she made mistakes, like tonight when she'd let Jacks touch her. But she would not let him touch her again.

She needed to find the youth stone soon, but didn't want to return to the dinner. She would have preferred to dance barefoot in the snow than sit back down at the table next to Petra Youngblood.

Evangeline hoped the dinner was lively enough that no one would notice as she crept back out of the portrait door. The dining hall was certainly louder than when she had left. Booming voices mingled with slightly drunken laughs and glasses sloppily clinking together.

"Miss Fox—" Her name was followed with a tap on the shoulder by an object that felt like a feather.

Evangeline turned.

Kristof Knightlinger of *The Daily Rumor* stood before her, smiling. As usual, he was dressed in black leather pants and a shirt with a frothy jabot.

Her stomach instantly dropped at the sight of him.

"It's such a delight to find you here." He took the feathered pen he'd just rapped against her shoulder and waved it about excitedly. "You look radiant! It's so good to see you with so much color in your cheeks. Of course, now I have to ask if anyone in particular put that flush there?"

Kristof shot a questioning look toward the portrait door she'd just stepped out of.

"Oh no," Evangeline said. The only thing that could make

this night worse was if Kristof Knightlinger wrote in the papers that she'd been off trysting with Jacks. If Apollo read that news, he might go from being forced to hunt to actually wanting to hunt her. "I was just exploring some of the secret passages. Definitely nothing newsworthy—" She hesitated, fearing that maybe she was taking it a little too far.

She didn't know Kristof Knightlinger well, though his scandal sheets were generally favorable toward her. Even when she'd been wanted for murder, he'd seemed to doubt her guilt. She didn't think he was malicious. But he definitely didn't wait for all the facts before he released a story—he actually seemed to enjoy printing rumors more than facts.

Evangeline couldn't let him print anything about her. With Apollo currently hunting her, the consequences could be deadly if Kristof wrote in the paper that she was here, even if he didn't mention Jacks.

She would have loved to flat-out ask him not to refer to her presence at all, but she feared that would only pique his curiosity.

"I didn't make it that far. I heard some noises that made me think I might have been interrupting others. I'm actually a little embarrassed, so if you could keep this just between us, I would be so grateful."

"Oh, my dear! Of course, your secret explorations are safe with me." Kristof brushed the feathered pen across his lips as if to seal them shut. But Evangeline feared that might not be enough.

Evangeline considered telling Jacks about her run-in with Kristof—and that there was a chance he might mention her in his paper. But the last thing she wanted to do was seek Jacks out.

All she wanted was to crawl into bed and sleep. It had been an impossibly long day, and she was exhausted. Climbing back up to her guest room on the fourth floor felt akin to scaling a mountain.

And yet, after cleaning up, putting on a nightgown, and climbing into bed, Evangeline couldn't sleep. Every time she closed her eyes, she flashed back to the hallway with Jacks. Her skin went hot, and then she was wide awake.

She wasn't sure how long it went on, but eventually she gave up on sleep. She lit several candles and went to the trunk where she'd packed a few books, including *The Rise and Fall of the Valors*.

The last time she'd looked at the volume, the cover had been blank, but tonight it seemed to be coming to life again. She watched the lavender fabric darken until the entire book was the color of damp plums. Seconds later, a new set of metallic words shimmered across the front: *The Inglorious History of House Slaughterwood*.

Evangeline felt a thrill at the words, but knowing how tricksy this book could be, she tried not to get her hopes up as she returned to her bed and opened the cover.

An ancient piece of newsprint fluttered out.

It looked so old she feared it might crumble in her hands, but the waxy paper was surprisingly sturdy. The print was old-fashioned and difficult to read, but the words at the top were quite familiar.

The Daily Rumor

MONSTER!

By Kilbourne Knightlinger

Here ye, my dear Northerners. There has been another monster attack! Last night, the mighty Lord Bane Slaughterwood had his throat ripped out.

The Valors continue to swear that they did not create any monster. But for ye who haven't been counting, this be the third violent attack on House Slaughterwood. And all these attacks began after the unfortunate death of our beloved Castor Valor—whom many speculate was killed by Vengeance Slaughterwood during the tragic slaying of House Merrywood.

It could still be coincidence that this monster is now coming after Slaughterwoods. There have been other vicious attacks, which have led many to speculate these monstrous murders are not targeted. But some fear that these attacks are only because the Valors do not have control over the abomination they have created.

The writing turned into gibberish after that, no doubt because of the curse. But thankfully, the original script stayed intact as Evangeline reread.

There was no date on the article, but she imagined this news had taken place after the story that Jacks had told her in the carriage—and it seemed to confirm everything Jacks had said.

It mentioned both the tragic slaying of House Merrywood and the death of Castor Valor.

Evangeline tried not to jump to conclusions—this was a scandal sheet, after all—but she couldn't help but wonder if this was the information she'd been looking for. She'd wanted to know why the North had turned on the Valors, and this seemed to explain it. Their son had been killed, and they had created a monster in revenge. The article even used the word *abomination*.

Could this be the same abomination that many believed was locked up in the Valory?

But that didn't quite make sense to Evangeline. Everything she'd read about the Valors made it sound as if they were magical and powerful—they would have no need to create a monster for revenge. But perhaps the rumor that they'd created the monster was enough to get people to turn on them.

Evangeline knew firsthand just how powerful rumors could be. And she could easily imagine a family like the Slaughterwoods starting the rumor—especially if Aurora Valor had left Vengeance at the altar for another man.

She looked once more at the book in her lap. It was open to a table of contents that appeared to list names of Slaughterwood family members:

Bane Slaughterwood

Vengeance Slaughterwood

Venom Slaughterwood

Ruin Slaughterwood
Malice Slaughterwood
Torment Slaughterwood
Belladonna Slaughterwood
Glendora Slaughterwood

The list went on for several pages.

Evangeline started with Vengeance, hoping to get more answers about the Valors, and compare the book's account with the story Jacks had told her in the carriage.

Unfortunately, the pages were blank.

She flipped back to the table of contents, and this time, it was Glendora's name that caught her eye. She hadn't been in Jacks's story, but she had been married to Vengeance, and there were large portraits of her throughout the castle, so perhaps Evangeline could learn something.

Glendora's entry opened with a picture of her in a coffin. Her eyes were closed, and her face was aged with countless wrinkles.

The words *Glory in Death* were printed beneath the picture and above it a span of years that suggested she'd died at the age of eighty-six. The entry on the following page was a surprisingly opinionated piece of history, and Evangeline wondered if the story curse had given the words a bit of extra flavor.

*Glendora Slaughterwood,
also known as Glendora the Good.
Mother of many. Wife of Vengeance.
Beloved by almost everyone.*

—+—

Poor, poor Glendora the Good, everyone adored her, except for her husband, Vengeance. Glendora was all goodness and joy and honesty—and she gave birth to so many babies. Without Glendora, there would be no Slaughterwoods left. But none of that mattered to Vengeance.

He pretended that he loved her, he commissioned statues and paintings and had minstrels write songs about his wife's goodness, all to hide that Glendora was his second choice, and not nearly as beautiful as his first choice, the girl who'd left him at the altar: Aurora Valor.

Pretty, pretty Aurora Valor. When they'd been engaged, Vengeance had loved Aurora's beauty. He'd drunk it up like poison until it ruined him for anyone else.

Glendora made babies, she threw parties and hunts, and turned the small Slaughterwood Estate into a glorious manor with grounds full of flowers and rooms full of mirth, but it was never enough to win Vengeance's heart. He was forever in love with the ghost of a girl who'd—

Evangeline stopped reading and returned to the line about flowers and *mirth*. Her fingers shook with excitement as she rushed to pull out the page of clues that the previous key had written.

Just as she'd recalled, the flowers had been drawn by the words *One for Mirth*. She knew it could be just a coincidence—a lot of people planted flowers. But hadn't LaLa said something about Glendora having a famed winter garden? The passage also described Glendora as generous and good and joyful. Perhaps she was just a kind person—as Robin Slaughterwood seemed to be—or perhaps something magical had made Glendora that way.

Evangeline took another look at Glendora's picture. It was in black-and-white, faded with age, but it was clear enough to see the woman wore a long heavy chain with a jeweled pendant.

Could this be the mirth stone?

Evangeline felt a burst of excitement, followed by a bolt of hope that Glendora had been buried with this stone—since the drawing showed her in a coffin.

She considered telling Jacks of her discovery, but after the events of that evening, he was still the last person she wanted to see.

With another shiver, Evangeline grabbed a robe and threw it on. She had no idea of the time, but she imagined it was several hours until sunrise, which gave her a fair amount of time to covertly search for Glendora's grave, and Evangeline knew exactly where to start.

Glory in Death—the words printed beneath Glendora's picture were also the words that had been written on the wall of the secret corridor that Evangeline had ventured into earlier that night. And she'd reached it via a portrait hole that had been home to a picture of Glendora.

27

The trebuchet in the dining hall looked even more horrid in the dark—a giant slumbering beast that might follow Evangeline to the portrait of Glendora and then rip her from the room before she could slip through the passage.

She gripped her gold dagger, which she'd tied to her robe. She thought she heard a movement, but the trebuchet remained inanimate as she scurried past on slippered feet in search of Glendora Slaughterwood's grave.

With only the moonlight pouring through the stained-glass panels of the dining room, it was a challenge to find the right painting. All Evangeline could see were Glendora's eyes, still sad, as she opened the frame.

She paused before stepping through, wondering briefly at Glendora's sorrow. If she had possessed the mirth stone, she should have been much happier, but perhaps Glendora hadn't been in possession of it at the time of this picture?

Evangeline hoped that was the case as she entered the corridor. Thankfully, torches still burned, lighting her way as she traveled the same path she'd taken earlier that night.

Her stomach clenched as she reached the spot where she'd found Jacks with the Darling girl. The dusty air smelled faintly of apples, and she half expected him to step out from the shadows.

Again, she thought she heard something.

But all she saw were spiders crawling along the walls over the words *Glory in Death*.

The air changed when she turned a corner. Sconces appeared between the torches—dirty glass filled with skeletal stems and a few dried petals. The scent of apples vanished, and all she could smell was stale dust that made her think of dry bones and dead flowers.

The unsettling fragrance thankfully lessened as she neared the monument. An enormous thing, watched over by two statues of weeping angels and covered with a layer of dust that made her think no one had visited in a very long while.

Evangeline held her breath as she approached, preparing to feel the magic of the mirth stone. But perhaps the coffin was dampening the arch stone's power?

The casket appeared to be made of marble, a fact Evangeline confirmed when she tried to shove the lid aside and it wouldn't so much as budge.

"Need a hand?"

Evangeline jumped as Luc appeared from out of the shadows, with a thin gold crown atop his head and a high-collared coat that looked as if it had been sewn together with pure swagger.

"Luc, what are you doing here? Were you following me?"

"I heard you came to the party after all, so I decided to join you." He flashed a crooked smile. "I was going to sneak into your bedroom, but then I saw you sneaking out, so I suppose I *sort of* followed you."

"You can't keep doing this."

"Why not? I used to do it all the time. I mean, not the following part, just the sneaking into your bedroom." He looked at her through his long and lovely lashes. But Evangeline didn't let herself get caught in his gaze like the last time they'd met.

"Is this because I'm a vampire?" he pressed. "Or are you still mourning your dead husband?" Suddenly, Luc was sitting atop the coffin, dangling his legs and looking far more harmless than she knew him to be.

Although she really didn't think he would bite her. When she took a moment to look past the princely swagger, Luc seemed to be more lonely than hungry, just like the last time she'd seen him. Evangeline was not an expert on vampires, but she wondered if being a vampire meant more than just thirsting for blood. Vampires didn't age. They remained unchanged throughout time. Perhaps this wasn't just physical; maybe their hearts were like that as well, making it harder for them to move on from things in their past.

"It's not because you're a vampire," she assured him. "In fact, there's something I need to do before the sun comes up, and I could actually use your vampire strength."

This seemed to brighten his mood. He grinned down from atop the coffin as Evangeline eyed the heavy marble lid, letting her gaze linger.

Like Evangeline, Luc was very curious. It only took a few moments before he asked, "What do you want in the coffin?"

"Help me open it and you'll see."

Luc jumped off the tomb, shoved the heavy lid, and turned to her with a satisfied smile as the marble thunked to the ground. "Can I bite you now?"

"No, Luc, I'm *never* going to let you bite me."

"Never say never, Eva." He flashed a hopeful smile made of fangs before peering into the box. "Are you sure this is the right coffin?"

"Positive," said Evangeline. Yet she felt a stab of worry as her gaze followed Luc's. Glendora Slaughterwood's body was all dust and teeth. She'd died so long ago there were no bones or clothes or necklaces. And there was still no feeling of magic. There was no tingling, no prickling, no sudden bursts of mirth.

But Evangeline had to believe there was more.

She took a deep, nervous breath and dug her hand into the murky gray dust that was Glendora Slaughterwood.

"Eva! What are you doing?" Luc clearly thought she'd lost her mind. He grabbed onto her shoulders, tugging her back from the coffin, but thankfully, she'd already caught hold of something that felt like a chain.

Evangeline pulled free of Luc and shook the dust off the rock dangling at the end of the chain until she was holding a butterscotch-yellow stone that looked as if it were made of shimmering sunlight.

Luc eyed the gem askance, obviously not thinking it was as pretty as she did. "I could get you nicer jewelry than that."

He grabbed for it.

Evangeline clutched the necklace tighter, feeling that familiar swell of protectiveness, followed by a wash of relief. This had to be the mirth stone. Perhaps she just hadn't felt it as strongly because she already had a hopeful disposition.

"Thank you, Luc." Hopping up on her tiptoes, she pecked him on the cheek and started back down the corridor.

"Wait," Luc cried. "There's a costume party tomorrow night. Will you be my date?"

Evangeline stopped halfway down the hall. If she went with Luc, she could avoid Jacks. At least until he showed up and found her with Luc.

Of course, that thought also tempted her because she imagined Jacks would not be happy to see her on Luc's arm, especially if the youth stone was near and working its jealous magic.

"I wish I could say yes," Evangeline said. "I just fear that wouldn't be a wise idea." As much as she enjoyed frustrating Jacks, this was LaLa's party, and she wouldn't make a scene. "But I promise to save you a dance."

Evangeline tucked the sunshine-yellow mirth stone underneath her nightgown, where she could feel it safe against her chest as she climbed up the stairs to her guest room. It was actually a bit of a relief that the stone didn't feel more powerful. After the tendrils of envy she'd felt from what she imagined was the youth stone, she'd been a little nervous about what the mirth stone might do.

She'd feared it might make her drunk with happiness, or so giddy with joy that she lost all sense of urgency.

But for now, if anything, she felt uneasy. Her skin prickled with an uncanny sense that made her slow her steps as she reached the fourth floor of Slaughterwood Castle.

It was quiet, so still she could almost hear the flickering of candles in sconces. Then she saw it—a streak of moonlight hair attached to a shadowy figure darting quickly down the hall. *Petra.*

Evangeline felt the same wrench of discomfort she'd experienced every other time she'd seen the girl. Then she felt it again as she wondered if Petra had come from Jacks's room.

Evangeline ran to the other end of the hall to look down the corner that Petra had just turned. But it was already empty.

It was tempting to wonder if she'd just imagined her. It was so late it might have actually been early. And Evangeline was starting to feel fatigued again. The rush of finding the mirth stone had started to wear off, leaving her tired. And yet she knew what she'd seen. She just couldn't understand why she'd seen it. *What was Petra doing sneaking around at this hour?*

Evangeline's mind flashed back to earlier that night. Jacks had said he'd thought Petra looked familiar. Then Petra had warned Evangeline about Jacks; she was the one who'd revealed to Evangeline that Jacks had snuck off with another girl.

Petra had seemed to dislike Jacks, and yet Evangeline couldn't shake the idea that Petra had just come from Jacks's room.

Evangeline supposed she could stand there in the hall, wondering until the sun came up, or she could simply knock on Jacks's door.

Her knuckles hit it three times. Softly at first, but when he didn't answer, she knocked once more, louder.

Jacks, she thought silently.

Again, he didn't answer.

Was he just asleep? Or was he ignoring her?

If Petra had visited him, he had to be awake.

Evangeline considered knocking again, but if she made any more noise, she might wake others. However—

She looked down at her finger. If she cut herself, she wouldn't need to knock.

Using her dagger, Evangeline pricked the tip of her finger and unlocked Jacks's room.

She knew right away that he wasn't there.

The fire was dead, and the sun was already coming up,

shining through the frosted windows and revealing that the four-poster bed had not been slept in. The creamy quilts on it weren't even wrinkled.

But Jacks had clearly been in this room at some point. Apple cores were piled high on his desk. There were also heaps of clothing strewn across chairs and lounges.

From the look of it, Jacks had brought more clothes than she had. There were breeches and belts and piles of boots. She knew it would have been better not to touch anything, but she couldn't help running her fingers over a pile of velvet doublets in various shades of blue, black, and gray. They were soft, and they smelled good, too.

She would never admit it to him, but she was feeling a little too tired to lie to herself, and she had to admit, she loved the way Jacks smelled, like apples and magic and crisp, cold nights that made her want to curl up in a blanket.

She wandered to the bed. It didn't smell like him, but it was soft when she perched on the edge of it. And the pillows felt amazing, fluffy and downy, and just leaning on them allowed Evangeline's body to relax.

She closed her eyes, just for a second. Or maybe just for a minute. . . .

Evangeline wanted to snuggle deeper into her blanket and ignore the shadow that had fallen over her. She didn't much feel like dealing with shadows, especially irritable ones. This shadow was cold and close, and she sensed that it was in a foul mood. Perhaps, if she just kept her eyes shut, it would go away.

"How long do you plan on pretending you're asleep?" drawled the shadow.

Evangeline reluctantly cracked one eye open.

The shadow was closer than she'd realized, as if he'd been about to stumble into bed until he'd seen her there. He'd already done away with his doublet: his shirt was half unbuttoned, his golden hair vaguely tousled, and his silver-blue eyes looked more threatening than usual, as if he might still join her in bed.

Her heart tripped at the thought, and then it stumbled again as Jacks's lids lowered and his gaze skated over her body. His eyes traced the way she curled in his bed, one hand tucked underneath her head, the other pressed to her chest, clutching the blanket to where her night robe had slipped open.

Slowly, his mouth slid into a grin. "Now you're obsessed with my shirts?"

Evangeline felt it then, the buttons on her blanket—or rather his shirt, which she'd been cuddling like a blanket.

Her cheeks pinked immediately.

His eyes glittered with amusement. "Were you missing me last night?" Jacks leaned against the bedpost and stroked one hand slowly up and down the wood as his eyes trailed back to her legs and the part in her robe.

Mortification was not a strong enough word for how she felt just then. Evangeline thrust the garment aside and rose on her knees until the two of them were nearly level. Her pulse briefly fluttered as she met his eyes. Up close, they were a little too powerful for her liking, but she refused to look away.

"I came in here to look for you after I saw Petra outside your door."

"Who is Petra?"

"The girl from the dinner last night, the one with the moonlight hair. Who is she to you, Jacks?"

He shook his head, brows drawing together. "I don't know her."

Evangeline eyed him warily. She was tempted to believe him. But she also knew better than to trust her judgment when it came to Jacks. "You said she looked familiar last night. And she's the one who told me that you snuck off during dinner."

What remained of his amusement instantly vanished. "I don't know who this girl is, but you should stay away from her."

"Why? If you don't know—"

"I don't like her," Jacks cut in.

"Why? Because she doesn't like you?"

"No one likes me," Jacks answered swiftly.

"We both know that's not true," Evangeline challenged. "Plenty of girls appeared to like you last night."

"They liked Lord Jacks. But, as you know, Little Fox, I am not Lord Jacks." For a second, Jacks's entire face changed, any hint of humanity slipping away as he looked at her with eyes as dead as Chaos's. "I'm the person who'll kill this Petra girl if she goes near you again. So you should stay away unless you want her dead."

28

For tonight's ball, everyone was supposed to dress as part of a famous couple from throughout Northern history. Evangeline had been excited about the theme and the idea of dressing up until she'd found the costume that LaLa had left for her.

The dress was peasant-girl pretty, with a sweetheart neckline, puffed sleeves, and a knee-length skirt that cinched at the waist with a wide pink ribbon, which formed a cheerful bow in back. The fabric was a simple yellow eyelet, dotted with pink and white flowers and dancing foxes, which made it clear who she was supposed to be. The Fox.

Given Evangeline's situation with Apollo, it felt a little bit morbid to be dressed as the Fox from *The Ballad of the Archer and the Fox*. But she tried to be optimistic. The dress was a gift from LaLa—under other circumstances, it would have been a thoughtful one. And truth be told, although it made her a little nervous, the dress did remind her of what she was there to do: break the Archer's curse on Apollo and find the missing stones. Hopefully, she'd find the youth stone tonight. Then all she would need to find was the truth stone.

The thought recentered Evangeline as she laced up her slippers, which had come with rose-gold ribbons that tied up all the way to her calves. She then put on the mirth stone and tucked it safely into her bodice.

She doubted Jacks would approve of her wearing the stone, but it didn't matter since she hadn't told him about it—not yet anyway. She probably should have mentioned it when she'd been in his room, but she hadn't wanted him to take it and lock it up inside a box.

The stone didn't seem to be harmful. It hadn't made her feel reckless like the luck stone, or envious like the youth stone. If she hadn't felt so possessive of it when Luc had tried to snatch it, she might have suspected it wasn't magic at all.

The old clock on the fireplace mantel gently ticked closer to eight. The ball was officially beginning, but Jacks hadn't arrived to collect her.

Evangeline worried her lip. They hadn't actually talked about attending the ball together. So perhaps he wasn't going to go with her. Maybe he was going to go with one of the Darling girls? She didn't like that idea at all.

Maybe he was still asleep? He'd seemed tired when he'd found her in his bed. She imagined he'd dozed off after that, and she knew from experience how intense his sleep could be.

Evangeline decided to check on him. His room was to the left of hers, and right away, she saw that his door was already cracked.

She probably should have knocked, but her curiosity got the best of her. She peered through the crack instead.

Jacks was awake, and he looked ready to go. Although if he was ready for the party or a battle, she couldn't quite tell.

He wore two swords strapped to the back of a smoke-gray shirt with sleeves shoved up past his elbows. She could see the muscles in his forearms before her view was blocked by dark leather gauntlets that matched his tall boots and his low-slung belt. There were no weapons in his belt, but when her gaze drifted to the thighs of his fitted black breeches, she saw two leather straps where he'd secured a series of shining daggers.

Evangeline didn't know who he was supposed to be, only that her heart was hammering as she watched him stand in front of the fire. In one hand he held a white apple; the other was clenched into a white-knuckled fist.

It was then she realized he wasn't alone.

29

LaLa stepped into view.

She was a bright contrast to all of Jacks's dark, dressed like a mermaid in a sequined teal skirt that fit through the knees until it flared out around her feet. Her arms were covered in sequins as well, all the way from her fingers to her shoulders, where they attached to the pearl straps of a seashell top.

Her brown stomach was decorated in more pearls and gems for a truly glamorous effect. She looked all Fate and magic. She also looked as if something was very, very wrong. In one hand she held a crumpled piece of newsprint, in the other a goblet that she took a long drink from.

"Why aren't you at your party?" Jacks drawled.

"I read something you should see." LaLa thrust the newsprint at Jacks's fisted hand.

He flicked it a dirty look. "I don't read the scandal sheets."

"You should read this one." LaLa took another nervous sip

of her drink. "Kristof wrote an article that says Evangeline is here. He didn't use her name, but he described a certain pink-haired princess."

Evangeline's stomach wrenched with dread. She leaned closer, fearing what else the article might say. She hoped it didn't mention the tryst, but it was bad enough that it had revealed her location. If they stayed, Apollo would surely arrive, but if they left, they might not find the youth stone, which she was certain had to be here.

"There's also a Wanted post warning that Tiberius has escaped the Tower," LaLa went on. "I would guess he's probably on his way here right now, along with Apollo."

Jacks shot LaLa a murderous look. "Whose fault is that?"

"I did what I had to do." LaLa's voice took on a hard edge. "She wasn't going to open the arch."

Evangeline staggered back. She must have misheard them. LaLa was her friend. LaLa couldn't have been the one to place the Archer's curse on Apollo.

But LaLa had told Evangeline to open the arch. And Jacks had asked LaLa to break the spell on Apollo. Maybe this was why—because LaLa was the one who'd cast it?

Evangeline looked down at her fox-girl costume. Perhaps it hadn't been by chance that LaLa had given her this gown. Maybe it had been an intentional push?

She didn't want to believe that LaLa would betray her. Then she remembered the day she'd visited LaLa's flat. At one point, LaLa had taken Evangeline's hand and spoken words of gibberish.

Evangeline had thought it was the story curse, garbling her speech, but what if that was when LaLa had cursed her and Apollo?

Evangeline watched through the cracked door as Jacks turned and faced the fire. For a second, all Evangeline could see was the angry roll of his shoulders as he spoke into the flames. "If she dies, it's your fault."

"She won't die if you get her out of here now." LaLa finished off her glass of wine. "Can you keep her safe?"

Jacks shot her a glare.

"Don't look at me like that. I saw the way you looked when you arrived here with your arm around her shoulders."

"How did I look?"

"Like you would kill for her."

"I would kill for a lot of things."

"Just be sure you don't kill *her*," LaLa said. "I've also seen the way you two look at each other. Last night when I walked into the dining hall, I was half-terrified you were going to kiss her in the middle of the party."

"I thought you knew me better than that." Jacks's glare slowly dissolved into a smile, and then his eyes flashed with the same primal look he'd given Evangeline last night. "I'm just giving her what she wants. But don't worry, she is not what *I* want. All I want is for her to find the stones."

"And you think I'm cruel." LaLa's shoes clacked angrily against the floor as she turned toward the door to leave.

Evangeline staggered back another step, and then she fled before either of them could discover she'd been listening.

If there was any mirthful magic in the stone around Evangeline's neck, then it wasn't working, because it hurt—everything hurt. She had believed LaLa was her friend. She thought LaLa cared, but it seemed LaLa was just like Jacks—all she wanted was to open the arch.

Evangeline's chest was heaving by the time she reached the Slaughterwood ballroom.

At the open doors, servants handed out goblets of dark red wine and sweet mead. It would have been wiser not to take one—she needed to find the truth stone and the youth stone before Apollo or Tiberius found her.

But Evangeline just wanted to drink until it felt better or until she didn't care that it was all suddenly worse—that there really was no one she could trust.

She grabbed a goblet and downed it quickly. Then she replaced it with another full drink to make sure she had enough.

Tonight, the goblets were wood, their stems twined with aged bronze vines and trumpet flowers that smelled of apples and blood.

Her footsteps faltered.

The scent made her think of the Prince of Hearts' church, but thankfully, Jacks had not entered the woodsy ballroom yet. She really didn't want to see him.

She was wounded by LaLa. But she didn't even want to think about what Jacks had said.

I'm just giving her what she wants. But don't worry, she is not what I want. All I want is for her to find the stones.

The words made her feel so naive. Repeatedly, she'd told herself not to trust him, she'd told herself he didn't care. But a part of her had really started to believe that he didn't want to keep her alive just because he needed her to open the arch.

Even now, after hearing him tell LaLa he didn't care, that he didn't want her—that killing her wasn't a risk because he was only pretending to be attracted to her—she still wanted to think he was lying.

Evangeline took another deep drink from her goblet and wove her way deeper into the costumed crush, determined to disappear in it.

Thankfully, she was not the only fox tonight. There were a number of others dressed as foxes with pastel peasant gowns, or dressed as actual foxes with furry ears and tails attached to tawny dresses. The Archer costume was just as popular. Some of the other couples Evangeline didn't as easily recognize, but she saw a number of Honoras and Wolfrics, Vengeances and Glendoras, mermaids—and a few mermen—along with captive sailors in billowing shirts who looked as if they'd been plucked straight from carvings of the gateway arch to the North. There was also a girl dressed as the Sun dancing with another girl dressed as the Moon. And in the middle of everyone was a handsome young man costumed like a dragon who twirled a girl who looked like glittering treasure.

It might have just been all the wine coursing through her, but for a moment, Evangeline didn't feel as if she were in a ballroom, she felt as if she were in the center of a hundred stories. Love stories and tragedies and tales with endings lost to time. And suddenly, her worries felt lost as well, swept away by a feeling that her life was one of those stories. She'd known it vaguely, but it wasn't until then that the enormity of it hit her.

She'd married a prince, she was part of a prophecy, and right now, she was searching for magic stones that could change the fate of the world. Of course, people would tell stories about her—they were already telling stories—it had just never occurred to Evangeline that these stories were bigger things, pieces of history currently being formed.

But unlike some of the doomed characters around her, Evangeline still had a chance at finding a happy end to her story.

Never mind that the odds were not currently stacked in her favor, not with all the curses and betrayals and murderous, lying princes. None of that meant she was doomed. Evangeline still believed that every story had the possibility for infinite endings, and she was going to find one of the good ones—as soon as she found the next two stones.

Excited sounds wove through the ballroom.

"Look who's here," people whispered. Followed by words like *young, attractive, unattached.*

Then, loudly, "Eva!"

A second later, Luc was there, striding up to her with a feather in his cap and a quiver of gold-tipped arrows at his back. "I knew you'd be the Fox."

Evangeline couldn't help but smile. Luc was, of course, dressed as the Archer, a gesture that she'd have found terribly romantic months ago—and a part of her still had to concede it was very sweet of Luc. Even though Luc had been cursed by Marisol, turned to stone by Jacks, and then transformed into a vampire, he still held on to some of his humanity. *Unlike Jacks.*

"I believe you owe me a dance," Luc said.

"Not tonight, vampire boy."

Evangeline stiffened at the sound of Jacks's low voice. Then she shivered as he stepped into view, looking like an angel of death with the swords still strapped to his back. "This dance is already taken."

"Yes, by me." Luc flashed his fangs.

Jacks merely laughed. The sound was musical and very much at odds with the voice Evangeline heard in her head. *I'll give you a choice. Dance with me, or watch me use one of my swords to chop off his head.*

Evangeline gritted her teeth and glared up at him. "Is this how you always get dance partners? By threatening to kill the other suitors?"

"Don't test me tonight, Little Fox." Jacks's free hand flexed as if to grab a sword. But then he wrapped it possessively around her waist instead.

Her rib cage tightened and her pulse raced, but she knew it wasn't Jacks. It was the wine, and the mirth stone, and the anger she still felt for the multiple ways he'd betrayed her. "You need to let me go."

"That's not an option." His eyes flickered down to hers as if by accident, as if he meant to keep her at a distance, but he couldn't help but pull her in. "You're in danger again. We need to leave."

"No, Jacks—I'm not going anywhere with you. I heard you and LaLa. I heard everything you said. I know what she did to Apollo. I know you kept it from me. And I know—" She tried to say that she knew he didn't want to be touching her right now. But she couldn't manage those words. Instead, she pressed her hands to his chest and shoved.

And then she turned and ran.

30

The ballroom was spinning. Musicians were playing fiddles on the ceiling. Dancers were floating in the wine-soaked air. And LaLa's sequins were everywhere.

At least that's how it felt to Evangeline as she fled from the dance floor and away from Jacks.

She caught a glimpse of LaLa on the arm of Robin. He looked blissful now that she'd arrived. Since leaving Jacks's room, LaLa had traded in her goblet for a trident and her nerves for an adoring smile. But Evangeline wondered if it was all an act, as her friendship with Evangeline had been. Was LaLa like Jacks, using Evangeline to get whatever it was that she wanted from inside the Valory Arch?

Evangeline didn't want to believe that—it didn't feel like the truth to her. But her head was dizzy from the wine, her chest was tight with hurt, and it was hard to think clearly. All she knew was that she didn't think she could take another betrayal. She just wanted one person to trust. Was that too much to ask?

"You look as if you could use some fresh air," Petra said. She linked arms with Evangeline before she could nod.

Petra was dressed as one of the figures that Evangeline didn't recognize. She wore a very low-cut white chain-mail gown and a slender silver circlet around the crown of her moonlight hair. "Come with me," she coaxed. "I know a secret way out of here."

Evangeline's stomach clenched as Petra led her toward a fountain spilling sparkling mead. She still didn't like or trust this girl. But if she stayed in the ballroom, Jacks would catch up with her. She wasn't sure what had kept him from doing so already. But Evangeline didn't dare look behind her shoulder to find out. She'd talk to him again when the room wasn't spinning and she felt steadier on her feet—right now, it would be far too easy for him to knock them out from under her.

"Where's this secret passage?" she asked.

"Just over here," Petra said.

In Evangeline's head, it all happened quite fast. One moment they were at the edge of the dance floor. Then they were at the wallflower benches—empty since this wasn't the sort of party that wallflower types were invited to.

"I think it's this one." Petra grabbed one of the bench legs, tugging it away from the wall and pulling open a concealed door in the process.

"Through here," she said quickly, almost as if she were on the run as well.

Evangeline felt a flicker of unease. But instead of moldy stones and cobwebs, the other side was reassuringly bright. All torchlit white plaster walls formed of sculptures of Slaughterwoods from the past.

Or at least Evangeline hoped they were sculptures. A few carvings they passed looked so lifelike, Evangeline could all too easily imagine they were actual bodies buried in the white walls.

She slowed her steps, but Petra took her arm once more and urged her to continue forward.

"How did you know about this passage?" Evangeline asked.

"Oh," Petra said quietly. "I've visited here a hundred times."

"I thought you said you were lucky to get invited to this party?"

"I lied." Petra winced. "I mean—I just—" she stammered, an action that looked especially strange on her lips, as if floundering for answers was not a thing she often did. "I've been coming to parties here longer than you've been alive."

Evangeline felt another clench in her gut. Then she felt the mirth stone burning hot beneath her eyelet dress. Only now, Evangeline wasn't so sure it was the mirth stone after all. Before, she hadn't sensed much power from the rock, but now it was as if the stone were finally waking up; she could feel it coming alive with power. But this power didn't give her a sense of joy or mirth as she would have expected. She felt the searing burn of *truth*—she was wearing the truth stone—and she felt it telling her to get out, to leave, to flee, to run for her life.

The world finally stopped spinning, and she regretted her lack of thinking.

Of course Evangeline had been thinking—it was just that one of her thoughts had been that when Jacks finally found her, it would feel like triumph to see the look on his face when he discovered her with someone he'd warned her against. Now, his warning about Petra felt a little more merited.

She slipped her arm free of Petra's. "I'm going to go back to the ball."

"No, Evangeline. I'm afraid you're not." Petra flashed a knife and thrust it straight at Evangeline's heart.

Evangeline leaped back, barely dodging the blade. "What are you doing?"

"I'm not a bad person—but I don't want to die." Petra lunged again, and she might have struck, but her chain-mail gown was clearly slowing her down.

Evangeline skirted the blade and grabbed for the other girl's wrist. She'd rather risk a slice in the hand than one to the throat. But Petra's hair was everywhere. Instead of a blade or wrist, Evangeline caught a handful of her moonlit locks.

She yanked the hair. It was just one tug, but the entire glowing mane came off.

Evangeline gasped. It was fake. Petra's real hair was a pile of pink, made of strands of rose with hints of gold.

"Your hair! It's just—" Evangeline was going to say it was just like hers, but Petra didn't give her the chance.

She pulled a second knife from the folds of her gown.

Evangeline threw the wig at Petra's face, buying herself a heartbeat of time. Her head was telling her to flee. But she was getting very tired of people trying to kill her. Instead of running, she launched herself at Petra, grabbing her wrists while the girl was still blinded. "Why are you trying to murder me?"

The stone Evangeline wore surged once more with heat as she spoke.

Petra thrashed, still holding both knives, and shook the wig from her face. Sweat plastered rose-gold hair to her forehead, and anger mottled her cheeks as she fought both Evangeline and the power of the truth stone. "I know you're also a key. And if I don't kill you, you'll kill me for my stone."

"What stone do you have?"

"The youth stone—argh—" Petra glared at the chain around Evangeline's neck. "Stop asking me questions!"

"Stop trying to kill me—I'm not your enemy."

"Yes, you are." Petra's shoulders sagged, and for the briefest moment, she stopped her struggle. "I was just like you once. I was married to a prince until I was accused of a crime I didn't commit. Then I learned about the prophecy, and I thought I was special—that everything had happened to me for a reason. I was the key—the one girl crowned in rose gold who could unlock the Valory Arch." She shook her head and laughed without joy. "But neither of us are special, Evangeline. We are just tools others use. In fact, I bet they don't even let you use the stones that you've found. Chaos wouldn't let me use the one I managed to discover."

Evangeline tried not to react. Chaos had told her that the last key had died—he'd said it had happened because the luck stone had made her reckless. But Evangeline didn't think that Petra could be lying with the truth stone so near.

"How did you know I'm working with Chaos?"

"Because I worked with him. I found Chaos the luck stone," Petra said, "but he didn't trust me with it. He locked it away to keep *it* safe, rather than to keep *me* safe. So when I found the youth stone and realized that with it I could stay young and live forever, I faked my death and disappeared." Her smile turned triumphant. "It was only then that I learned what all four stones could do together. But I'm guessing they didn't tell you that part, did they?"

"Is that why you're trying to kill me? So that you can get all four stones?"

"No!" Petra's head reared back, and she looked entirely offended. "I just want to keep my stone. I'm telling you this so that you know you can't trust *them*. But . . . I can already see you're way too trusting." Petra's eyes shone with something sad, right before she pressed all her weight against Evangeline's hands and slammed her body against the opposite wall.

Her teeth clacked as her head hit one of the statues.

"Please, stop this—" Evangeline cried, still struggling to hold Petra's wrists. She didn't want to hurt her, but Petra wouldn't stop fighting. Petra bucked against Evangeline's grip and nearly slashed Evangeline's cheek with one of her knives, finally giving Evangeline the strength to grit her teeth and smash Petra's knuckles into the wall hard enough to make her drop both blades.

The daggers clattered to the floor, skittering in opposite directions.

Evangeline didn't want to scramble for one, but Petra didn't hesitate to dart for the other and stalk after Evangeline. She wasn't going to give up. Evangeline wondered if this was why she'd seen Petra sneaking around last night—if she hadn't been coming from Jacks's room but from Evangeline's because she'd hoped to murder her in her sleep.

The torches flickered with each step Petra took, smoke snaking through the shrinking space between them.

"Stop, please." Evangeline's hands were slick with sweat and dread, but she grabbed the other knife and held it like a shield.

"I'm really not a bad person," Petra repeated, and for a second, her eyes looked truly sorry, but she didn't stop her steps or lower the knife. "It's not that I want to do this, but as soon as I saw you here, I knew—"

Evangeline thrust her dagger into Petra's chest, right on the edge of her chain-mail dress.

Petra made the worst sound Evangeline had ever heard, or maybe it was just the awful ringing in her ears, the sudden flash of horror and regret that swallowed her as soon as she'd thrust the knife. This wasn't what she wanted. She wanted to pull it out. She wanted to take it back.

A laugh gurgled up from Petra's throat as blood leaked from her chest. "I was once like you . . . but now you're . . . just . . . like me."

31

Tears coated Evangeline's cheeks as she released the knife and backed away from Petra's body. Her unmoving body lay in a swell of blood. Evangeline had never seen so much blood. When she'd thought Apollo had died, there'd been no blood. He'd just stopped moving.

But Petra's blood was there. Red and thick and damning. Even with the knife still in her chest, the blood had soaked through her white chain-mail dress and oozed onto the floor.

Evangeline started to shake, or maybe she'd already been shaking.

She had killed her. She'd chosen her life over Petra's. It was just what Jacks had said would happen. She'd killed someone for the stones. She'd sworn she'd never kill anyone, but then the moment Evangeline had been given the choice, she hadn't failed to act.

Yes, Petra had attacked her, but she wasn't thrusting a blade when Evangeline had stabbed her. Evangeline brought her hands to her face, stopping when she saw there was blood on them as well. She wiped them on her skirt, but that almost made it worse, as if she were trying to wipe away not just the blood but what she had done.

"Little Fox!" Jacks's urgent voice was accompanied by the sound of running.

Evangeline shook harder. She didn't want him to find her right now, especially not like this. She was shaking and covered in blood, and she felt too weak to face him. Yet she'd never been so relieved to see him.

"Jacks—" His name came out like a sob. She knew he wasn't a savior, but she didn't want a savior just then. She didn't want someone to hold her while she cried and tell her it would be all right. She wanted fury, she wanted rage, she wanted a villain to tell her she'd done exactly what she needed to do.

"What happened?" Jacks slowed his steps as he approached, eyes furiously going back and forth between the blood and Petra and Evangeline.

"I killed her—" Evangeline cried. Saying the words made it even realer, and the guilt was suddenly too much. Her chest was tight. She couldn't breathe. She could barely even stand. Then Jacks was crushing her to his chest. He held her like a secret, pulling her close to his pounding heart. She remembered her vow not to let him touch her. But if she pulled away, she felt as if she might break into a thousand tears.

Evangeline let herself lean against him as one of his hands

slid into her hair, gently pressing her head to his shoulder. The other hand was at her waist, fisting the ribbon tied around it as if he also knew that, were he to let her go, she would shatter.

She tried to hold back the tears, but she sobbed until his shirt went damp. "I'm a murderer."

"There is a knife in her hand," Jacks said. "She would have clearly killed you if you hadn't stopped her. You didn't do anything wrong."

"But it doesn't feel right."

"It never does." Jacks carefully released the ribbon at her waist and slowly rubbed a hand up and down the length of her spine.

Evangeline took a shuddering breath. She'd thought that she didn't want a savior, but maybe a part of her needed one. Or perhaps she just needed *him*. Another time, she would have felt guilty at the thought, but she'd killed someone tonight. In comparison, it hardly seemed wrong to want Jacks to hold her closer, until the hallway and the body and this terrible night disappeared and all that was left was the two of them.

Jacks's hand went suddenly still. "You should go back to your room now. Pack a bag you can carry. I'll be there to get you shortly."

"But—what about her—"

"I'll take care of the body."

Jacks let her go.

Evangeline felt numb as soon as his arms were no longer around her. It was tempting to fall apart again when she cast a look toward Petra, still on the ground with a halo of rose-gold hair exactly like Evangeline's. Petra's blood had stopped seeping, and her body did not stir, but Evangeline could still hear her accusing voice: *I was once like you, but now you're just like me.*

"She doesn't deserve your guilt," Jacks said. His eyes were flinty, more silver than blue as he gazed at the body. "There are heroes, and there are villains. She made her choice between the two, and she got the ending that came with it." Jacks said the words through gritted teeth, and Evangeline had the sudden fear that he wasn't just talking about Petra but himself.

"You should go now," he said.

For once, Evangeline wanted to do as Jacks told her, but she couldn't leave just yet. She took a wobbly step toward the body.

Jacks scowled.

"She was another key," Evangeline said.

"I gathered from the hair."

"She also had a stone—or she said she had a stone." Evangeline didn't look up to see how Jacks responded to this news or how he looked at her as she bent down toward the body. It felt so wrong to search Petra's corpse for the rock. But both Evangeline's life and Apollo's rested on her finding it.

Her fingers felt clumsy as she removed the first glove from Petra's hand. Evangeline hoped to find a ring or a bracelet, but Petra's arm was bare of jewels.

"Which stone did she say she had?" Jacks asked.

"The youth stone." Evangeline pulled off Petra's other glove, and gooseflesh covered her arm.

A shining golden cuff was hooked around her wrist, and in its center was a glowing stone the perfect blue of Jacks's un-earthly eyes.

Evangeline didn't want to touch it. She'd thought it was dangerous last night when it had made her half-mad with jealousy. Now she thought again of Jacks's warning when they'd first arrived: *If the stones are here, people are going to die at this party.*

Now someone had, but it wasn't just because of the stones' power, it was because of this quest to open the arch. Evangeline wondered once again at what it held. What could be so valuable or so dangerous that it would need to be locked with life-altering prophecies and magic stones that would require killing to retrieve?

"Evangeline." Jacks's voice was soft but urgent. "We can't linger here. You need to go pack. I'll take care of the stone."

There was so much blood on Evangeline's eyelet dress. One of the embroidered foxes was covered in a great smudge of red. She needed to take it off. She needed to change and pack. She'd killed someone, and because of Kristof's article, Apollo and Ti-berius could be on their way here to kill her right now.

But Evangeline was feeling overwhelmed.

What should she do first? Take off her bloody clothes? Wash the blood streaked on her face and the red staining her hands? Or should she pack? And what did one pack when one was fleeing for her life?

She'd brought so many party gowns to LaLa's, but she wouldn't use them now.

She needed a cloak and boots and—

Through the wardrobe mirror, she saw her door edge open.

Evangeline went very still, or she tried to, but her limbs were trembling again as she watched a leather boot step in—one that did not belong to Jacks.

"Eva, are you in here?" Luc's head poked through the door next. "I was worried about—"

He stilled as soon as he saw her, eyes going wide and fangs coming out at the sight of the blood on her dress and face.

Her chest erupted with panic. "Luc, you should go—"

"But you're bleeding!" He sounded concerned, but his eyes were on fire with hunger. "What happened?"

"It's not my—" Before Evangeline could finish, pain lashed down her back in horrible streaks. "Argh!" It hurt so much she couldn't breathe. She doubled over, barely able to remain on her feet as she felt the skin on her back split open.

"Eva!" In a flash, Luc had an arm wrapped around her waist to keep her from falling to the floor. But it didn't stop the pain.

It burned. It ached. It bled.

She glimpsed a lengthening of fangs, but there was nothing she could do to push away from Luc—the pain was all she could think about. At first, she didn't know what was happening. She thought maybe she was being punished for killing Petra. But then she remembered Apollo and the mirror curse. Someone must have been torturing him, and by default torturing her. She could feel blood seeping through her dress as she cried out again. "Ahhh—"

"Oh, gods, Eva—your back." Luc's voice was thick with hunger, and the arm around her waist felt almost painfully hot.

"Get away from her!" Jacks roared from the doorway.

Evangeline tried to tell him it wasn't Luc who'd done this—Apollo was being tortured, and he needed to be saved—but she could only moan. She couldn't even see beyond the sword Jacks was holding—it took too much strength to keep her eyes open.

"Hey—it wasn't me," Luc protested, but his voice sounded dim and far away. "Something has possessed her."

"Apollo," Jacks muttered.

"She's possessed by her dead husband?" Luc dropped her on the ground.

Jacks growled.

Evangeline crumpled into a ball, her back hurting so much the fall didn't really matter.

"Look at me, vampire boy, and listen very carefully, or Evangeline will die," Jacks gritted out. "You need to go and find Chaos. Fast."

"Oh, he's not very happy with me right now. I was supposed to stay away from Eva—"

"I don't care," Jacks cut in. "Evangeline dies tonight unless you tell Chaos to find Apollo, get him out of danger, and make sure his wounds are healed. Can you do that?"

"Yes."

"Then why are you still here?" Jacks spat.

A whoosh of Luc's footsteps followed.

"Evangeline—" Jacks's low voice sounded distant, but he must have been there because she could feel him. She could feel the cool of his arms sliding gently under her legs and carefully under her neck as he cradled her to his chest.

"It hurts, Jacks."

"I know, love. I'm going to take you somewhere safe."

32

Another lash ripped across Evangeline's skin, making her cry out. It hurt like hell and fire. She was dimly aware of biting down, and she feared it was on Jacks's neck.

"It's all right," he rasped. "I've got you. Just stay with me, Little Fox." He kept pressing Evangeline to stay awake when all she wanted to do was pass out.

There were minutes where the agony was so intense she couldn't breathe. Pain would lash across her back. Her limbs would buck. Her teeth would bite. Her whole life would feel like hurt. Then she'd feel Jacks smoothing the damp hair from her forehead or pressing a cool hand to her cheek.

Her head lolled against his shoulder. They were in a sled, and she was on his lap. He held her with her chest pressed to his, and his arm so low on her waist, it wasn't really her waist. But her back was made of fire—anything that touched it burned.

"We're almost there," he whispered.

She wanted to ask where *there* was, but her throat was too raw from crying out. All she could do was crack her eyes. The world was gray. Not night or day, just gray. Gray as death and covered in fog that tasted like smoke.

She wondered if perhaps this meant she was dying. Then their sled tumbled forward, speeding over a ravaged road, past the weathered sign that said *Welcome to the great Merrywood Manor!*

She couldn't believe Jacks had taken her here. She couldn't remember why. It hurt too much to think clearly. But Evangeline knew this was not a happy place, especially for him.

Sprays of ice and snow made her shake as Jacks drove the sled faster and harder, past the remains of the manor and deeper into the cursed Merrywood forest. Whenever she cracked her eyes, there were only skeletal trees and more hopeless gray.

The first green leaf daring to live among the gloom felt like a trick, a delusion of her breaking mind. But then there was another and another. A canopy of gorgeous green. Everywhere she looked now, there was sunlight, snow-dusted trees, and chirping blue birds, and she was half-afraid she'd lost her mind.

The flowers came next, in delirious shades of yellow and pink and mermaid teal. They lined a sloping road that led them down into a valley with an inn and a lake and an aged sign that read *Welcome to the Hollow!*

The name was unfamiliar. It must not have been a Great House, or maybe she just couldn't remember.

The sled rumbled past more carved signs that pointed toward places she couldn't quite make out until finally they stopped at an inn that couldn't be real. It had to be part of a dream.

The rooftop was covered in enormous cheery mushrooms with red caps that had tiny dragons dozing upon them. Then there were the flowers, so large they were the size of small children, with bright-colored petals in every shade, which seemed to perk up as the two of them arrived.

Jacks picked her up in one quick swoop and carried her inside the inn.

Her skin immediately tingled from the warmth, inviting her to keep her eyes open. It was a fight—her wounded body begged her to rest—but she wanted to know why it smelled of spiced ciders and fresh-baked bread and how it managed to feel like home, though even in her current state she was certain she'd never been here before.

Near the door towered a brightly painted clock with jeweled pendulums. But instead of hours, it seemed to have names of food and drink. Things like *Dumplings & Meat, Fish Stew, Mystery Stew, Toast and Tea, Porridge, Ale, Beer, Mead, Wine, Cider, Honey Pie, Brambleberry Crisp, Forest Cakes.*

She half expected an innkeeper with a long beard and a jolly laugh to greet them as they entered. But it was only Jacks's heavy boots that swiftly crossed the rough floorboards.

What is this place? she thought.

Jacks didn't reply or even seem to hear her thought as he

started up the stairs. Whatever magic worked here must have severed their link, or she was just too weak.

There were candles glittering light and fires burning in hearths, but not a single person appeared. Fairytale images covered all the closed doors on the second floor: a rabbit in a crown, a knight holding a star-shaped key, a pastry goblin tossing sweets.

Jacks hurriedly carried her past them all. Then up two more flights of stairs until he reached a pair of old glass doors that opened to an even older arched bridge that led into a thick cluster of snow-tipped trees.

"Stay with me a little longer," he murmured, and then he opened the doors.

Evangeline pressed her head to his chest, bracing for the return of cold, but instead of feeling ice, the chill felt like sparkles against her skin, giving her a small measure of relief.

It was then she also realized, although she was still in pain, she'd not experienced a single new slash or lash since they'd arrived at whatever this place was. She wondered if perhaps it was some sort of new magic that only lived here, or if Apollo was being cared for, too. She remembered Jacks telling Luc to ask Chaos to get Apollo to safety, and she hoped that was happening now.

More snowbirds chirped a cheery tune as the bridge ended at a rounded door tucked high inside the branches of a tree.

Jacks took a deep breath, and Evangeline felt his chest moving against her as they stepped through the door and into a smallish loft. There were no fires or candles, and yet somehow the place was warm and bright with the sun shining through all the many windows. So many windows carefully nestled between branches in a way that made it difficult to see where the glass began and the tree ended.

There might have been some furniture, but her vision was so hazy around the edges it was hard to be entirely sure.

The bed merely looked like a pile of old quilts in faded patterns. Jacks carefully placed her head on a pillow and laid her on her stomach. The blankets were as soft as they looked, but she still hissed from the pain that prickled across her injured back.

"Sorry, Little Fox." He brushed back the hair that had stuck to her forehead, and it felt a little like a fever dream. Or maybe she was really dying and that's why Jacks was being so sweet.

"I'll be right back." His voice was soft.

Her eyes drifted shut, then she heard his steps, featherlight, as if he didn't want to wake her.

Her lids fluttered open. She'd expected he would return with some sort of healer. But it was only Jacks with his arms full of supplies.

He set them on the wooden floor near the bed, and then he carefully smoothed her hair away from her back and shoulders. "I need to cut off your dress."

That was all the warning she got before she heard the tear of a knife as it sliced through her blood-soaked gown from her shoulder blades down to the dip in her waist.

For a second, she forgot how to breathe.

Her head grew even lighter at the feel of Jacks's hands gently peeling her dress away from her back. The process was excruciatingly slow. Several times, Jacks quietly hissed through his teeth, and she imagined what a mess her back must have been. But he didn't say a word about it. He just went on to carefully clean her wounds, wiping them with cool, damp cloths. It stung every time the cloth touched a gash. But then his fingers were soothing her by grazing the uninjured side of her ribs, sometimes with his knuckles, other times with his fingertips, and it was all she could do not to gasp.

"You're good at this," she murmured. "Do you often travel with girls who've been flayed?"

This earned her a soft laugh. "No." Then quietly, as he ran a cloth along her lower back, just below the dip in her waist, "Would you be jealous if I did?"

I'm not a jealous person was what Evangeline intended to say, but instead the words "Of course" came out.

Jacks laughed, louder this time.

Embarrassment surged through her. "That's not what I meant to say."

"It's all right. I'd probably kill another man if I found him with you like this." Jacks's hands pressed harder as they went to her shoulders and, one by one, ripped off the sleeves of her dress so that what remained of the gown completely fell away.

She made a sound somewhere between a squeal and a gasp. "Was that really necessary?"

"No, but everyone should have their clothes ripped off at some point."

She imagined Jacks was mostly trying to distract her from all the pain, yet she blushed all the way from her cheeks to her chest.

Out of the corner of her eye, she thought she saw him smile.

And for a second, nothing hurt.

He strode away from her and returned a few moments later with a folded bundle of cloth that smelled a little like a forest, clean and crisp and woodsy. "You'll want to prop your arms on this."

"For what?"

"I need to bandage you now."

Her stomach dipped as she realized what that meant: to dress her back, he'd have to wrap the cloths around her bare stomach and *chest*.

"I can close my eyes," he said, "but then I'll have to feel my way around your body."

Evangeline felt fresh butterflies along with the strange feeling that, unlike with his earlier comment, Jacks wasn't joking now. The thought made her slightly dizzy as she rested her elbows on the pile of cloth.

She briefly closed her eyes, but all that did was make her more aware of Jacks's breath against her neck as he hovered over her back and put a cool hand under her bare stomach. He was helping to lift her from the mattress, but all she could think was that his fingers were splayed across her naked skin.

"Don't forget to breathe, Little Fox, or the bandages will be too tight."

She breathed and tried to focus on the snow that fell on the other side of the windows like feathers, floating down in dreamy flakes, as Jacks started wrapping the cloth around her. He was gentle with the bandage, but a little careless with his hands—every time he wrapped the fabric around, she felt his cool fingertips brushing her stomach or ribs and occasionally her breasts.

Every touch brought a rush of electricity to her skin, and she found herself wanting to lean in. It was absurd—she was injured, and he was merely tending to her wounds. But it didn't feel like that; it felt like *more.* Or maybe she just wanted it to be more—maybe she wanted *him.*

She immediately tried to banish the thought. She couldn't want *Jacks.* But it was hard to think of all the terrible things he'd done while he continued bandaging her. She felt his breath against her neck, and she wished for a second their story could have a different ending.

The thought was instantly followed by a hot flash of guilt and a memory of Apollo telling her he wanted to try.

But then she could feel Jacks's hands again, and she wished that it was Jacks she was trying to save instead of Apollo.

She closed her eyes, forbidding all thoughts of Jacks and willing herself to just think of Apollo—or really anything except for Jacks. When she opened them again, she focused on the twisting branches that helped form the walls of the cozy loft. It was then that she noticed the vertical line of notches on the wood. The sort that children made to measure their height.

There appeared to be about five years' worth of measurements, with five names carved beside them:

Aurora
Lyric
Castor
Jacks

She wasn't sure what made her heart stop—the fact that his name was on this wall, or that another name appeared near the top, during the final year: *the Archer.*

33

Evangeline's already-light head started spinning. If Jacks's name was on this wall along with the *other* members of the Merrywood Three, then he must have been telling her the truth all this time. He wasn't one of the Merrywood Three.

She felt a shock that Jacks had been so honest. But there was also a swirl of disappointment that she had been so wrong. But maybe she hadn't been entirely wrong. Even if Jacks hadn't been a member of the Merrywood Three, they had clearly been friends. They must have all taken holidays here. And maybe whatever had happened in the past still had something to do with why he wanted to open the Valory Arch.

To open this arch, Jacks had upended her life, he'd brought her to the North, he'd cursed someone so she'd get married, he'd turned her into a fugitive, and he'd no doubt done countless other things, and she wanted to know why.

He'd never answered her before, so she doubted he'd tell her now. But maybe she could get him to reveal something that might give her more of a clue as to what he wanted. "Can you tell me about the names carved into the wood?"

Jacks's fingers stilled. "I forgot those were here."

His wrapping of the bandages grew rougher. Evangeline winced as he pulled on the cloth.

But she wasn't going to be deterred. "Why are those names here?" she pressed.

"We used to measure our heights on this wall."

"I gathered that, Jacks. I'm curious who all of you were to one another. You said you weren't part of the Merrywood Three, but you didn't mention being friends with them."

"I was only friends with Lyric and Castor."

"What about Aurora and the Archer?"

"Aurora was a pest, and I wouldn't say that the Archer was my friend." Jacks finished with the bandage, tying it tight enough to make her catch her breath.

"Why—"

"You should go to sleep now," Jacks cut in.

"I'm not tired anymore," she lied.

He gave her a withering look. "You were just flayed."

"Exactly, and I'm feeling very awake." She was actually feeling a flood of fatigue. With Jacks's hands no longer on her, there was not quite so much adrenaline. But somehow she managed to smother a yawn with a smile as she said, "If you want me to sleep, tell me a bedtime story."

"This isn't a bedtime story, Little Fox."

"Most fairytales aren't."

The frown lines around Jacks's mouth deepened. "This isn't a fairytale, either. Fairytales have heroes. But all the heroes in this story died that day at Merrywood Manor." Jacks looked back at the notches on the wall, his gaze turning far away and a little lost, making her think that the past was not a place he visited very often. "We were all a little like you back then, stupid enough to believe that if we did the right thing, it would all work out. Lyric was good, Castor was noble, and I—"

He paused and shook his head darkly, as if he didn't think much of his former self.

"I tried to be the hero that day at Merrywood Manor when Vengeance attacked. I wasn't there when it happened. When I arrived, everyone was dead except for Castor."

Evangeline watched regret wash over Jacks's face.

"He'd been stabbed in the back, and I foolishly thought I could save him. His mother, Honora, was the greatest healer in all the North. And I believed if I could just get him to her fast enough, then she could mend him. But . . ." He trailed off. She could see on his face he hadn't been fast enough. "Life is not a kind storyteller. And I'm not meant to be a savior."

Jacks turned to go.

"You're wrong." Evangeline reached out and grabbed his hand. Her grip wasn't as strong as she would have liked. Exhaustion was starting to take a deeper hold on her, but she held as tight as she could. She wanted to remind him that he'd held her as she'd cried, he'd carried her as she'd bled, he'd bandaged her wounds. But her head was growing so heavy, all she managed to say was "Tonight, you saved me."

"No, I stopped you from dying. That's not the same thing." Jacks pulled away and abruptly left.

Evangeline didn't remember closing her eyes, but when they opened again, the loft in the tree was dark, and she feared she was alone. She didn't know if Jacks had even returned to check on her after taking the supplies. She wanted to think he wouldn't leave her when she was injured like this, but he'd done similar things before.

"Jacks," she whispered.

When he didn't respond, she tried it louder. "Jacks?"

The floor beneath her creaked, but there was nothing else. It was just Evangeline, a pile of blankets, and lingering pain.

Gingerly, she pushed up on two arms. Her entire back smarted at the movement, but it wasn't horrible, and she couldn't ignore the pressure inside her that said she needed a bathing room.

Another push to her knees and—

She remembered her lack of clothing. There were only the bandages around her chest and a blanket that had just fallen from her hips.

Jacks had clearly returned at some point. He must have removed her blood-soaked dress entirely while she'd slept. She couldn't blame him. But suddenly, she was very relieved he wasn't there as she fumbled around with the bedding until she found something soft that felt like a shirt. He must have left it. It smelled of him; of apples and magic and cold, moonlit nights.

He really did smell good.

She slowly put the garment on and then rose on shaking legs. There were no burning candles to guide her, but thankfully, there were the starry lights outside. It wasn't much, just whispers of gold, but it was enough to make out the edge of the loft, where an old rope ladder led to another darkened room below.

She felt better than she would have expected, but she was still terribly sore and not anywhere close to strong enough to climb down a loose ladder.

That left the outside bridge Jacks had carried her across.

She prepared for the chill of the snow against her bare legs, the dark of the night, and the terror of crossing a sky-high bridge she could barely see. But she wasn't prepared for the wonder of all the little lights that looked like stars. A midnight army of sparkles. They warmed the air and tickled her skin and made her feel as if an adventure was about to begin.

She only hoped this adventure involved a bathing room, because she had no idea where she was going when she reached the doors at the end of the bridge.

Unlike the tree loft, the inn was still bright and as warm as she remembered. There were happy flickering candles on the walls, and she could feel the rising warmth of the roaring fire burning in the hearth of the open entry that lived below the many levels of rooms.

She didn't know what it was about this place, if it was just the sparkly lights outside or the reassuring crackle of fire, but with every step she took, she felt as if she'd left the pages of the traumatic story that was her life to visit a lost fairytale land where time and troubles both stood still.

She knew she couldn't stay here forever. But for a strange second, she was glad she was injured and that she needed to rest—because she wasn't ready to leave.

Evangeline felt even better after taking care of a few needs in the bathing room. It felt incredible to wash her hands and her face and run a comb through her hair, although it didn't do much to tame the torrent of pink and gold. But she could hardly worry about her hair when she was traipsing around in nothing but a shirt. It looked like the same one Jacks had worn the night of the costume party. Although the dark sleeves he'd rolled up to his elbows were hanging past her hands, while the hem made it down to just past her thighs.

She needed to get back to the loft before someone saw her in her state of undress—because surely there had to be someone else here tending the fires.

The hallway outside the bathing room smelled once again of spiced apple cider and warm loaves of bread, making her stomach rumble. The scent must have come from the tavern downstairs next to the entrance.

Evangeline bit her lip. Although she was feeling better, it would hurt to climb up and down four flights of stairs—not to mention, she was practically naked. But the bread and the cider smelled amazing enough to push aside those concerns.

After making her slow descent, she found a lovely entry on the first floor. She could see the rounded door that Jacks had carried her through last night. It was carved with decorative mushrooms like the ones that she'd seen on the roof. Above it, someone had carved the words *The Hollow: Inn for Travelers and Adventurers.*

To the left of the door were the stairs she'd just climbed down. Next to them was the wall with the roaring fire she'd seen from above. There were also notches and hooks shaped like branches, where it appeared travelers could hang cloaks and weapons—it seemed swords and knives weren't allowed in the tavern, which was to the right of the main door. The entry was open, and Evangeline could smell the sweet, spicy cider wafting through.

First, she stepped closer to the peculiar clock she'd noticed last night. She'd thought perhaps she'd imagined it in her daze, but it was just as she'd remembered. Bright and colorful and labeled with foods and drinks instead of numbers. The golden hour hand currently pointed to *Dumplings*, the minute hand pointed to *Cider*, and the second hand pointed to *Honey Pie*.

Evangeline felt a sudden craving for honey pie, but once

again, she found herself distracted by another sight. Right next to the meal clock, carved into the wood, were two names: *Aurora + Jacks.*

Her stomach dipped down to her toes.

"Having fun snooping?"

34

Evangeline spun around at the sound of Jacks's voice. She wanted to say she was just hunting for bread and cider—and that she wasn't disturbed at all to see Jacks's name paired with Aurora's—but the words would not come.

Jacks was standing in front of her, in just a pair of dark trousers that were scandalously low on his hips. Evangeline felt flustered at the sight of him without a shirt. The ridges of his abdomen were marble smooth. He was perfect—except for the reddened row of bite marks trailing down his neck to his shoulder.

"Did I do all of that?" With a flash of mortification, she remembered biting down on him, but she'd thought she'd only done it once.

"You really don't recall?" Jacks cocked his head to the side, and she swore it was just so she could get a better view of where her teeth had marked his skin.

She wanted to say she had no memories of biting Jacks's neck, no intense flashes of digging her teeth into his shoulder, but once more, the words refused to come.

"I'll cover them up. If you give me my shirt back." Jacks's eyes glittered as he let his gaze drift lower, past the meager buttons of the top she wore and down to her very naked legs.

She'd been warm before, but now her skin was on fire. She didn't really think he'd take the shirt, but she never knew with Jacks.

His mouth inched up playfully, and he took a deliberate step toward her. "Speaking of things we don't remember, I do have a question about something." He traced a line down her neck with his finger and took hold of the chain at her throat.

It felt like being tossed into a barrel of ice water. With all that had happened, she'd forgotten that she had the truth stone.

"Don't!" she cried.

But Jacks's fingers were faster. They plunged down her shirt and made her gasp as he pulled out the glowing gold rock.

"What do we have here, Little Fox?" His voice took on a mocking lilt. "Was this a gift from Luc?"

"No!" she said, and she might have laughed with relief that he didn't know what it was and then again at the disturbed look on his face. "Are you *jealous* of Luc?"

"I thought we already covered that yesterday. I'm always jealous. And so are you," he added with a smirk. His eyes cut past her then to the names on the wall she'd been looking at: *Aurora + Jacks.*

And she couldn't deny it. The feeling wasn't as strong as it had been in the presence of the youth stone, more of a prickle than a burn, but it was there. She shouldn't have been jealous. Aurora Valor was dead, and from what Evangeline had gathered, the circumstances around it were tragic. But in every book she'd read, Aurora was always described as the most beautiful girl to ever live. Last night, Jacks might have told Evangeline that Aurora was a pest, but here Jacks's and Aurora's names were linked together.

"Were you in love with Aurora?" she asked.

"No. I didn't even know this was here." He actually frowned, and she felt a little better. Which, again, made her feel silly.

Even if he had loved Aurora, it shouldn't have bothered her. But it seemed the delirious feelings of attraction that she'd experienced so strongly yesterday hadn't completely vanished.

It could have just been that Jacks was still standing a little too close, in only a pair of trousers, while she wore nothing but his shirt—and the necklace, which he still had yet to let go of.

She probably should have told him what the rock really was. But he'd certainly put it in another iron box, and there were so many questions she wanted to ask him.

Although it probably would be best to wait until Jacks wasn't gripping the stone. She wasn't quite sure how the stone worked, but she remembered that when she'd asked Petra questions she didn't want to answer, the rock had flared with heat and she'd been compelled to tell the truth. If the stone warmed now, Jacks might know it was magic and steal it away from her.

"I'm hungry," she announced. Then she pried Jacks's fingers from the stone and started toward the tavern.

The Hollow's tavern was just as welcoming as the rest of the curious inn, with lots of wood and candles and one wall of windows that looked out on a lake, which appeared as if it were full of stars instead of water. It was all glitter and night-glimmer, and she was already wondering what it would look like in the day.

Evangeline hadn't noticed the lake upon her arrival, but given the condition she'd been in, she imagined there were lots of things she hadn't noticed.

Like the rest of the Hollow, the tavern was empty of people, but every table and seat at the bar was set with fresh meals. Evangeline could see the steam rising from the food as she and Jacks sat at a cozy nook in the corner, near a clever triangle window that looked out upon the starry lake.

Their meals matched the ones that the hands on the clock had pointed to. There were two earthenware bowls of meat and dumplings, with thick slices of bread, mugs of spiced cider with dollops of cream, and dishes of honey pie.

It all smelled amazing, like the best parts of home and the sweetest of memories. She knew there were questions she still needed to ask, but she couldn't resist sipping the spicy cider and taking a bite of one perfect dumpling.

Jacks smiled at her, a rare curve of his lips that looked genuinely happy. "You like it?"

"Yes," she moaned, and she couldn't even be embarrassed. She hadn't finished her first dumpling yet, and she already had a feeling she'd be stealing a bowl from one of the other tables.

"Did you make all of this?"

Jacks raised a concerned brow. "You think I cook?"

"No, I suppose not." And it really didn't make sense that he would have fixed *all* this food. "I'm just trying to figure out what this place is." She took a bite of honey pie, and it tasted like a dream. "Why does everything feel so different here?"

"Long ago, before the fall of the Valors, an enchantment was placed on the Hollow to protect it from a threat. But magic often has unintended results. In the case of the Hollow, this enchantment didn't just keep the Hollow safe from one threat, it protected it from all curses and kept it unchanged throughout time."

"And that's why the food is all laid out like this," she said.

"Like clockwork," he said wryly as his long fingers tore a piece of bread and tossed it into his mouth.

She didn't think she'd ever seen him eat something that wasn't an apple. In fact, since they'd arrived, she hadn't even seen him eat one. It made her think again of what he'd just said about the Hollow being a place that was protected from all curses. She wasn't sure if that had anything to do with Jacks's apples, but it did make her wonder about something else. "Did you bring me here because I'd be protected from the curse that binds me to Apollo? Is that why the slashes stopped as soon as we arrived?"

Jacks nodded once. "I imagined the mirror curse would be put on pause if you were here. And I had hoped you'd heal faster. The magic of the Hollow is fueled by time—what feels like hours here is really days elsewhere—so people tend to heal quickly."

"Why didn't you just bring me here before, when you first learned about the curse on Apollo?"

Jacks tore at another piece of bread. "I don't ever come here. The Hollow used to be my home." His eyes turned a bleak shade of blue.

Evangeline felt the urge to say she was sorry, but she wasn't sure what for. All she knew was that her heart had cracked when he'd said the word *home*.

What had happened to change things? How had he turned from a boy with a family and friends into a Fate? And why did he no longer want to come here? To her, the Hollow felt warm and wonderful, but it clearly didn't to Jacks.

"When was the last time you were here?"

"Right after I became a Fate." Jacks's countenance shifted as soon as the words were out.

It was like watching a spell break apart.

The fire crackled, and the tavern grew hotter as Jacks's entire body tensed. He dropped the bread, hardened his jaw, narrowed his eyes on Evangeline, then slowly lowered his stormy gaze to the chain around her neck. And this time, he didn't ask if it was a gift from Luc.

"I think you've been naughty, Little Fox." He made a tsking sound with his tongue. "Where did you find the truth stone?"

"I took it from Glendora Slaughterwood's grave." The words were out before she could stop them.

And then, before she could ask him something in return, he fired another question. "And you didn't think to tell me about it?"

He sounded hurt or angry; it was hard to tell.

She felt a stab of guilt, but not that guilty as she realized he was now using the power on her, forcing her lips to spill the words, "I did think about telling you, but I didn't want you to take the stone away."

His hand shot across the table and took hold of the rock in his fist. For a second, she thought he might pull it clean off.

"Don't, please—" Her entire body tensed, and then another truth she didn't mean to say slipped out. "I just want to understand you, Jacks."

He looked at her as if she was making a mistake, features softening with something like pity, and then he ripped the stone from the chain.

"Jacks!" She scrambled to chase him as he left the tavern, but he was too fast and she was still slow from her injuries. She'd never catch up. There was also a part of her that didn't want to catch up, not when he was upset like this.

But she couldn't let him go. She wasn't sure how close she had to be for the truth stone to work, but there was still a question she had to ask and an answer she needed confirmed. She shouted at him as he left the tavern. "Why do you want to open the Valory Arch?"

A frustrated growl came from Jacks's throat. His footsteps halted just past the door. Then, almost too low for her to hear: "I don't want to open it at all."

35

J acks didn't want to open the Valory Arch. It was all Evangeline could think about as he disappeared up the stairs.

The revelation was so unexpected and incomprehensi-
ble, Evangeline fell into the nearest chair. Her back was throbbing again, and now her mind was spinning with this news.

Usually, Jacks just twisted the truth rather than lying, but
he'd told her very clearly before that he wanted to open the
Valory Arch. Hadn't he?

Evangeline swore he'd said it, but when she thought back
to the last time she'd asked him about it, she just remembered
him saying: *I'm flattered you've taken such an interest in my wants.*

She thought back further to when she'd first learned about
the existence of the Valory Arch. She'd asked Jacks what it was,
and he'd told her that she didn't need to worry about it. But he
never actually said that he didn't want to open it. Which begged
the question once again: What did Jacks actually want?

In the hall, the clock with all the meals chimed, and the hand that had pointed to *Cider* creaked its way to *Mead*. Before Evangeline's eyes, the earthen mug in front of her shifted to a tall glass filled with sparkling golden liquid the same color as the truth stone Jacks had just taken from her. And it struck her like a bolt of lightning, sharp and electric and painful. Jacks didn't want to open the Valory Arch—he just wanted the four stones.

Tiberius had said that together the Valory Arch stones possessed great power, and Petra had hinted that when all four stones were together, they were capable of impossible things. It must have been this power that Jacks wanted all along.

Was he even going to let her use the stones to open the arch and save Apollo?

Given how quickly he'd taken both stones after she'd found them, she suddenly doubted he'd ever planned to let her use them. Was this the real reason why he hadn't wanted to tell Chaos where they were going? Because he'd planned to keep the stones for himself?

Evangeline looked toward the rounded door of the tavern— she wasn't sure if Jacks would be returning soon, but she didn't plan to sit there and wait for him.

His last revelation might have left her with more questions than before, but she had learned one thing: the Hollow was Jacks's former home. If anywhere had more answers about Jacks and what he was truly after, this might be the place.

And it would be nice to find some more clothes.

Although no one was there, Evangeline still felt a little

too exposed as she climbed up to the second floor, with all its fairytale-covered doors, in nothing but Jacks's shirt. She was also starting to feel terribly achy and tired.

The first door she opened was carved with a picture of a pastry goblin tossing sweets. The room on the other side was even more delightful, decorated with apothecary jars full of colorful candies. The pillows on the bed all looked like sweets as well—wrapped taffy, gumdrops, and fluffy marshmallows. It felt tempting to lie down, just for a minute. She could almost hear the bed say, *If you sleep here, your dreams will be sweet, too.*

But Evangeline wanted answers—and clothing—more than she wanted sleep.

After opening an empty wardrobe and an empty desk, she dragged herself into the next room. This door possessed a picture of a knight with a star-shaped key, and even more stars lived inside the room, hanging from the ceiling and covering the quilt and the carpets.

She peeked inside the wardrobe—which had star-shaped handles—but it was sadly empty of both clothes and answers to mysteries.

"You don't give up, do you?" Jacks asked.

She spun to find him in the doorway, arms crossed over each other as one shoulder leaned casually against the frame.

He had come back to find her—she hadn't expected that. He'd seemed upset when he'd left. She'd thought he'd shut down again and disappear. But there he was, watching her from the doorway.

He'd put on a clean shirt—soft blue, with sleeves shoved up to the elbows, and most of the buttons done except for the ones up top, which allowed a clear view of the fading bite marks she'd left on his neck. Earlier, she'd felt so bad about them, but now she thought he deserved them.

"You lied to me." She hated that she sounded more hurt than angry and that his cold expression didn't shift.

"About what?" he drawled.

"You don't want to open the Valory Arch." She glared, hoping it hid just how much this betrayal stung. "You just want the stones."

He shrugged one shoulder, unapologetic. "I would think that would make you happy, since you've been so afraid of opening the arch."

"But I need to open it to find the cure for the Archer's curse. Were you even going to let me do that?"

Jacks didn't answer, which was practically the same as no.

It shouldn't have hurt. Even if he'd said yes, she wouldn't have believed him.

It all brought a new swell of fatigue as she started toward the door.

Jacks shot an arm across the frame, trapping her in before she could cross.

"Let me go, Jacks."

"You should get some rest, Little Fox. You look exhausted."

"I feel fantastic," she said. At least she could lie now that the stone was gone. And if she tottered on her feet as she said it, it was only because she was angry, not because her legs were starting to feel as weak as string.

She took another step and swayed.

Jacks groaned and scooped her up, one powerful arm swooping under her legs and the other behind her neck.

And suddenly, she was boneless. She knew she needed to fight him, but her body refused, mistaking his arms for somewhere safe. She hated that he could be both so gentle and so maddening. She knew that he needed her alive to find the last stone, but he didn't need to carry her; he could have left her in a guest room bed or simply let her crumble to the ground. He'd let her turn to stone before. Why couldn't he be more unfeeling now? He didn't need to hold her close to his chest as they stepped outside, protecting her from the chill.

"I'm still mad at you," she grumbled.

He sighed as they crossed the bridge. "I thought you were always mad at me."

"I almost forgave you last night."

"That would have clearly been a lapse of judgment."

"I was dying, and—" Evangeline stopped herself as he carried her into the tree loft.

She didn't know why she was arguing with him. He was right: what he'd told her earlier about the stones confirmed that she couldn't trust him. But despite being mad at him for lying, for tricking her again, she still felt impossibly drawn toward him; it didn't matter that nothing could ever come from it. The wanting from last night *still* hadn't gone away. If anything, it was even stronger. And she couldn't believe the inexorable pull she felt was entirely one-sided.

She looked up at his unreadable eyes as he lowered her into the bed. "Do you still think of me as just a tool?"

Jacks frowned. "I try not to think of you at all."

In Evangeline's dream, Jacks was sitting in the shadows at the end of an old wooden dock, overlooking the same lake she'd seen from the tavern. The one that had been full of stars. Only now there were no stars, just a gem-bright sky, trapped in the final moments of a sunset. All pink clouds and brilliant strands of glowing yellow and orange.

She watched as Jacks skipped a rock across the mirror-smooth surface of the water. *Plink. Plink. Plink. Plink. Plink.* When it disappeared, he tossed another.

He didn't look up as she approached. His back was to a post, hair tousled and dark *brown*.

Evangeline's steps faltered.

From a distance, she'd thought Jacks had been cast in shadow, but now it was clear the young man at the end of the dock was not Jacks.

"You're a difficult one to track down." The young man turned from the lake, and when she saw his face, her breath caught in her chest.

She thought at first that he looked familiar, but it might just have been that he was incredibly handsome, clean-cut jaw, dark eyebrows over hypnotic eyes, and a charming smile that made her heart take an excited little tumble.

"Who are you?"

Ignoring her question, the handsome stranger leaped to his feet with one agile move. His clothes were rough and rugged, the kind meant for forest adventures, but his movements were graceful and slightly predatory.

Evangeline felt a flicker of caution. She told herself this was just a dream, but this was the Magnificent North, and she feared that dreams were like fairytales, a little bit true and not entirely trustworthy.

He dropped his brilliant eyes to her very naked legs. Evangeline was still only dressed in Jacks's shirt, and she flushed from her toes to her cheeks. But she tried not to let it show in her voice as she asked the handsome stranger once again, "Who are you?"

His eyes glittered with his smile. "Why don't we just stick with the Handsome Stranger."

Her heart did an embarrassed flip. "You can read my thoughts."

"No, but it's the truth. I am incredibly handsome." He sauntered forward a step, cocking his head as he took in her face instead of her bare legs. "I can see why Jacks likes you. You're a bit like her, you know?"

"Like who?" Evangeline asked.

The Handsome Stranger rubbed his jaw. "He wouldn't be

happy if he knew I said this, but if you're not careful, you'll end up like her as well."

"Like who?" Evangeline repeated.

"His first fox."

36

Birds were chirping and the sun was shining, but all Evangeline wanted to do was fall back to sleep and hear more about the first fox.

She closed her eyes, but she was too alert, and she had a feeling she already knew who this other fox was. If she believed the Handsome Stranger from her dream, then Jacks was really the Archer.

Evangeline had considered it before, but she'd dismissed the idea, even before she'd seen Jacks's name and the Archer's both etched onto the wall. A fact that had also made her doubt what the Handsome Stranger had said.

She would have asked Jacks about it, but Jacks wasn't in the loft. And before she brought the question up, she wanted to be sure about it. All she had was the word of this Handsome Stranger.

The last "helpful" stranger that she'd met—Petra—had tried

to kill her. And given the number of others who'd tried to murder Evangeline as well, it wasn't unreasonable to imagine this Handsome Stranger wanted the very same thing—planting ideas in her head that would make her distrust Jacks.

Evangeline decided to dismiss the idea entirely and push all thoughts of the Handsome Stranger away as she made her way out of bed and then down to the cozy tavern to eat. She half expected this part of the Hollow to have been a dream as well. But just like yesterday, she sat down at a table and her food appeared before her like clockwork.

The only thing missing was Jacks.

As she ate, she kept expecting to look up and find him leaning in the doorway.

It was tempting to panic when she finished her meal and he still hadn't appeared. But the Hollow was the sort of place that made it very difficult to hold on to any panic.

Everything about the whimsical inn inspired curiosity instead of fear. In a third-floor bathing room, Evangeline found the most delightful copper tub, reminiscent of the clock in the hall. It had lovely jeweled handles and a faucet that could pour out different-colored waters in a variety of scents:

Pink honeysuckle
Lavender rose
Green pine needle
Silver rain

She'd mixed the rain and honeysuckle, and now she smelled like a sweet and stormy day. She'd not expected to be able to take a bath, but her back was fully healed.

It was actually a little disappointing. Now that she was healed, she imagined that Jacks would want to take her from this place as soon as he returned. There was still one more stone left to find.

But Evangeline wasn't feeling particularly driven to find it. As she'd noted earlier, the Hollow was not a place where it was easy to hold on to panic or fear, and her entire search for the stones had been inspired by fear. She wasn't afraid right now. In fact, she couldn't remember a time where she had been more at peace. And she knew, somehow, that Apollo was safe as well.

Without Jacks or anyone else, she kept expecting the Hollow to feel lonely. But strangely, Evangeline didn't feel empty or alone. The Hollow felt like the safest place she'd ever been. She found herself wishing that she could share this enchanted place with her parents. Her father would have loved all the magical wonders, and her mother would have adored all the fairytale rooms.

On the fourth floor, Evangeline finally uncovered a wardrobe full of dresses that made her think of butterflies in gardens and the feel of holding someone's hand.

From them, she chose a soft cream dress with golden embroidery and a thick pink ribbon that tied around the waist, matching the trim on the sweet, puffed sleeves.

All she needed now was slippers.

She imagined finding a magical pair of shoes as she rummaged through the floor of the wardrobe. Surprisingly, there were no spiderwebs or balls of dust, just boxes of gloves and ribbons, along with a curious little book.

It was the first book she'd found in the Hollow, and the side of it was locked. Evangeline searched for a key, until she remembered that she could simply use her blood.

The lock opened with a click, and the first aged page was covered in a very old-fashioned handwritten script.

Property of Aurora Valor
Do not read unless you wish to die shortly thereafter.
I have cursed this book!
Cease your reading if you value your life.
This includes you, Castor!

Evangeline felt a thrill as she read the words. She'd found the diary of the mysterious Aurora Valor. Perhaps this would provide more clues about Jacks's past—since he'd clearly known Aurora.

The bit about the book being cursed gave Evangeline brief pause, as did the undecipherable words at the very bottom, which were the only ones written in the language of the Valors. But according to what Jacks had told her, curses couldn't touch her in this place. The writing also looked a touch juvenile, which made Evangeline guess that the book wasn't truly cursed.

She carried the diary downstairs to read before the fire in the tavern.

In the journal's first few pages, there was quite a bit of complaining about her brothers, paired with mentions of weather and meals and clothing that made Evangeline imagine Aurora had either led a very mundane life or she still was trying to dissuade readers by including only boring details.

Evangeline didn't come across Jacks's name. She skimmed ahead searching for any mentions of him until the style of writing turned more sophisticated and the content became more interesting.

Father set a date for the wedding. I cannot believe he's forcing me into this. He would never force Dane, Lysander, Romulus, or Castor—and if you're still reading this, Castor, stop! I was serious about the curse.

I suppose Vengeance is handsome enough, but I feel nothing for him aside from revulsion when he brags too much about himself and his collection of swords.

I've tried telling Mother and Father that I don't love him, but Mother promises I'll grow to love him, and Father tells me I'm too young and I know nothing of love. But I do know love. I know it so deeply, it's hard not to fill the pages of this book with my feelings for my truest love. But I dare not write about him, for although this book is cursed, I fear someone could read it and before my curse strikes them down dead, they could pass on what I've written to my father or to Vengeance.

LaLa keeps telling me that I should just marry Vengeance. But I don't think she's ever really liked me. I don't think she believes I'm good enough for her brother, which is fine, as I don't think she's good enough for my brother.

The entry ended there. Evangeline flipped through the rest of the journal. There were, sadly, only a few more pages with writing, but none of them were nearly as interesting as what this page revealed.

The journal confirmed the story Jacks had told about Aurora and Vengeance. But what struck Evangeline was what the entry had revealed about LaLa. The journal didn't mention the name of LaLa's brother, but Evangeline had a sinking feeling she knew who LaLa's brother was, because she knew who Aurora's true love was—*Lyric Merrywood.*

Evangeline felt a sharp pain as she thought about the horrible fate that had befallen House Merrywood. She knew she was supposed to be upset with LaLa for putting the Archer's curse on Apollo and her, and she was—but her heart was also breaking at the thought that LaLa hadn't just lost her brother but her entire family.

It was almost too much to process. Evangeline was a little surprised Jacks hadn't mentioned this when he'd told her about the destruction of the Merrywoods, but given how private Jacks was about his past, she could understand how he could also be careful with the pasts of others. Of course, that hadn't stopped him from being nasty to LaLa about her choice of fiancé.

It all made a mind-spinning, terrible sort of sense.

Evangeline wondered then if this story had anything to do with LaLa's desire to open up the Valory Arch. Evangeline still didn't know what LaLa wanted, only that she wanted it badly enough to curse Apollo and her.

The clock in the first-floor hall struck *Porridge*.

Evangeline dropped the book—both from the sound and the shocking realization that a full day and night had passed while she'd been reading and wandering about the Hollow.

Jacks had said time worked differently here. But it wasn't just that the time had gone so quickly, it was that she'd been so unaware of its passage. And Jacks was still gone.

The front door to the Hollow swung open.

Evangeline spun toward it, expecting Jacks to step through.

But it seemed the door had been opened by a gust of wind.

The only creature who entered was a lost-looking little dragon, coughing tiny gold sparks as he hopped inside.

He was blue and shimmering and so adorable, Evangeline couldn't help but smile at the sight of him looking curiously around.

Dragons weren't meant for indoors, but this glittery little fellow didn't want to leave. She kept the door open for a full, freezing minute, but the tiny dragon just flew toward the clock, bumping his little head as he tried to get to the jeweled pendulums—over and over. Evangeline eventually scooped him up and brought him with her to the tavern.

The tables were once again magically set with steaming bowls of porridge and fresh cups of chocolate, which the tiny dragon kindly kept warm for Evangeline. She imagined he didn't want to be tossed back outside and was trying to make himself useful.

The dragon seemed to worry every time her eyes cut toward the door. But she wasn't thinking of throwing her new little friend back into the cold. She was looking for Jacks. And now she was starting to feel just a little nervous.

Lunch was much the same. In between bites of food, Evangeline found herself gazing toward the doorway for Jacks.

She reminded herself that Jacks was a Fate. He could control people's emotions. He could kill with a kiss. He could handle himself.

But by dinner, Evangeline started to worry again that something might have happened to him. He'd been gone for nearly two days now. He'd disappeared before—he'd left her at Chaos's castle for ten days—but he'd written a note letting her know he was leaving. This time, he'd just gone.

She thought of the last thing he'd said to her: *I try not to think of you at all.*

Had he left to prove that point?

Whether he had or he hadn't, there was a queasy feeling in her stomach that wouldn't settle, despite the warmth of the Hollow. She wasn't afraid, but she wasn't at peace.

Evangeline stirred her cider and shoved her food around her plate.

Halfway through her meal, the tiny dragon suddenly darted behind her cider mug. The last broken heart scar on Evangeline's wrist prickled, and she turned toward the tavern doorway to find Jacks had returned.

He was breathtaking without even trying as he leaned in the doorframe with windswept golden hair and a crooked cape.

"Where have—" She broke off almost immediately.

Jacks wasn't leaning in the doorway, he was gripping it for support.

"Jacks!" She ran across the tavern, horrified as his cape slipped from his shoulder, revealing a great stain of sparkling gold and red blood.

37

"What happened?" Evangeline gasped.

"I was just being myself." Jacks staggered back, half collapsing on a bench in the entry.

Snowy air blew inside from the cracked-open door. She knew she should shut it, but she went to him first. She'd never seen him injured, and it was surprisingly terrifying.

"Jacks—" She shook his cold shoulders, gentle but firm. She didn't know much about tending to injuries, but she recalled he hadn't let her pass out when she'd been bleeding. "Please, stay with me. I don't know what to do."

The glittering blood was spreading across his doublet, turning the smoky gray to red. Her chest clenched at the sight of it; she wished she hadn't just sat in the tavern, she wished she'd gone out looking for him. As a Fate, Jacks didn't age, but he could die if injured badly enough.

She needed to mend him quickly. She needed to take off his doublet, clean the wound, then stitch it up.

"Is the weapon still in there?" She reached for his cloak to push it farther back.

"It's fine." Jacks grabbed her wrist, stopping her hand from exploring. "I just need a blanket . . . and some sleep."

He tugged her toward him as if intending her for the blanket.

"Oh no—I'm not a quilt." She braced her free hand against the wall, stomach tumbling as she looked down on his hazy blue eyes. "I need to stitch you up first."

It took two pulls to free her wrist. Even injured, Jacks was incredibly strong. She could still feel the imprint of his cold fingers as she dashed into the tavern.

Behind the bar, she found liquor and then a number of cloths, which she desperately hoped would do for now. She could clean him first, then search for thread and needles.

"You're wasting your time, Little Fox." Jacks leaned against the doorway, clutching his side. "It's just a knife to the ribs."

"I suppose it's going to heal on its own?"

"Yours did."

"After you tended to them."

His mouth twitched up at the corner. "Only because I wanted to take off your clothes."

A vivid image of Jacks's hands on her skin flashed before her eyes.

Of course, she was almost certain he was joking. He seemed

delirious. His eyes were losing focus, and he was swaying on his feet.

Evangeline didn't know how she got him up a flight of stairs. Fortunately, there were endless available rooms at the Hollow. She helped him into the closest one, a suite that smelled of fresh pine needles. The carpets were deep shades of green, the bed was made of thick cuts of wood, and the sheets were crisp and white. A fire kicked to life in the hearth as soon as he half fell onto the bed.

Jacks's bleeding had thankfully stopped, but he seemed exhausted. Before he shut his eyes, she saw that they were webbed with red, and even the blue was tinged with it. She wondered if he'd slept at all the past couple of days.

It felt strange to worry about Jacks, but she doubted anyone else did, including himself. His chest barely rose and fell as he lay across a pile of snowy white quilts.

Evangeline hastened out to retrieve a basin of water.

When she returned, Jacks had kicked his boots onto the wood floor, but he still wore his cloak and bloody doublet.

"Are you going to tell me what you were doing?" she pressed.

"I already told you," he muttered. "I was just being myself. Other people were being their horrible selves, and as you can see, it didn't end well."

"Where were you?"

"Stop asking such difficult questions."

He groaned, eyes still closed, as she undid the cloak to get to the wound. She hung the garment on a chair near the roaring fire to dry. Snow had left it damp, and she imagined it was also wet with blood, though the fabric was too dark to see.

Jacks's doublet was lighter, a soft dove gray, save for the parts near his ribs that were stained red. She cut the garment off.

His chest moved slowly up and down.

She peeled the doublet away, careful not to brush his bare skin with her fingers. Yet Evangeline felt as if she were holding her breath as she started to clean the ragged gash of blood across his ribs.

It would need to be stitched. Or it should have—

Evangeline paused her ministrations as she watched Jacks's skin knit together before her eyes. It was still painfully red, and she imagined it could easily open again with friction, but the gash was healing; it would not kill him.

The relief she felt was enormous.

By the time she finished bandaging him, he appeared to be asleep, closed eyes half-covered in tousled waves of golden hair. She briefly debated staying with him as he rested.

She was relieved he was back and that he was safe. More relieved than she should have been. She kept reminding herself Jacks was dangerous. But he didn't look that way now—he looked like a sleeping angel, which was probably why she needed to leave him.

She ran her fingers through his soft hair, just once.

He leaned into her hand. "That feels good," he mumbled. "You feel good, too." He hooked an arm around her waist and drew her onto the bed.

"Jacks—what are you doing?"

"Just for tonight." He tightened his arm, holding her even closer, until her chest was pressed against his bare skin.

"You're injured," she breathed.

"This makes me feel better." He spoke against her throat and finished with a lick that made her head begin to spin.

Now would have been a really good time to untangle herself. His mouth closed over her pulse.

She tried to tell him this was a bad idea, but a soft sigh came out instead. If his lips felt like this on her neck, she wondered how they'd feel on her lips.

Her eyes closed, and her breath went shallow. She shouldn't think about Jacks's lips on hers. And yet she couldn't help but wonder if maybe she could kiss Jacks here, in the Hollow, in the one place curses couldn't touch them. The idea was painfully tempting. But even if Jacks's kiss couldn't kill her here, that didn't mean it wouldn't ruin her in other ways. "We shouldn't do this," she said.

"I'm just asking you to stay the night." His lips left her neck as he murmured, "You won't even remember."

Evangeline tensed in his arms. "What do you mean, I won't remember?"

"I mean . . . it's just one night," he said softly. "In the morning, you can forget it. You can go back to pretending you don't like me, and I can pretend that I don't care. But for tonight, let me pretend you're mine."

She melted at the word *mine*. For a dizzying second, she

couldn't think. She couldn't bring herself to pull away, and yet she couldn't tell him she would stay.

"If it's easier, you can pretend, too," he whispered. "You can pretend that I'm still Jacks of the Hollow and that you want to be mine." His mouth pressed against her throat once more and slowly traced a blissful line up her neck, to her ear. Then his teeth nipped her earlobe.

She gasped. The bite was sharp and a little painful, as if he wanted to hold her and punish her, too. But he didn't have to punish her. This was already torture because she wanted it so much. She wanted him to want her, even if he was half-delirious in his wanting.

"I'm not delirious." His voice was husky with something like sleep, but when he looked down on her, his eyes were clear and lucid.

And Evangeline felt as if she were tumbling into them.

When she was a child, her mother had once told her a story about a young woman who'd been playing hide-and-seek in a forest with her love. The young woman had been running through the trees, searching for a place to hide, when she'd fallen through a crack in time. It was just a tiny crack, a hairline fissure that should have plopped the young woman a few seconds into the future—or perhaps into the past. But Time had seen the young woman and fallen instantly in love. And so, instead of landing in the future or finding herself in the past, the young woman continued to fall through time. She fell and fell and fell, trapped by Time until the end of Time.

Evangeline knew that feeling now. More than two weeks had passed since she'd jumped off that cliff with Jacks, and somehow she felt as if she were still falling, plummeting toward something uncontrollable with nothing but Jacks to hold on to.

She knew Jacks was far too dangerous a person to truly fall for. But she could no longer deny that it was happening. She couldn't deny that she wanted him. Just enough to keep her from pulling away every time he touched her. Enough to keep his name near the tip of her tongue even when he wasn't in the room. The physical attraction had always been there, but her pull toward him had been increasing ever since the night they'd jumped off that cliff together.

Because she'd never actually stopped falling.

Her blood rushed faster and her heart stuttered. She tried not to move, hoping he wouldn't be able to tell as they lay in that bed, chests pressed close and legs tangled together. Everything between them felt as fragile as a raindrop that would cease to exist when it touched the ground. But the Hollow also felt like the sort of place where raindrops never touched the ground.

Jacks slowly ran a hand up and down her spine. "Have you decided to stay?"

"I thought you already heard what I was thinking," she whispered.

"I want you to say it out loud." His words were low and quiet; she wouldn't have heard them if she hadn't been so close. And it struck her how intimate words could be, how they could be spoken only once, for only one person, and they would never be heard again, they would disappear like a moment, gone almost as soon as you realized they were there.

Evangeline's heart was still racing, and she wondered now if it wasn't scared or nervous but if it was just trying to catch up to all the moments before they disappeared—before *he* disappeared. She knew it would happen; it always did, Jacks always left, which made this even more foolish, and yet right now, she didn't want to be smart. She just wanted to be his.

She meant to say, *For tonight, I'm yours,* but all that came out was "I'm yours."

38

That night, the Handsome Stranger was in the Hollow's tavern, standing just a few feet away, throwing darts at a painted board on the wall and hitting the red bullseye every time.

"I know," he said. "It's hard to believe I'm so handsome *and* so talented."

Swish.

He hit another bullseye, with all the ease of a young man who was either incredibly skillful or incredibly used to things happening the way that he wanted.

"Why are you haunting my dreams?"

"'Haunting' implies that I'm dead. Do I look dead to you?" He placed a hand over his chest and gave her a bewitching smile.

She still hesitated to trust him, but the sense of familiarity was back. The way he looked at her felt like a dare she'd received once before. He was a name on the tip of her tongue that she couldn't quite recall. A feeling that she couldn't put a name to.

"Who are you?" she asked.

"I still prefer Handsome Stranger."

Evangeline gave him a sour look. "Why not just tell me?"

He pulled at the back of his neck. "I would, but that might make Jacks a bit jealous, and given how close you two are becoming, that wouldn't be a good idea. Although getting cozy with Jacks isn't too smart, either."

The stranger raised two condescending brows.

"What I do with Jacks is none of your business," Evangeline snapped.

The Handsome Stranger frowned. "I'm not trying to upset you, Evangeline, I'm trying to save your life."

"Why do you care about my life?" she asked suspiciously.

The Handsome Stranger threw another dart, hard enough to cut through one of the other darts in the bullseye. "You need to be careful with Jacks. I don't think he's in his right mind right now."

"He's right." LaLa stepped into the tavern dressed in a sleeveless gown that appeared as if it were made of treasure, with a belt around her waist that looked like a crown, and a full skirt covered in sparkling jewels.

"What are you doing here?" Evangeline asked.

"Yeah—this is my dream!" The Handsome Stranger tossed a dart at LaLa.

She batted it away with a scowl. "We're on the same side, you nitwit." Then she turned to Evangeline with a face that looked like an apology.

"I came to say I'm sorry—about Apollo. I felt so guilty. I had hoped to talk to you about it and explain everything before you ran off from the party. Jacks had promised he wouldn't tell you what I did—"

"He didn't tell me," Evangeline cut in, too tired to be polite to the person who'd cursed her husband to hunt her down and kill her. "Jacks never said a word. I overheard the two of you talking."

"Oh." LaLa worried her lip between her teeth. "I suppose I owe him an apology for stabbing him with that butter knife, then."

"You're the one who stabbed him?" Evangeline was begrudgingly impressed. It would take a lot of strength and determination to seriously wound someone with a butter knife.

LaLa shrugged a shoulder. "It was probably an overreaction, but it wasn't just because I thought he'd told you everything. He was being nasty about my engagement—"

"From what I've heard, you deserved it," the Handsome Stranger interrupted.

"Don't you dare lecture me, too," LaLa spat. "You're half the reason we're in this mess. If you hadn't—"

LaLa broke off as the Handsome Stranger vanished. *Poof!* He simply disappeared, leaving nothing but a dart that fell to the floor.

"What happened to him? And why did you just say he's half the reason we're in this mess?"

"I'm not sure we have enough time for me to explain everything." LaLa frowned at where the dart had fallen on the floor. "Jacks probably removed him, and I imagine he'll do the same to me soon. So you need to listen carefully."

"But this is my dream," Evangeline protested.

LaLa sighed. "I don't have time to explain how Fates can manipulate dreams. You're just going to have to trust me."

"Why should I trust you after everything you've done?"

LaLa gnawed on her lip, looking unusually nervous. "I never wanted Apollo to kill you. You really are my friend, Evangeline. I just made a rash decision the day I learned that you could open up the Valory Arch but that you weren't planning on doing it. It was a horrible mistake. But I really didn't want you to die. That's why I put the mirror curse on both of you—I thought, if Apollo actually hurt you, he'd be injured as well, and then he couldn't keep hunting you. Everyone knows he's a terrible shot, so I didn't ever believe he'd hit you in the heart with an arrow."

As apologies went, it was far from the best one Evangeline had ever received, and yet it felt earnest. LaLa looked up at her with pleading eyes, and Evangeline could see they were also rimmed in red and splotches of smeared kohl. LaLa had looked so sparkling and perfect when she'd first stepped into the dream, but the longer Evangeline watched her, the more she could see the signs of anguish all over her pretty face.

Evangeline knew from her experience with Jacks that Fates had different moral lines from those of humans, which made it easier to forgive LaLa. But Evangeline still felt wary of her friend. She could believe LaLa didn't want her dead, but it was troubling to know that she'd been all right with her being hunted down. "I want to know why you did it. What's in the Valory that you want so badly?"

"Evangeline, we don't have time for this," LaLa said. As she spoke, gems fell from her skirt onto the floor. "The dream is already starting to fracture."

"I don't care," Evangeline said. "I can forgive you for what you did, but if you want me to even think about trusting you again, I need to know why you did it."

"The Valory is either a treasure chest that protects the Valors' greatest magical gifts—or it's a magical prison that is home to an abomination that the Valors created." LaLa twisted her mouth as if the words had come out all mangled.

"Stupid story curse," she muttered. "I'm afraid, since I'm not actually in the Hollow, I still can't tell you what's inside the arch."

"Well, you need to tell me something," Evangeline said. She still wasn't sure she could believe anything LaLa told her, but she wanted some sort of explanation.

"I might be able to tell you a story." LaLa started to pace the tavern, her shining boots clacking against the wooden floor. "Once—there was someone I loved more than anyone else. He—" She broke off abruptly and wrenched her mouth as if she couldn't say what she'd originally planned. "He could shift into a dragon—a large one," she finally shoved out. "As you know, dragons like hoarding treasures, and I've always liked wearing sparkling things, and that was why he found me. He was flying in his dragon form, and he plucked me from the ground, thinking I was treasure."

LaLa's face turned wistful as she picked a gem off her glittering skirt. And Evangeline remembered a young man who looked like a dragon at LaLa's party, dancing with a girl costumed like treasure. "Were there people who dressed like you and your dragon at the ball?"

"Yes. It's an old story," LaLa said. "Most people in the North know the bit I just told you, but they don't remember who the dragon was—" LaLa's mouth contorted once more, words failing her before she finally said, "My first love is the true reason I'm the Unwed Bride. My grooms never leave me. I always call things off with them because I've never been able to let go of my love. I chose to become a Fate because Fates aren't supposed to be able to love, and I wanted to stop loving him. I wanted to let him go. But I can't."

LaLa ran one hand up and down a brown arm covered in a brilliant dragon fire tattoo. Evangeline had always thought the ink was because LaLa had so much spark to her personality, but now Evangeline knew the tattoo was for her very first love.

"I've tried to fall for others. But no matter how close I come to falling in love, there's still only one person that I want to give my heart to. And there's only one way for that to happen."

LaLa stopped pacing and looked at Evangeline with eyes full of sparkling tears. LaLa had once confessed she wanted love so badly she cried poison tears. At the time, Evangeline thought she understood. She desperately wanted love, too. But to have found true love and lost it, and yet still have a sliver of hope of getting it back, was another type of torture entirely.

"Your love is in the Valory," Evangeline guessed.

LaLa didn't respond, as if she couldn't even acknowledge the question. But Evangeline imagined she was right—locking a dragon shifter in the Valory fit with the version of the story that said the Valory was an enchanted prison that locked away magical beings.

"Why didn't you just tell me this story before when I came to your flat?" Evangeline asked.

LaLa's face fell further. "I never tell this tale. And I wanted to believe that I had finally fallen in love with someone else. I didn't want to admit that my shiny new engagement was another lie I was telling myself because I couldn't get over my childhood love. But then I suddenly feared that I was going to lose my only chance at seeing my true love again, and, well— you know the rest." LaLa's forehead creased with regretful lines. "I hope you can forgive me for cursing you and Apollo."

Evangeline hesitated. She was still hurt by what LaLa had done, but she also hurt for LaLa and all that she'd been through.

"Just promise not to do it again." Evangeline reached forward and gave her friend a hug. "We all make mistakes for love. I was so desperate to hold on to my first love that I made a deal with Jacks that turned an entire wedding party into stone."

This made LaLa laugh. "I didn't know Jacks could turn people into stone."

"He can't. Poison owed him a favor, and Jacks had him do it."

LaLa pulled away and gave Evangeline a peculiar look. "Speaking of Jacks, I'm afraid you might be in danger."

The ground started shaking as soon as she said *danger*.

LaLa cursed, and when she spoke again, her words came out in a torrent. "Listen to me carefully. You've been missing for weeks, Evangeline. We all thought you were dead until Jacks appeared a few days ago. I think he has the mirth stone and it's clouding his judgment."

The ground cracked. LaLa jumped back, and more stones fell from her gown into the growing fissure.

"From the look of this dream, it seems he's tucked you away in the Hollow," she rushed out. "I'm sure it feels like a haven right now, but as long as you are with Jacks, you're not safe." More of the ground began to crumble. "If you think you are safe—it's only because you're feeling the effects of the mirth stone as well. But you have to fight it. Find the mirth stone, get it away from Jacks, and get out of the Hollow, before—"

39

Evangeline woke up on a swallowed gasp that tasted like magic and cold. Her lips were on Jacks's throat. She felt a burst of panic, until piece by piece last night came back.

Jacks had returned. He'd been wounded. He'd healed. Then he'd asked her to stay. He'd tugged her onto the bed. He'd held her close. And then he'd said, *Let me pretend you're mine.*

She melted once more at the memory of how he'd said the word *mine*. It was only supposed to be for the night, but the pretending hadn't stopped. Light was bleeding through the windows, showering them in sunshine as they lay together, legs and arms entwined. One of his cool hands wrapped protectively around her waist, and the other had made its way up her skirt, holding her to him as if touching were a form of breathing.

They had moved closer as they'd slept, as if drawn by some force that she suspected was simply each other.

The thought made her chest feel light and bubbly. Or maybe it was just the feel of waking up so close to Jacks. This was what she wanted more than any stones. She just wanted to stay here with Jacks and forget everything else.

But you are forgetting, she thought.

Something else was there. She could feel it, right beneath the surface of her bliss.

Ignore it, she thought.

But the more she tried to ignore it, the more she started to remember. The dream in the tavern. The Handsome Stranger, the darts. LaLa. The warning about Jacks, the warning about the mirth stone. It all came back in a horrible rush. *He has the mirth stone and it's clouding his judgment.*

Evangeline closed her eyes and told herself it was just a dream. She didn't want to think that last night Jacks had only wanted her because of the stone.

It couldn't have been because of the stone. Jacks didn't have the stone. She'd taken off his shirt last night, she'd seen his chest. He wasn't wearing any stones. His judgment wasn't clouded. He wasn't lying in bed with her because of magic.

Unless the stone was in a trouser pocket?

Evangeline took a nervous breath. She still didn't think he had it—she didn't want him to have it, but it would be easy enough to make sure. One of her hands was on his back. All she had to do was slide it lower. . . .

Her fingers glided over his skin carefully. He was still cool to the touch and smooth and soft, and for a second, she almost forgot what she was doing. She could have easily traced her fingers up and down his spine or his back or the ridges of his stomach. But she let them drift toward his pants.

She bit her lip as her fingers slid lower and—

Jacks made a soft sound.

Her heart skipped a beat. Her fingers had barely dipped into his pocket—painfully slowly, she let them slide lower. The material was soft and the pocket was . . .

Empty.

He didn't have the stone. She nearly cried in relief.

Until she realized . . . she shouldn't be relieved. She should have wanted to find the mirth stone. It was the only stone still missing. Once she found the mirth stone, she could open the Valory Arch and break the Archer's curse.

But she hadn't really been thinking about the Archer's curse or Apollo. And for as long as she'd been here, she hadn't wanted to look for the mirth stone. She hadn't wanted to leave. She'd felt too content, too happy. She hadn't even felt guilt over killing Petra. She knew it was self-defense, but she should have felt *something*. She tried to feel sad, but even now, it wouldn't come. There were other thoughts she'd pushed aside; she couldn't even remember them now, but she knew they were there.

But was this because the mirth stone had clouded her judgment? Or had her attraction to Jacks clouded it?

Evangeline bit down on her lip as she slowly slid her hand out of Jacks's pocket, and before she could rethink it, she untangled herself from him and stumbled out of the bed. It felt like a mistake as soon as she was free of his arms. She wanted to go back to him—to wrap herself up in him. The pull was stronger than ever.

With every step she took from the bed, she felt as if she was doing the wrong thing. But Evangeline wasn't sure she could trust her feelings.

She forced herself to leave the room, to stumble back out into the hall.

The clock in the entry struck *Toast and Tea*.

The sound was as bright and light as the morning sun streaming in through the open tavern and casting light on the clock's jeweled pendulums, and the little baby dragon that was trying to reach them—pawing at the glass, kissing it, petting it with his tiny paws, in hopes of getting to the jewels.

"Oh no, darling—" Evangeline went to scoop up the beast, but she found herself opening the glass and reaching for one of the jeweled pendulums instead. It was so pretty and—

She pulled her hand back and staggered away—she knew this feeling.

This wasn't just a gem. She could feel the power pulsing through it, sweet and soft as a siren's call. This jewel was the mirth stone.

40

The awful truth pressed against Evangeline's chest, making it hard to breathe. LaLa had been right. The mirth stone was here. All this time, it had been clouding Jacks's judgment—and *hers*. Nothing she'd felt here was real. The sense of safety and happiness, the growing feelings she had for Jacks, it was all because of the mirth stone.

It should have been a relief. She was married to Apollo, and Jacks was not someone whom she could ever have a future with. He'd already found the one girl who'd made his heart beat, and it wasn't her. Evangeline wasn't Jacks's true love. But she found herself wishing that she were.

She closed her eyes, trying to clear her head, even though all she really wished to do was close the glass door of the clock and forget what she'd discovered. She'd come to the North hoping for a happily ever after, and being here with Jacks was the closest she'd come to feeling it. Ever since coming here, Jacks no longer felt like her enemy, he felt like her home.

Evangeline worried her lip. She shouldn't want any of this, because it wasn't real. But what actually made something real? If it was a lack of magic, then nothing in the North was entirely real.

Evangeline carefully scooped up the little dragon. Then she closed the door to the clock, securing the mirth stone behind the glass.

She knew what she needed to do—she just wasn't ready to do it yet.

In the tavern, Evangeline found thick stacks of toast, all accompanied by scrumptious cast-iron pots of Hollow marmalade, Northern lemon curd, Merrywood blueberry jam, and something thick and chocolaty. Her little dragon immediately claimed the chocolate pot.

Evangeline scraped some lemon curd onto a piece of bread, but she couldn't bring it to her lips. Her stomach churned as she thought about the mirth stone sitting merrily in the clock. Now that she knew it was there, the peace she'd felt before was shattered.

But the pull she felt toward Jacks was not.

She sensed him as soon as he stepped into the tavern. The air turned charged as if sparks had taken the place of half the oxygen. The broken heart scar on her wrist tingled pleasantly, and she felt herself smiling.

"Hello," he said, almost shyly, as he approached the table. He was barefoot and shirtless, and adorably tousled, with golden hair falling over sparkly eyes that looked as if they were still waking up.

"Hi." Her voice came out oddly shy as well, which only seemed to make Jacks smile.

"You didn't have to sneak out of bed," he said.

"I didn't sneak."

"Then why didn't you stay?" He casually slid into the seat beside her and turned to her with a wolfish grin. It was a smile like a fairytale, part villain, part hero, part impossible ever after.

She couldn't bear how much she loved it.

But then she remembered the stone. She imagined she'd feel differently if it was in an iron box, and she feared that Jacks would, too. That he wouldn't be looking at her as if he wanted to devour her instead of the breakfast.

"Tomorrow, I won't let you leave so easily." His eyes flashed with mischief, and he stole a bite of her toast.

The gesture was so simple and so comfortable, and all she could think was that it would be so easy to stay here. "I thought you said it was just one night."

"I thought you never believed what I said." He shook his head reproachfully and tugged her onto his lap.

"Jacks—" Evangeline put a hand against his chest. She could feel his heart was pounding, which surprised her. On the outside, he looked so casual and careless, but now she imagined he felt as nervous as she did. It made her want to pull him closer, to press her head into his shoulder and tell him all the things that she was trying not to feel.

She wrapped her arms around his neck, and for a second, she held tight. She held him as if he were hers and she were his, and there was nothing else between them. No curses. No lies. No past wounds or mistakes. She held him as if there was only now, as if nothing mattered but this moment. Then she let him go. She shoved off his lap with clumsy arms and even clumsier legs that stumbled as she tried to step back.

"Evangeline . . . what's wrong?" A line creased between his brows.

"This isn't real, Jacks. You and I, we're under the influence of the mirth stone."

"You think you would only feel this way about me because of a rock?" Jacks's mouth clamped shut. For a second, he looked angry, but when she looked in his eyes, all she could see was hurt.

Evangeline wanted to take the words back. She didn't want to cause him pain. She didn't want to do this at all. But she knew they couldn't stay here, even for another day, because she feared one day wouldn't be enough—*there would never be enough*. If Evangeline stayed here with Jacks, she would be like Petra, holding on to him the way that Petra had held on to her youth and her stone, willing to do whatever she needed to keep them.

"I don't think, I know." She picked up the empty cast-iron jar of chocolate along with the lid. "I found the mirth stone this morning. It's in the clock in the hall."

"Evangeline—"

She heard him jump up from his seat, but she didn't turn around. The sooner she did this, the better off they'd both be.

She ran to the hall.

"Wait—" Jacks grabbed her hand and spun her away from the clock. His face was pale, and his eyes were glassy with red.

She hated that she'd hurt him, but she shuttered her expression. In a minute, they'd both feel differently. Jacks wanted the stones more than anything else, and she wanted to save Apollo. She wanted a happily ever after—and she wanted it to be real and true and not because of magic.

"Whatever it is, Jacks, you won't feel the same in a minute."

He swallowed hard and clenched his jaw. "You have no idea what I'm feeling now."

He looked at her lips, and the most tortured expression she'd ever seen crossed his face.

When Jacks wanted something, it was with an intensity that could break worlds and build kingdoms. That was the energy pouring off him now, as if he wanted to destroy her and make her his queen all at once.

And it was oh so tempting to let him. Magic crackled in the sliver of space between them. Golden and electric and alive. It felt like the end of a fairytale, when one kiss had more power than a thousand wars or a hundred spells.

Evangeline imagined drawing closer, pressing her lips to Jacks's and spending eternity lost in one neverending kiss.

"This isn't real, Jacks." Each word hurt to say, but Evangeline knew that although the words were painful, at least they were true. "This place, it's the enchantment of a fairytale without any of the curses or the monsters. But there are still curses and monsters out there. Apollo is still out there—"

"Apollo is fine," Jacks cut in, angry as he said the prince's name. "Chaos found him—and I saw him when I was away. Apollo is comfortably locked away in Chaos's castle, where no one else can hurt him and he can't hurt you."

"But he also can't live like that. And we can't live like this." Evangeline pulled her hand from Jacks's, and before he could stop her, she turned toward the clock. She opened the door to the pendulums, snatched the mirth stone and shoved it into the iron jar.

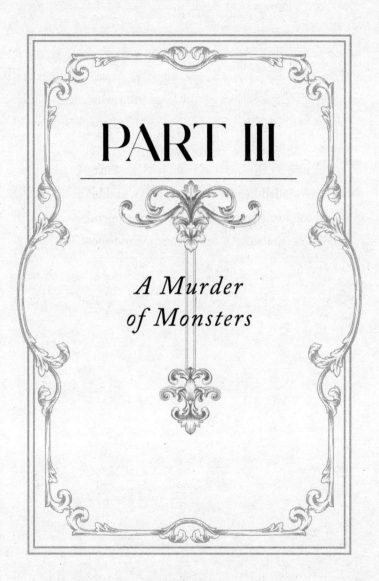

PART III

*A Murder
of Monsters*

41

As soon as the mirth stone was removed from the clock, its ticking ceased. The Hollow turned silent, and the air in the entry went cold as tombs at night.

Evangeline knew places weren't truly alive, and yet she felt as if the Hollow were dying. Candles blew out. Cracks wounded the floors. Dust appeared on the stairs where before there had been gleam and shine.

The Hollow might have been enchanted to keep out curses, but it seemed the rest of its magic had come from the mirth stone.

Even the little dragon changed. He started pawing at the entry's doorknob as if he couldn't wait to leave.

Evangeline would have loved to have kept him, but she opened the door and let him fly out into the cold. On the other side of the entrance, the snow no longer sparkled. Instead, it was wet and icy, and it bit at her cheeks before she shut the door.

A pit formed in her stomach.

She didn't even want to look at Jacks. If the Hollow was this cold, she feared what she'd see when she turned back to him. Although a tiny part of her hoped that nothing had changed, that although the Hollow had been altered, Jacks had stayed the same.

"You can turn around, Little Fox." His tone was brisk, and at the sound of it, her spark of hope burned out. "You don't have to worry about any more unwanted declarations from me."

And he was right; when she turned, the red was gone from his eyes. His jaw was still tight, but it looked annoyed instead of pained.

"I told you that you'd feel differently," she said. The words hurt, and she tried to push the ache aside. Chaos had told her that she'd feel the power of the stones stronger than anyone else. It seemed she hadn't stopped feeling the mirth stone's influence yet, but hopefully, the lingering feelings would be gone very soon. They'd clearly already departed from Jacks.

"You were right," he answered. "I feel like leaving now. I'll fetch the other two stones. You should find a cloak."

Evangeline discovered a gold cloak lined with thick white fur in the same wardrobe where she'd come across Aurora Valor's journal. She took the cloak and changed into a matching white dress with embroidered gold flowers and a bodice laced up in sunset-pink ribbons. She decided to pack up the diary as well. She wasn't really sure why—after the last entry she'd read, almost all the pages were blank. And it wasn't as if she needed the book to find any more stones. She and Jacks now had the mirth stone, the truth stone, and the youth stone, and Chaos already had the luck stone.

Evangeline felt a prickle of something like trepidation as she remembered what Petra had said before she'd died. *It was only then that I learned what all four stones could do together. But I'm guessing they didn't tell you that part. . . .*

"Ready?" Jacks said.

She spun around to find him in the doorway, standing straight as a soldier, clad in a long dark travel coat that looked as forbidding as his expression. She knew the mirth stone had taken all the joy from this place, but she'd have thought he'd have been at least a little happier now that they'd located all four stones. Instead, Jacks looked almost angry as he watched her.

"Aside from opening the arch," she asked, "what do all four stones do when they're together?"

"It's a little late to worry about that," he said sharply. His tone was no colder than it had been a hundred times before, and yet she felt the sting of it as he turned from the door.

The sled was ready to go when Evangeline stepped outside. Cold winter air whipped her hair across her face as she looked around at the Hollow. The flowers lining the road, which had been so bright when she'd arrived, were now wilted and covered in frost. She thought she remembered cheery mushrooms and flowers on the rooftop as well, but now it was just a series of boards that looked as if one storm might tear them away.

"We should get going," Jacks said.

Evangeline climbed onto the sled beside him. It was as white as snow, with a wide bench that would have allowed for another passenger. This was the amount of space between her and Jacks. And she was achingly aware of the distance.

She didn't want to keep glancing at him and hoping that he would look back at her. She didn't want to feel anything for him at all, especially not this callous version of him. But her heart would not stop hurting.

She kept thinking the pull she felt toward Jacks would vanish now that the mirth stone had been put into a box. But she could not let go of it.

The ride back to Valorfell was brutal—it was frigid and silent, save for the galloping of the horses drawing the sled.

She wondered if Jacks truly felt nothing or if he was just trying to hide what he felt. She was the one who'd insisted on taking the mirth stone from the clock so that they could leave and open the arch. And she would do it again.

She didn't regret her choice.

She just hated that it hurt so much. She hated that all she wanted was to reach across the carriage and take Jacks's hand.

But she didn't dare move.

Even if Jacks did still feel a flicker of something for her, he was choosing not to show it.

They left the sled at the cemetery gates to travel the rest of the way to Chaos's castle on foot. Jacks had two of the stones in his satchel, and she still had the mirth stone sealed inside the cast-iron jar.

She was surprised he let her hold on to it. Unless he really didn't have any lingering feelings, and the very thought of them appalled him so much that he didn't want to carry the stone, even sealed away.

Two sad marble angels guarded the entrance to Chaos's underground castle—one of the angels mourned over a pair of broken wings while the other played a harp with broken strings. She'd seen them several times before, but usually, it was during the night. The sun was still out now, shedding grainy light on the statues, and for the first time, they'd reminded her of the angels guarding the Valory Arch. She wondered if there was some sort of connection she was missing.

"Now that we're back, I'm sure you're eager to see your husband," Jacks said, "but don't go looking for him. Until the Archer's curse is lifted, Apollo is a danger to you."

"I already know that."

"Well, I know how much you like tempting death, so I thought I'd remind you," he snapped.

Shaking her head, Evangeline used her blood to open the door.

This earned her another glare from Jacks as they stepped through.

"What's wrong now?" she asked.

"You have no sense of self-preservation. Did you not listen when Chaos told you that you shouldn't shed blood when you're in a vampire castle?"

"It's still daylight. The vampires are asleep."

"Which gives you several hours to die before you can open the arch."

She lifted her chin defiantly. She almost added that she'd lived here for nearly two weeks on her own—she didn't need his caution. But there was still a part of her that couldn't help but wonder if his worry wasn't just about the arch. "I thought you didn't care about opening the arch. I thought you only wanted the stones."

"I do," Jacks said without hesitation. "But I gave Chaos my word that I wouldn't use them until after he opened the arch and removed his helm, and he can't do that until it's dark. So why don't you go be a good little key and lock yourself safely inside of your suite."

Evangeline seethed. She still suspected maybe Jacks was trying to annoy her to hide any feelings he still had, and if that was the case, then he was succeeding.

"Don't worry, Jacks, I would never inconvenience you by dying." She stalked off toward her room. It was tempting to look for Apollo just to make Jacks mad. She also imagined that once she saw the prince again, it would be easier to stop thinking of Jacks. Because right now, it felt impossible.

Evangeline passed the courtyard where she'd found him playing checkers, and it made her think of the conversation she'd overheard him have with LaLa, the one that made it sound as if he'd spent his time away from her searching for a cure to the Archer's curse. Hearing that conversation had made her dare to think he cared, but now she wished that he'd just been playing games. It was so much easier not to like him when he was being selfish.

Tears prickled at the corners of her eyes.

She swiped at them, refusing to cry for him. But it was so hard. All of it hurt. It hurt to want him. It hurt to be rejected by him. It hurt to breathe. It hurt to cry. It hurt even more when she tried not to cry.

Her head was throbbing and heart was heavy by the time she reached her room. It was cold and dark, but she only lit a few of the candles before collapsing into bed.

She was still clutching the iron jar with the mirth stone. It would have been so easy to take the lid off. And really, what harm could it do? The stone took away pain, and she was in so much pain.

Evangeline's fingers hovered over the lid. Then she gently knocked it off.

42

The relief was sweet and instant. Evangeline's shoulders relaxed, her eyelids closed, her chest felt as if she could finally breathe without all the weight pressing on it.

The wanting was still there. When she closed her eyes, she found herself straining to hear a knock on the door followed by Jacks's low voice. But instead of falling apart at the silence, she felt a quiet sort of hope. She could not believe Jacks didn't care for her. She couldn't believe his feelings for her were only because of this stone. She—

She was being delusional.

Evangeline forced herself to put the lid back on top of the iron jar. Then she shoved it under her pillow so that it was out of sight. No matter how much she wanted to numb the heartache, living in a delusion was not the answer. It would be better soon. Once she opened the arch and broke the Archer's curse, things would be different with her and Apollo—that at least was a guarantee. But what kind of different would it be?

A shudder racked her body. It was tempting to reach under the pillow and take out the stone again. Just until it was time to use it. But maybe she needed to feel this pain to get over it.

Evangeline hugged her pillow as she closed her eyes.

Time moved in that slow sort of way when it seems as if it's not moving at all. There was no change in the light or the temperature, until suddenly there was. The air thickened. A second later, she felt feather-soft fingers brushing her hair away from her cheek.

"Jacks—" Her heartbeat skipped and her eyes fluttered open—and she swallowed a cry.

Apollo leaned over her bed. His hand stilled at her cheek, or was it her neck? Was he about to choke her?

For a second, terror paralyzed her. Then she scrambled to her knees. She needed to get away.

"Don't be scared—I'm not going to hurt you, Evangeline." He said her name like a plea as he placed one knee on the bed, followed by the other, until he was kneeling before her. His eyes were liquid brown, not red. She knew how quickly his gaze could change, but right now he looked so haunted, so alone, so desperate, so wounded.

It felt a little like looking in a mirror and seeing her own emotions reflected back.

She knew she needed to run from him, but she didn't want to hurt him more than he was already hurting.

Carefully, he cupped her cheek. She stilled, but she didn't pull away. He kept his word. He didn't hurt her. If anything, his touch dulled some of her pain.

He stroked her jaw.

His hand was warm and gentle. Although there was a slight tremble to his fingers, as if he was frightened, too.

The touch still felt good, but maybe it wasn't a wise idea, after all. "Apollo—this isn't safe."

He laughed, loud but brittle. "Nothing has been safe since the moment I laid eyes on you. And yet I don't want to look away."

He kissed her then.

For a moment, she forgot how to breathe—she forgot how to kiss. But Apollo was patient. His lips moved reverently across her mouth, soft brushes over her lips until she began to relax and lean in.

She'd kissed him before, but never like this. When Apollo had been under Jacks's spell, his kisses were like fever dreams, hot and hungry, as if he wanted to taste more than just her mouth. This kiss was more like an invitation to dance.

And Apollo was a very good dancer. Slowly, his hand slid into her hair, tilting her head as she parted her lips. Butterflies moved inside her, and she wrapped her arms around the back of his neck.

He smiled against her mouth.

"You don't know how much I've wanted this." He took her lip between his teeth, kissed her again and then bit down, rough enough to draw blood.

"Sorry," he murmured.

"No—it's good." It reminded her of Jacks. But she pushed that thought away. She nipped Apollo back. He grinned again and kissed her harder as his hands worked off her golden cloak.

Her breathing hitched as the garment fell away.

She knew this was a bad idea, but Apollo felt so good. Each touch felt as if he worshipped her. Once her cloak was gone, he started to undo the ribbons at her chest as he pressed her back against the bed. "Tell me if I go too fast."

He kissed her gently, once on the lips, then on the jaw, trailing warm kisses down her neck as his hands grabbed her breasts and then her throat.

Instantly, her eyes flashed open.

"I'm sorry," Apollo rasped. This time, he didn't follow it with a kiss.

The terror inside her grew wings as his eyes turned from brown to red and his hands began to squeeze.

43

Evangeline turned into a thousand pieces of panic. She kicked Apollo between the legs, but he was too heavy on top of her for her kicks to be effective. She was pinned to the bed by his body.

She tried to scream as his fingers crushed painfully against her windpipe.

Then he was choking, too—sputtering and coughing and losing his grip thanks to the mirror curse.

Evangeline could barely breathe, but as Apollo pulled away, she managed to grab the jar with the mirth stone and crawl out from under him.

Clumsily, she rolled off the bed. Everything was a blur. The dark room spun, candles flaring and smoking all at once. She was wheezing, stumbling on her legs. But somehow, she remembered the lever next to the bed.

She pulled on it with all her might. A cage immediately

crashed down around Apollo. Bars clanked loudly into place, imprisoning him.

With a growl, he grabbed the bars. His face was feral, eyes still glowing red, but his words were a plea. "I'm sorry, Evangeline. I really don't want to hurt you!"

"I know." She staggered back. Into—

Jacks.

Veins pulsed in his neck; murder flared in his eyes as he glared at Apollo.

"Go," he ordered Evangeline.

"You can't hurt him," she panted, and she tugged on Jacks's shirt to get him to leave. "If you hurt him, it also hurts me. Remember?"

Jacks groaned something like, *"Someday I will kill him."* He put an arm around Evangeline.

"Get your hands off my wife!" Apollo cried.

Jacks pulled her closer and urged her toward the door.

Evangeline felt horribly torn. She couldn't go back to Apollo—not when he was like this—but leaving with Jacks felt like a different sort of agony. He was always there to rescue her, and then he always left.

He was rough as he took her from the room, only pausing to slam the door behind them before he turned to her again.

"What did he do to you?" Jacks's jaw tensed when he saw the blood staining her lips.

"I'm fine—I just—" *I just need you to hold me.* She wasn't able to say it. She wasn't even sure she projected the thought.

But then Jacks picked her up. She clung to him and buried her head in his shoulder.

He held her so tightly it hurt, but this pain she didn't mind. She'd let him crush her, let him break her, just as long as he never let her go. This was what she wanted, and she refused to believe that he didn't want it, too.

She could feel his heart pound against her chest as he carried her into the room next door to hers. It was a mess. There were apples and cores all over the desk. The sheets on the bed were thrashed. The fire was burning more than just logs. Clearly, she wasn't the only one upset after they'd returned from the Hollow.

He kicked the door shut and brought her to the bed. "Little Fox, when I saw you, I thought—"

He broke off as he set her atop all the twisted sheets. Then he fisted her hair in his hand and tugged until she was looking up at him. His face had all the agony of a fallen star, broken and beautiful, with eyes so blue, the color of everything else looked dull.

Deliberately, his gaze fell to her lips.

Her breathing turned ragged, and she wished just once that he could kiss her.

He leaned closer and gently twisted her hair, angling her head as he brought their mouths incredibly close.

"You're still bleeding." He licked the center of her lips, soft and agonizingly slow. His tongue felt like heaven and hell. Like everything she wanted and all she couldn't have. She had to stop herself from leaning closer, though she doubted Jacks would let her. She could feel his fingers against her scalp, holding her in place, keeping her lips just shy of his.

But maybe it was close enough. Maybe they didn't have to touch. She could live like this as long as she could live with him.

Then he let her go. He dropped her hair and stepped away from the bed, making her skin go suddenly cold.

"What's wrong?" she said. She could see him shutting down again, wiping the emotion from his face—the anger, the lust, the fear, the pain, the longing. It was just like the Hollow. This was what he'd done when she'd put the mirth stone in the pot. He'd shuttered all his feelings. He'd pretended everything had been because of the stone.

She'd suspected this was the case, but she hadn't been certain until now.

"I have to go," he said coldly.

"No—" She shoved up from the bed. This time, she wasn't going to let him get away with shutting her out. "What are you so afraid of?"

A flicker of something like regret flashed in Jacks's eyes.

"What is it?" she pressed.

Jacks raked a hand through his hair. "Do you still want to know what the stones do when they're together?"

"Yes," she said. But suddenly, she felt nervous. This was the answer she'd been waiting for. The one she'd been begging for. All this time, she'd been dying to know what Jacks really wanted. For a while, she'd been afraid of it, because she didn't want him to hurt anyone. But now from the way he looked at her, she suddenly feared the only person his answer would hurt was her.

Jacks crossed over to his desk and picked up a white apple. He tossed it as he said, "When the four stones are combined, a person has the power to return to any moment in their past. It can only be done once. Once the stones have been used for this purpose, they'll never have the power to be used like this again."

For a second, it didn't sound so bad. Lots of people had moments they wanted to change. That day alone there were several things Evangeline would have done differently. "What moment do you want to go back to?"

Jacks looked at the apple in his hand as he answered. "I want to return to the moment I met Donatella."

"The princess who stabbed you?"

He nodded tightly.

For a second, Evangeline was speechless. Of all the answers, she did not expect this. She quickly flashed back to the night that she and Jacks had spent together in the crypt, when he'd finally told her the story of Princess Donatella—how he'd kissed her and it should have killed her, but instead, it made his heart beat. She should have been his one true love, but Donatella chose another and stabbed Jacks in the heart.

"Why would you want to go back for her?"

Jacks worked his jaw. "She was supposed to be my one true love—I want another chance at that."

"But this doesn't make sense," Evangeline said. "Why go to all this trouble for a girl who *you* don't love?" Because Evangeline knew Jacks didn't love Donatella. She might have believed it before, when she'd first heard the story, but Evangeline couldn't fathom it now.

Jacks never talked about her, and on the rare occasions he did mention her, he didn't sound as if he loved her.

"Is this just because you didn't kill her? Or do you really want to be with her?"

Jacks's nostrils flared. "This is a pointless argument." He bit down hard on his apple. "And you won't remember this anyway."

Fresh panic gripped Evangeline. This was the second time he'd said that. The first time, in the Hollow, he'd made it sound as if he hadn't really meant it, but now, Jacks's voice was clear and hard.

"Why are you saying I won't remember?" she asked. Although she feared she already knew. If Jacks went back in time, it wouldn't just change his life, it would also alter Evangeline's. That's why he was saying she'd forget, because if Jacks created a new reality, none of this would happen. They would never even have this argument.

Everything that had occurred between Jacks and Evangeline since she'd come North had been a result of Jacks's search for the arch stones. But if he managed to use them and rewrite his history, then he wouldn't need to find them again—he wouldn't need her.

Suddenly, Evangeline felt sick.

Jacks looked as if he didn't care at all.

"If you go back in time, how much of my life will change?" she asked.

Jacks took another bite of his apple. "Your life won't be entirely different. Time doesn't wish to be changed—most things will reset themselves, unless someone actively fights to alter them. From what I've gathered, you'll still find your way here—it just won't be due to me. I imagine Chaos will accomplish bringing you here on his own. So, don't worry, pet, you'll still be a princess, and you'll still have Apollo."

"What about you? Will we ever meet?"

"No." And if Jacks felt anything about it, the emotion didn't show.

"Will you still remember me?"

"Yes," he said with equal indifference. "But I'll make sure our paths never cross."

"But you just said my life wouldn't change."

"It won't." He took another bite of his apple. "You'll find another way to stop Luc's wedding. Poison, I imagine."

"That wasn't what I was talking about." Tears prickled at the corners of her eyes. She couldn't believe that Jacks didn't care that she would forget him. That this moment and every other moment between them would be erased. That Chaos or Poison would simply replace him—that is, if his *theory* about her life staying mostly the same was correct. If he was wrong, there were so many other directions her life could take.

Although she wasn't worried about that just then. All Evangeline cared about was that she was going to forget about *him*.

Her breath was short, and her heart was pounding—she feared that at any moment it might just give out. And he was standing there eating an apple.

But she knew he felt something. She no longer believed anything that had happened between them in the Hollow was because of the mirth stone. The mirth stone didn't create bliss; all it had done was mend wounds and take away fear.

What was Jacks afraid of? What was his wound?

She was supposed to be my one true love—I want another chance at that. That's what he'd said when Evangeline had asked why he wanted to go back to be with Donatella. He hadn't said he loved her. He just wanted her because he believed she was his only chance at love. It really was because she was the one girl he hadn't killed with his kiss.

"What if you're wrong? What if Princess Donatella isn't your only chance at love? You said that if I opened the Valory Arch, there was something inside that could cure the curse on Apollo. What if there's something in there to help you, too? Maybe there's a way that you can find *another* true love."

Jacks ground his jaw and dropped his apple into the fire. "That's not how it works."

"Why won't you at least try? Why is your only solution to go back in time for a girl who doesn't love you?"

Jacks's eyes turned into a storm.

Evangeline probably should have stopped there, but this was her last chance. If he went through with his terrible plan, she wouldn't even know they'd ever met. Slowly, she walked toward where he stood and tilted her head to look up at him.

"If you really believe this is what you want, then you're lying to yourself."

"I'm not lying to myself," Jacks snarled.

"Then tell me this is what you truly want. Swear you want this more than anything else and I'll never mention it again."

Jacks grabbed her by the shoulders and looked directly into her eyes. For a minute, he didn't speak. He just looked at her, at the remaining blood still on her lips and the dried tears staining her cheeks. "I swear this is what I really want." He spoke each word like a vow. "I want to erase every moment you and I have spent together, every word you've said to me, and every time I've touched you, because if I don't, I'll kill you, just like I killed the Fox."

Evangeline's heart stopped.

She searched Jacks's eyes, but all she saw was darkness, and all she felt was the press of his hands. He held on to her the way a person might grasp the edge of a cliff, knowing once they let go, there was no taking hold again.

And Evangeline could no longer avoid the truth she hadn't wanted to see. Jacks was the Archer from *The Ballad of the Archer and the Fox*. That was the reason why he'd known so much about the Archer's curse and why he'd been so insistent there was no way to break it, why he'd said he wasn't *friends* with the Archer. He *was* the Archer.

Evangeline had feared it was true as soon as the Handsome

Stranger had mentioned the first fox. But she'd dismissed it because she hadn't wanted to be right. She hadn't wanted *that* to be Jacks's story—*she* wanted to be his story.

A tear slid down her cheek as she tried to imagine Jacks as the Archer, fighting not to hurt the girl he loved and failing. No wonder he was so damaged and cruel. No wonder he'd perfected the art of not caring.

"Sorry to break your fairytale, Little Fox, but ballads don't end happily, and neither do the two of us."

His hands dropped from her shoulders, and he started for the door.

"I'm not that fox!" Evangeline cried.

"You don't understand." He tossed a dark look over his shoulder. "Every girl is another fox. You want to know how the story really ends? You want to know the part of the tale that everyone forgets?"

Evangeline told herself to shake her head. For so long, she'd wanted to know the end of this story, but now she wanted to forget it all. She wanted Jacks to simply be the Prince of Hearts again—the heartsick Fate looking for true love—rather than a fallen hero who'd found the love of his life and killed her.

"I thought you just told me how the story ended," she said.

"I told you that I killed her, but I didn't say how." A dangerous intensity slipped into Jacks's voice. "I didn't tell you that I ran away, that I tried to leave her so I wouldn't hurt her. I didn't know if I really loved her, or if my feelings were all from the curse, because it wouldn't let me stop thinking about her. But she had more faith in me than I did. She chased after me. She was convinced I really loved her and that I could fight the curse. And I did. I never laid a hand on her. I overcame the Archer's curse. But it didn't matter, because as soon as I kissed her, she died." Jacks's mouth twisted bitterly. "Since then, every girl I've kissed has died, except for one. And you are not that girl."

44

Evangeline was beginning to fear that time was fueled by emotions and that things like dread made it move faster. There was a curvy black glass clock atop the fireplace mantel in Jacks's room that she didn't notice until after he had left her. Now she couldn't take her eyes off the timepiece. Her palms started to sweat as she watched the spinning of the second hand, twirling faster and faster each minute.

Soon it would be nightfall. Soon she would forget him. She would forget this version of her life. She might even have an entirely different life, and she wouldn't know this life had ever existed.

She would know he existed, but he would no longer be Jacks, he would just be a mythical figure: the Prince of Hearts. She would forget that he'd been Jacks of the Hollow, and the Archer, and, for the span of one night, *hers*.

How could he take all of that away from her? She hated him

a little for it, which made it marginally easier. But it still felt wrong. Evangeline had always believed that every story had the potential for infinite endings, but this didn't feel like the way their story was supposed to end. She hadn't met Jacks just to forget him.

She needed to convince him of this before he used the stones.

The door to the room creaked open. Evangeline looked away from the clock to find Chaos standing in the doorway.

He was dressed more like a prince than a warrior, in a velvet doublet of deep wine red with an elegant cream shirt underneath. His gloves were brown leather, his pants were dark, and the sword strapped to his side was gold. The weapon looked more decorative than necessary, as if tonight were some sort of special occasion. She supposed, for him, it was.

In his hands, he held a small iron chest, which must have concealed the luck stone, the youth stone, and the truth stone. She still had the jar with the mirth stone in her hand, and for a terrible second, she wished that she had lost it.

"Ready, Princess?"

"No," Evangeline blurted. She would never be ready to have her life erased and replaced. "Don't we need to wait for Jacks?"

She stole what she hoped was a covert glance down the hall in search of the errant Prince of Hearts.

"He won't be joining us," Chaos said. "I'm going to bring him the stones after you've opened the arch."

"He's not even planning on saying goodbye?" Evangeline felt

her hopes crumple like paper wings that had made the foolish mistake of thinking they could fly.

"He said you wouldn't remember anyway," Chaos added softly, as if he knew it was the opposite of consolation.

"Do you think what he's doing is a good idea?"

The vampire rubbed the jaw of his helm. "I think we should get going."

"I'll take that as a no."

Chaos sighed, one part impatient, one part beleaguered. "I don't ever think time travel is a good idea. I've lived long enough to know that the past doesn't like to be changed. Jacks believes his plan will work because he only wants to alter one thing. But Jacks's reason gets clouded when he wants something badly enough. I believe the only way that time travel works is if the past hasn't had time to settle. The further back you go, the more Time fights against changes. And given the vindictive nature of Time, even if Jacks succeeds in changing the past, Time will no doubt make sure he loses something else in order to pay for it. So you are correct, I think he's making a mistake."

"Then help me change his mind!"

Chaos shook his head ruefully. "You're not good for him, either, Princess. This is a better mistake for Jacks to make than *you*. If he were to stay for you, he would kill you, and your death would kill him. Trust me, Evangeline. If you care about Jacks, the best thing you can do for him is let him go."

"That doesn't feel like the best thing," she said. But a part of her couldn't deny that maybe Chaos was right. Months ago, she'd felt as if Luc was the person she was meant to be with. She'd clearly been wrong about that, and if she was wrong about Jacks, the consequences would be far worse.

"Ready now?" Chaos asked.

Reluctantly, Evangeline nodded.

As she and Chaos walked down the hall, she kept hoping to hear the rhythm of Jacks's boots or the crunch of his teeth biting into an apple.

But there were only the sounds of her slippers, the occasional groan of an opening door, and the growing realization that she might never see Jacks again. He was not going to change his mind. He was going to go through with his plan to change the past and both of their lives along with it.

Evangeline felt numb by the time she entered a dark carriage with velvet seats that looked as if it had never been used. She supposed that for a vampire with preternatural speed, a carriage ride would feel painfully slow, but to her, it felt impossibly fast.

Just before they reached Wolf Hall, the carriage rolled past a row of ancient headless sculptures that made Evangeline think of the Valors, and she felt a sudden chill. She still didn't know what the Valory held.

When LaLa had told her the story of her dragon shifter, it had made Evangeline think the tale about it being a prison was true.

According to Jacks, the Valory held a cure for the Archer's

curse that had been cast on Apollo, but it supposedly held no remedy for Jacks's fatal kiss.

Evangeline looked across the coach at Chaos, who believed the Valory would let him finally remove his cursed helm. The vampire was currently stroking the jaw of it, his hand moving over the intricate carvings of images and words.

Something prickled at Evangeline then, as she remembered what he'd once said about the words—the ones that belonged to the language of the Valors. *It's the curse that prevents me from removing the helm.*

"I'm curious," Evangeline said. "If the Hollow is protected from all curses and your helm is cursed, why didn't you ever just go to the Hollow to remove the helm?"

Chaos waited a beat before saying, "If I stepped foot in the Hollow, I would cease to exist at all. The Hollow was enchanted specifically to keep it safe from me."

"But I thought you and Jacks were friends."

"We are, but when I first became what I am, I was not quite in control of myself."

Evangeline flashed back to the newsprint she'd read at Slaughterwood Castle: *But some fear that these attacks are only because the Valors do not have control over the abomination they have created.*

She sucked in a gasp as suddenly it all linked together. "You're the monster that everyone thought the Valors created."

"The Valors did create me."

"They did?"

"Did you think they were as blameless as the stories say?" Chaos laughed, but there was nothing happy about it. "The Valors made a great number of mistakes. But you don't have to worry, Evangeline. I have not been a monster for a long time. I just want to unlock the Valory, and get this helm off."

The carriage reached the snow-kissed grounds of Wolf Hall seconds later.

Then it was as if Evangeline blinked and they were at the royal library, opening the door to the room with the Valory Arch.

45

The room was just as Evangeline remembered: crumbling floors, gray walls, fossilized air that scratched at her throat, and a giant arch guarded by a pair of warrior angels, one sad and one angry. Both had their stone swords drawn over the center.

The last time Evangeline had been here, the angels had not moved, but this time, she swore they flinched when Chaos stepped into the room.

With a click, he unlocked the small iron trunk holding the first three stones.

The air immediately changed, glitter swirling through the room like dust.

The stones in the box were glowing, gleaming, shining, practically singing in their splendor. So was the mirth stone in her hand. Evangeline hadn't even realized she'd lifted the lid on her jar, but now the stone was in her palm.

For a second, time seemed to pause, and she wondered what would happen if instead of placing the rock in the arch, she placed it in the box with the other stones and used them to go back in time.

Jacks had said the stones could only be used once for that purpose. If she did it first, he would never have the chance.

She knew that Chaos had warned that Time was vindictive and didn't like to be changed, but with the mirth stone in her hand, it was hard to feel truly afraid. Her skin prickled with magic as she pictured going back in time and meeting Jacks before he found Princess Donatella. Then she saw her parents. She imagined going back and saving both their lives. If her mother had lived, Evangeline's father might not have died of a broken heart. Her family would be whole again.

For a dazzling minute, she saw images of her parents alive again and smiling. She saw the curiosity shop open and Jacks holding her. She pictured a happier life where she never had a stepmother or a stepsister. A life where she never had to go North to look for love. Where Apollo was never cursed and she was never hunted. Where Luc never turned into a vampire. She could change her life and find one of the many infinite endings she'd always believed in.

"Don't forget what we've come here for," said Chaos.

"Don't worry." Evangeline closed her palm over the mirth stone. She was still tempted, but as much as she hated the choice that Jacks was making, she didn't want to take it away. Instead, she hoped, one final time, that he would make a better one.

With a deep breath, she put the mirth stone in the arch. For a second, she waited for something magical to happen, for the stones to glow brighter or the angels to attack, but everything stayed just as it was before.

She put the luck stone in next. Again, nothing changed.

Her palm started to sweat when she placed the youth stone in the arch and the only thing that moved was a swirl of glitter-dust.

"I don't know if it's working," Evangeline said.

"It will work." Chaos's voice was tight, and his fingers were tense as he handed her the final stone.

Evangeline felt like a bundle of nerves as she held the final stone in her hand. Everything that she'd done and experienced since coming North had led to this moment. If she believed in fate, she might have thought her entire life had led her here. She didn't like that idea at all, and yet she couldn't deny the sense of inevitability that seemed to fill the ancient room, as if Destiny were somehow standing silently behind her, holding its breath as it waited for the end of a story that it had set in motion centuries ago.

She put the last stone in.

Finally.

The word was whispered in her thoughts from the arch. She could feel it breathing, brushing wind against her skin. It was waking up. *It was working.*

Chaos held out a small gold dagger, and Evangeline carefully pricked her finger.

As soon as she touched her blood to the stones, the room exploded in light, brighter than the first time she'd touched the arch. The angels glowed like a slice of sun. Evangeline had to shield her eyes until the angels dimmed.

When she could see again, the warrior angels had lowered their swords, and behind them waited a thick wooden door with an iron knocker shaped like a wolf's head.

Chaos pressed one gloved hand against the door, as if to test that it was real. Then he turned his head back to her. "Thank you, Evangeline."

He took his dagger and sliced off a lock of her pink hair.

She jolted back. "Why did you do that?"

"Don't worry, you're the last person I wish to hurt right now." He quickly returned the dagger to his belt. "The hair is to break the curses on you and Apollo—just wait out here while I go inside."

"What's inside?" Evangeline asked.

But Chaos had already opened the door and slipped through to the Valory.

The stone angels on either side of the arch shuddered as he entered. She remembered once more that he was the abomination many believed to be locked away behind the arch.

If that was the case, she wondered what was actually inside. The heavy door was still cracked. Chaos hadn't properly shut it behind him. Clearly, he wasn't afraid of something sneaking out to get her.

Evangeline stepped closer just to peek. With the arch still

glowing as bright as daylight, the other side appeared dim at first, a world of sepia shadows.

It took her eyes a moment to adjust. She half expected cages and prisoners, but there was only a domed vestibule of sandstone walls with flickering orange and red torches that lit a series of halls. It looked like the entry to an ancient temple, but it could have been a vault. The story about the Valors locking away their greatest magical treasure could have been true after all.

She knew Jacks didn't believe that there was anything in the Valory that could allow him to have another chance at love. But what if he was wrong?

Evangeline took a step inside.

She understood why Chaos had warned her away from Jacks earlier—she'd seen a glimpse of Jacks's heartache when he'd talked about his dead friends and killing the Fox. Evangeline didn't want to be another heartbreak, and she didn't want to die. But she refused to believe that meant she had to let Jacks go. There had to be another way.

She felt a rush of anticipation as she stood inside the Valory's entry. At a glance, the halls snaking out from the vestibule all looked the same—arched doorways made of ancient redstone brick, and floors covered in surprisingly thick stretches of gold-threaded carpet.

This was definitely not a prison. Evangeline listened to each hall. Two were quiet, but she thought she heard footsteps echoing down the third. That must have been the one Chaos had gone down.

Quietly, she crept forward, following the sound. Halfway down the hall, sconces turned from iron to gold, art appeared on the walls, and then she saw a door.

The door was tall and wide, and fairytale-bright light spilled through, allowing her to spy through the crack and see the other side with ease.

Evangeline inched forward, about to open the door all the way, when she caught sight of Chaos on the other side. He was peering down at a row of people lying on the floor holding hands. Their clothes looked ancient, like something out of storybooks—lots of deep-dyed wool gowns and braided gold rope, pewter breastplates and spiky pauldrons.

Evangeline didn't know what to make of it all until she glimpsed a face among the group, one that she'd seen once in a painting. The girl was even prettier than she'd looked in the portrait, and Evangeline instantly recognized her as Aurora Valor.

It was then she noticed the gold circlet crowning the head of the petite woman beside Aurora. The woman's skin was a darker shade of olive, her hair was gleaming silver, and her face was serene. She must have been Aurora's mother, Honora Valor.

The man lying beside Honora looked more battle-worn than handsome. He also had a crown on his head, and Evangeline imagined he must have been Wolfric Valor.

The family on the floor was the Valors.

They were what had been locked away in the Valory, not their treasure or their prisoners. Evangeline nearly staggered back at the realization. This was not what she had thought she'd find.

But it made perfect sense—and it actually fit both of the stories she'd been told about the Valory. If the Valors had been trapped here, then the Valory was a sort of prison, one that locked away the Valors' greatest magical treasure—because it contained them.

No wonder Chaos wanted it open. If the Valors had cursed him to wear the helm, then it stood to reason that they could take it off. Evangeline wondered then if Honora was one who could break the curse that was placed on Apollo. Jacks had said she was the world's greatest healer.

It all made perfect sense—except Jacks's belief that the Valory did not contain a loophole for him. If Honora could cure Apollo of the Archer's curse, then maybe she could help Jacks, too.

Just then, the queen began to stir from her place on the floor. She was graceful, even as she stood on unsteady legs. Chaos seemed to watch her with bated breath, as if she might disappear. And Evangeline found herself doing the same.

"Is that really you?" Honora had a slight accent that spoke of times before and a voice just as delicate as her appearance. "Castor?"

Evangeline leaned closer, unsure she'd heard the name right. Castor was dead. Jacks had told her how he'd died. Except now that she thought back, Jacks hadn't finished the story. He'd just ended by saying he wasn't meant to be a savior.

Evangeline watched as Honora embraced Chaos. "How long has it been?" she asked.

Chaos said something too low for Evangeline to hear. But she thought she caught the words "I've missed you, Mother."

Honora started sobbing.

Evangeline felt like a terrible intruder, yet she couldn't look away. If she was putting this together correctly, the Valors hadn't created a monster to avenge Castor's death—he'd *become* the monster. Chaos was Castor Valor. *This* was why he really wanted to open the arch. Not just to take his helm off. He wanted to save his family. He missed them. He loved them.

It hit Evangeline then, how she could save Jacks. It was so simple, she cursed herself for not considering it before. Love was how she could save him. She didn't just care about him or want him. She loved him. She just needed to tell him that.

The thought terrified her a little. He'd already rejected her; it was tempting to fear he would do it again. But that was the whole problem: fear. Jacks was only rejecting her because he was afraid that he would kill her. But if she told him that she loved him, hopefully it would be enough to make him want to stay and try for more than what he was settling for.

Some of her ideas about love might have changed since coming North, but she still believed it was the most powerful force in the world. If two people really loved each other and they were willing to fight for that love, if they were willing to go to war for each other, day after day, then it didn't matter what they were up against. Love would always win as long as they never stopped fighting for it.

If Jacks loved her the way she loved him, they could find a way to make it work.

It didn't matter if he stayed forever cursed. Although a part of her couldn't help but believe that maybe her love would be enough to break his curse. She knew the stories said that Jacks only had one true love—and he'd already found that girl—but the stories also twisted the truth. The Valory proved that.

With a surge of hope that felt like wings powerful enough to soar to the moon and stars and beyond, Evangeline started to turn around. She needed to find him, she needed to tell him how she felt. She—

—startled to a halt as a flash of blinding light came from the room with the Valors.

Chaos made a sound that might have been a sob, pained and deep.

Evangeline turned back to the cracked door, just in time to see the cursed helm on Chaos's head was now broken.

He wrenched it off with a roar and threw it across the room. The helm crashed so hard against the wall that it shattered as it fell to the ground.

"Finally," he said, his voice somewhere between a cry and a roar. And for the first time, Evangeline saw what he looked like. He had a face that made her breath catch in her chest. Glittering eyes, clean-cut jaw, smooth olive skin, and a smile that made her heart flip.

"The Handsome Stranger," she gasped.

Honora and Chaos both turned her way.

Evangeline froze in the doorway.

"Looks as if we have a visitor," Honora said, angling her head in a way that could have been either curious or wary.

"Mother, this is Evangeline," said Chaos. His voice was different without the helm, all velvet without the smoke, more similar to the voice he'd used in her dreams. "She's the one who unlocked the arch."

Suddenly, Chaos was at the door, opening it wider and giving her a smile that rivaled any immortal's she'd ever met. "I truly can't thank you enough." He took her hand and gently kissed it.

Without his helm, Chaos was a different kind of monster, possessing all the charm of a prince and the power of a vampire. It made Evangeline a little breathless as he smiled down on her. His eyes were the most arresting shade of green, a thousand different facets, all shimmering with magic until they flared with heat.

Evangeline caught her mistake too late—she shouldn't have looked into his eyes. Before she could scream, Chaos's smile turned to fangs, and then those fangs were on her neck, tearing into her throat.

46

Everything was teeth and breathless pain.

Evangeline tried to escape. She tried to cry out.

She thought she heard Honora cry out as well. But Chaos didn't release her. One of his hands held her neck while his lips drank her blood. He drank and drank, draining her with violent pulls of his mouth and tongue and the occasional scrape of teeth, piercing more skin and drawing more blood.

She could feel it rushing from her veins to his mouth, leaving so fast her heart couldn't keep up.

Honora started pleading.

Evangeline tried to hit Chaos, but she couldn't muster the strength to move her hands. She couldn't even open her eyes. Her body was heavy, and her head was light. All she could feel were Chaos's teeth, cutting deeper to take even more—

"Castor, no!" Jacks shouted.

The vampire was wrenched away.

Evangeline started to fall, and then Jacks was there. Her eyes were too heavy to open—but she could feel him. He held her with the type of intensity that only happens when a person wants something that isn't quite theirs.

But she was. She just needed to tell him she loved him.

"Evangeline—" His voice was hoarse. "Come back to me. . . ."

I'm not dead, she tried to say. But there was something wrong with her throat. And it seemed Jacks couldn't hear her thoughts.

He silently held her tighter and pressed his forehead to hers. She wasn't sure if he was crying or if she was, but there was wet on her cheeks. It felt a lot like tears. And then she felt . . .

Nothing.

THE END

A tormented scream pierced the night like a blade. The sky bled, and darkness fell instead of stars, erasing lights across the Magnificent North.

The story curse that touched most Northern tales and ballads watched. This tragedy would certainly be a tale one day—and, from the look of it, was already cursed.

The girl was dead. If her lifeless body had not confirmed it, then it would have been made clear by the horrible scream of the Fate who held her in his arms. The story curse was familiar with pain, but this was agony, the sort of raw grief that was only seen once in a century. The Fate was every tear that anyone had ever shed for lost love. He was pain given form.

"I'm so sorry, Jacks. I—" The vampire looked down at the girl he'd just killed; he scrubbed a hand over his jaw, and then he fled.

The Fate didn't move. He didn't let the girl go. He looked as if he never would. He continued holding her as if he could return her to life with the force of his will. His eyes were wet with blood. Red tears fell down his cheeks and onto hers. But the girl didn't stir.

The other sleeping immortals were starting to wake, but the girl remained unmoving. Dead. And yet the Fate continued to hold her.

"Bring her back," he said softly.

"I am sorry," said the queen who'd just awoken. She was a petite thing. She'd tried to pull her son away from the girl, to stop his unnatural feeding, but her hands were not strong enough. The queen could not fight immortals physically, but she had an iron will forged of mettle and mistakes. "You know I cannot do that."

The Fate finally looked up. "Bring her back," he repeated. For he also possessed an indomitable will. "I know you can do it."

The queen shook her head remorsefully. "My heart breaks for you—for this. But I will not do this. After bringing back Castor and seeing what he became, I vowed to never use that sort of magic again."

"Evangeline would be different." The Fate glowered at the queen.

"No," she repeated. "You wouldn't be saving this girl, you would be damning her. Just as we did to Castor. She wouldn't want that life."

"I don't care what she wants!" roared the Fate. "I don't want her dead. She saved you, you need to save her."

The queen took a shaky breath.

If the story curse could have breathed, it would have held its breath. It hoped the queen would say yes. Yes to bringing her back, to turning her into another terrible immortal. Despite what this Fate believed, the girl would be horrible—the ones with endless life always were, eventually.

"I am saving her," the queen said quietly. "It is kinder to let her die a human than to sacrifice her soul for immortality."

At the word *sacrifice,* something sparked in the Fate's cold eyes. He held the girl tighter, carrying her in his bloodstained arms as he stood and started down the ancient hall.

"What are you doing?" A crack of alarm showed in the queen's implacable face.

"I'm going to fix this." He continued marching forward, holding the girl close as he carried her back through the arch.

The angels who'd been guarding it now wept. They cried tears of stone as the Fate set the girl at their feet and began wrenching stone after stone from the arch.

"Jacks of the Hollow," warned the queen. "Those arch stones can only be used one time to go back. They were not created for infinite trips to the past."

"I know," Jacks growled. "I'm going to go back and stop your son from killing her."

The queen's face fell. For a moment, she looked as old as the years she'd spent lying in a suspended state. "That is not a small mistake to fix. If you do this, Time will take something equally valuable from you."

The Fate gave the queen a look more vicious than any curse. "There is nothing of equal value to me."

44

Evangeline was beginning to fear that time was fueled by emotions and that things like dread made it move faster. There was a curvy black glass clock atop the fireplace mantel in Jacks's room. Her palms started to sweat as she watched the spinning of the second hand, twirling faster and faster each minute.

Soon it would be nightfall. Soon she would forget him. She would forget this version of her life.

The door creaked open. Evangeline looked away from the clock to find Chaos standing in the doorway.

He was dressed more like a warrior than a prince, in red velvet and leather and gilded weapons. There was only one other time she'd seen him in something aside from leather armor, yet she couldn't shake the sense she'd seen him dressed like this before. "Ready, Princess?"

"No," Evangeline blurted. She would never be ready to have her life erased and replaced. "Don't we need to wait for Jacks?"

She stole what she hoped was a covert glance down the hall in search of the errant Prince of Hearts.

"He won't be joining us," Chaos said. "I'm going to bring him the stones after you've opened the arch."

"Actually, I changed my mind." Jacks swaggered down the hall, a stunning young woman at his side. She had painted red lips, shimmering black hair, and a slip of a dress that didn't even look like enough to be a nightgown.

Evangeline felt a surge of jealousy and confusion.

"What is she doing here?" Chaos gave a tight nod to the girl in the slip.

Jacks shrugged. "I thought you might need a snack when you get your helm off."

Chaos made a sound like grinding teeth. "I'll be fine."

"I'm sure you will. But—"

"No," Chaos said sharply.

"What if we just leave her in the carriage?" Jacks waved a thoughtless arm at the girl. She didn't even move. Doll-like, the girl stared straight ahead, clearly under Jacks's control.

"I agree with Chaos," Evangeline said. "I won't let you drag this poor girl around."

"I'm hardly dragging her around." Jacks flashed a dimple at the girl. "Isn't that right, pet?"

"I'm happy to be here," the girl said cheerfully. "I've always wanted to meet a vampire. I wore this dress so there would be lots of places—"

"Get rid of her," Chaos interrupted. "Evangeline doesn't want the girl to come with us."

Jacks glared at Evangeline, but something about it was off. The firm set of his mouth was angry, but his eyes were filled with something else—pain. *You're picking the wrong thing to be stubborn about,* he thought to her.

Why do you even care how I feel? she thought back tartly. *It's not as if I'll remember any of this anyway.*

Jacks worked his jaw.

She hoped that he would argue with her—she hoped that he would fight for her. She hoped despite everything that he would choose her. But after dismissing the girl, Jacks and Chaos and Evangeline walked in silence to the carriage.

The ride to Wolf Hall was excruciating. Evangeline's heart felt especially fragile in her chest as they drew closer to the castle. These were her last moments with Jacks, and although he sat across from her, he wouldn't even look at her.

He stared out the frosted window as if he wished the night were already over and the past were already changed.

Evangeline wished he'd have second thoughts about his plans, but he looked more unyielding than ever. She wished she knew what to say to make him change his mind, but she didn't want to *convince* him to do anything. She wanted him to make the choice. And she feared she was running out of time.

Instead of time moving like sand slowly pouring through an hourglass, she felt as if the hourglass had cracked open and all the sand was quickly spilling out. She didn't know if it was her fear or if it was something else, but she kept losing moments.

She didn't recall arriving at Wolf Hall, but suddenly, they were there. Then, it was as if she'd blinked and they were back at the library door with the wolf head on it, ready to enter the room with the Valory Arch.

45

The room was just as Evangeline remembered—crumbling floors, gray walls, fossilized air that scratched at her throat, and a giant arch guarded by a pair of warrior angels.

With a click, Chaos unlocked the small iron trunk holding the first three stones.

The air immediately changed, glitter swirling through the room like dust.

Evangeline stole a look back at Jacks. Once she opened the arch, the stones would be his to use as he pleased. She wished that he'd change his mind, that this night wouldn't end with her forgetting him. But he was still refusing to look at her. As if one glance her way might change his mind, and then the whole world might come crashing down around them.

Reluctantly, she looked away, and one by one, Evangeline put the first three stones in the arch. They looked duller than she'd remembered. She hoped that maybe they'd already been used to change time. Then she instantly felt guilty. Evangeline hated the choice that Jacks was making, but she didn't want it taken away from him. Instead, she hoped, one final time, that he would make a better choice. With that, she put the fourth stone inside the arch.

Welcome back, it whispered.

Chaos held out one of his daggers, and Evangeline carefully pricked her finger.

As soon as she touched her blood to the stones, the room exploded with light. The angels glowed like a slice of sun. Evangeline had to shield her eyes until the angels dimmed.

When she could see again, the stone angels lowered their swords, and behind them waited a great wooden door with an iron knocker shaped like a wolf's head. Chaos pressed one gloved hand against the door as if to test if it was real. Then he took his dagger and sliced off a lock of her pink hair.

She jolted back. "Why did you do that?"

"The hair is to break the curses on you and Apollo—just wait here while I go inside."

"I think Evangeline should just leave." Jacks gave her a bloodshot glare.

Evangeline felt briefly stunned. *Was this supposed to be his version of goodbye?* And when had his eyes become so red? She told herself not to worry, but she suddenly felt as if something was very wrong. "Jacks, are you all right?"

"No." In a flash, his red eyes narrowed. His mouth pulled

tight, and his voice turned to venom. "I'm confused as to what you're still doing here. Do you think you're still needed?"

"Jacks—"

"I know my name. There's no need for you to keep repeating it."

Evangeline flinched at the malice in his tone.

Even Chaos looked surprised. Then, as if not wanting to be a part of their final argument, he slipped through the door to the Valory.

Evangeline and Jacks were alone.

A muscle throbbed in Jacks's neck as he continued to hold her gaze. "What are you still doing here, Evangeline? Did you expect a teary goodbye?" He sneered. "I've told you before that you are nothing but a tool to me. Now your purpose has been fulfilled."

Embarrassment burned her cheeks. But she couldn't bring herself to move. Evangeline didn't know what she'd expected. She'd hoped that Jacks would change his mind, but even if he didn't, there was no reason for him to be like this after all that they'd been through. "Why are you being so cruel?"

"Because you won't leave!" Jacks shouted. "And if you stay, you will die. Chaos hasn't fed in hundreds of years. I know he thinks he can control his hunger, but he can't. That's why they put the helm on him."

"You could have just said that. If you don't want me to say goodbye or you want me to leave, you don't have to hurt me to get me to do it."

"I'm not—I—" Jacks broke off abruptly. His eyes were no longer just red, they were blazing with fear. She'd never seen him look so terrified before. She'd been poisoned, shot, lashed across the back, and Jacks had always kept his calm until now.

With a great deal of effort, he took a deep breath, and when he spoke again, his voice was soft but uneven. "I'm sorry, Little Fox. I didn't want to hurt you. I just—"

He looked suddenly at a loss for words, as if whatever he said next might be the wrong thing. He'd never looked at her like this before.

"Jacks, please, don't use the stones tonight. Come with me instead."

He took a jagged breath. For a second, he looked torn. He raked a hand through his hair, his movements jagged.

Evangeline took a step closer.

He shuttered his expression and took a step back. "This doesn't change anything. I still can't have you in my life. You and I aren't meant to be."

"What if you're wrong?"

Jacks worked his jaw and clenched his fists.

Evangeline had once heard a tale about a pair of doomed stars, drawn across skies toward each other's brightness, even though they knew that if they drew too close, their desire would end in a fiery explosion. This was how Jacks looked at her now. As if neither of them would survive if they drew any closer.

"Evangeline, you need to go."

A thunderous roar poured out from the Valory, so loud it

shook the arch and the angels and the ground at Evangeline's feet.

"Get out of here," Jacks said.

She held his gaze, one final time, wishing she knew how to change his mind. "I wish our story could have had another ending."

"I don't want a different ending," Jacks said flatly. "I just want you to leave."

46

Everything hurt. It was the sort of pain that made it hard to breathe.

All Evangeline wanted was to run back to Jacks. But she forced herself to keep walking. She made herself exit the library and turn down the emptiest hall she could find, where no one could hear her cry.

She pressed her hands to her eyes as the tears flowed harder. She didn't want to cry. But it truly felt over. And it hurt. It hurt so much. It hurt in her chest, and it hurt in her heart. Because he didn't want her heart. The thought made her cry harder. She cried until she couldn't see straight, until she was in some unknown corridor, clutching her stomach and biting her arm, trying to silence the sobs as she sank to the floor.

Maybe it would be better to forget him. She hadn't wanted the forgetting before, but she wanted it now.

She wanted the pain to end. She wanted to forget his dimpled smile, his brilliant blue eyes, the way he called her Little Fox. And suddenly, her chest was tight at the thought she might never hear that nickname again. And she didn't want to forget. She didn't want to forget at all.

She didn't want the memories erased or rewritten; she wanted more of them.

She didn't want to say goodbye. She still wanted Jacks to change his mind. To find a way to another true love.

It hit Evangeline then, how she could save Jacks. It was so simple, she cursed herself for not considering it before. Love was how she could save him. She didn't just care about him or want him. She loved him. She just needed to tell him that.

Love was the most powerful magic of all. If he loved her the way she loved him, they could find a way to make it work.

It didn't matter if he stayed forever cursed. All that mattered was that he *stayed*, that he chose her instead of fear.

Evangeline started back toward the arch. She needed to find him; she needed to tell him how she felt before it was too late. She needed to do it before he used the stones and she forgot they'd ever met.

He couldn't have used them yet, because she still remembered him. Evangeline picked up her pace to a run, chest heaving and slippers slapping hard against the castle floors. She must have gone farther than she'd thought and stayed there longer than she'd realized. Wolf Hall was waking up. She could hear servants moving down other halls and see the flicker of freshly lit candles lighting her way back to the library.

It felt like forever before she reached the room with the arch.

The air still swirled with magic and hints of power that felt like a storm. The arch was the same as when she had left. The ancient door was still there, and so were all the stones.

Evangeline felt a rush of relief. If Jacks hadn't taken the stones, maybe he'd already changed his mind? Although . . . if he'd changed his mind, it seemed odd he'd have just left the stones for someone else to take.

Something was wrong. She knew it even before she noticed the drops of gold-flecked blood spattered across the wings of the warrior angels.

A tremor of fear moved inside her. What if Chaos had fed on Jacks? Or what if something else from inside the Valory had hurt him? She still didn't know what was inside of it.

Evangeline reached for the door. But it was already opening.

She jumped back.

"It's all right," Apollo said as he appeared in the archway, his broad shoulders nearly filling it.

Evangeline tensed and took another step back.

Apollo slowly raised his hands. "Please, don't be scared. I'm not going hurt you." He looked down at her with warm brown eyes; the red was gone, along with the anguish. "The curse is lifted, Evangeline."

"How?"

"A woman—she didn't tell me her name, but she was some sort of healer. She found me, cut some of my hair, said a few words I didn't understand, then I felt it vanish." Apollo took a shuddering breath. "As soon as it was lifted, I told her that I needed to find you, and she showed me an old arch that led me here." He looked around the ancient room as if trying to figure out where he was, but then his eyes quickly returned to Evangeline's.

They really were beautiful eyes, rich and brown, and when he looked at her, his gaze was so full of emotion it made her chest ache again. She didn't know what he wanted to say, but she knew she couldn't stay. She had to find Jacks.

And yet, it felt callous to just run from Apollo. He'd been cursed three times now. She had no idea if he even knew why. He didn't look haunted or desperate like the last time she'd seen him, but there was something terribly vulnerable about him as he stood in the door with his palms still raised and his smile fading. "I'm sorry," he said. "I never wanted to hurt you."

"It's not your fault—you were cursed."

"I should have fought it harder." Apollo slowly lowered his hands. "I shouldn't have come to your room last night. I should have run away so that I wouldn't hurt you."

He shook his head remorsefully. His dark hair had grown longer. It fell over one eye, making him look suddenly younger as he said, "I've had a lot of time to think. But mostly, I've just thought of you."

Evangeline's heart cracked a little. Weeks ago, this was what she wanted to hear Apollo, uncursed, saying: he wanted her. And a part of her still wished she could want it. It made far more sense to fall in love with the prince than with the villain.

But Evangeline didn't want love that made sense, she wanted love that made her feel, love that made her want to fight and hope for the impossible.

"Whatever you've thought, it's only because of the Archer's curse. Jacks said—"

"You can't trust anything he says," Apollo snapped, and for a second, he looked murderous.

Evangeline backed away a step.

Apollo scrubbed a hand down his face. The rage vanished, replaced by pain. "I'm sorry. I didn't mean to snap at you. He's just done so much to both of us. He's clearly used some of his magic to make you trust him."

Evangeline almost didn't reply. Apollo was justified in his anger. But she didn't want him blaming Jacks for crimes he hadn't committed. "I know he's done a lot of terrible things, but he hasn't used any magic on me, and if it weren't for him, neither of us would be alive."

"No, Evangeline. If it weren't for Jacks, neither of us would have ever been in danger." Apollo dragged a hand through his hair. "I wish he didn't have this hold on you."

"I wish he didn't, either," she confessed. And she would have told Apollo that she'd really tried to love him. But that confession almost seemed as unkind as some of the things that Jacks had done. "I'm sorry, Apollo."

He looked at her with wounded eyes. "I am, too." But there was something off about the way he said it.

A warning pulsed inside Evangeline, telling her she needed

to leave. But Apollo was too quick. She tried to dart past him, but he grabbed her and pressed her back to one of the stone angels, holding her in place with his chest and one heavy arm around her waist.

"Apollo—stop. Let me go!" She shoved against him.

"Shh, sweetheart." He stroked her hair, unmoved by her protests. "I didn't want to do this, but it's for the best."

He brushed his thumb across her temple, terrifyingly soft and sweet, and she felt the fight draining out of her limbs.

"What did you just . . ." Her head was too heavy to finish the question.

"It's all right. I've got you." His arm tightened around her waist.

She tried again to struggle, but she was pathetically weak—as if she were a ball of yarn trying to battle a great cat.

Apollo cupped her face with one large hand. His touch was soft, but it felt wrong, as if he wasn't just caressing her. It felt as if he were reaching into her, as if there were invisible fingers digging into her mind, taking things they shouldn't. *Memories.*

"No!" Evangeline tried in vain to struggle as she felt him snatch away the first night they met—the night Evangeline kissed him, up in the tree after Jacks had painted her lips with his blood. Although . . . the memory of that was fading as well.

"Don't!" she cried. "Stop!" But Apollo merely held her tighter.

"It will be better soon." He stroked her cheek, and the memory of the last time they'd been together, when they'd been kissing in the bed, when he'd wrapped his hands around her throat, when Jacks had stormed into the room and carried her away—it all disappeared.

There was a blankness in her mind. She knew something had been stolen, but she had no idea what it was.

With her body weakened, she fought to lock him out of her mind, to hide her remaining memories, but one by one he plucked them out.

The night in the crypt with Jacks . . . *gone.*

Marrying Apollo . . . *gone.*

Her friendship with LaLa . . . *gone.*

Apollo infected with the Archer's curse . . . *gone.*

Jumping off the cliff with Jacks—

"No!" she screamed.

. . . *gone.*

The wonder of the Hollow . . . *gone.*

Jacks bandaging her wounds . . . *gone.*

Jacks confessing he was the Archer . . . *gone.*

"Please, stop," she begged.

She held tight to the memories of her parents, of the curiosity shop, of all the fairytales her mother had ever told her. Evangeline tried to hold them in her head like a child with a precious blanket, as if they might protect her, since she couldn't seem to protect them.

"Please—stop! Please, stop!" she cried. "Please—"

She cried until her throat went raw. Until she wasn't even sure who she was begging.

She was crying so hard she could barely see.

But she knew that she was alone. Not just alone in this strange place but alone in the world. She felt it down to her bones.

Epilogue

Evangeline's back was pressed to something hard, and her knees were curled against her chest. She was in a ball on an unfamiliar patch of cold ground.

Where was she? How had she gotten here? All she could remember was crying until she wasn't sure why she was crying.

Now she just wanted to go home. She wanted a hug from her mother and her father. But then she remembered: both her parents were dead.

The tears started flowing again.

She still wanted to go home, but she was afraid she couldn't return there. Although no matter how hard she tried to remember, she couldn't recall why home was no longer safe. She just knew it was a place she couldn't go. But where was she now?

She looked up at a pair of stone angels, warriors, who appeared to be watching over her as if they could give her an answer, although it looked as if they'd been crying, too.

"There you are!" A finely dressed young man with strong, attractive features, dark hair, and a pair of concerned eyes rushed into the room. "I've been so worried."

In one gallant move, he picked her up and pulled her to a chest covered in a very fine velvet doublet.

She stiffened in his arms. "Who are you?"

"Don't worry. You're safe with me." He didn't let go of her, but he loosened his grip. "I would never hurt you, Evangeline."

He said her name with warm affection. She still didn't recognize anything about him. He looked a few years older than she was, although there was something in his gaze that made her suspect he'd been through a great deal. His brown eyes looked wounded and a little haunted, but they softened when he looked at her.

She wished she could remember him.

"I'm sorry," she said, her voice raw from all the crying, "but I have no idea who you are."

He smiled wider, which seemed an odd response to her confession. But his voice was nothing but soothing as he said, "I'm your husband. You've been through something terrible, but it's all right now. I'm here, and I'm never going to let you go."

Acknowledgments

My heart is bursting with gratitude as I write these acknowledgments. I continue to thank God every day that I get to write books and that there are people in the world who want to read them.

For this book, I had a very specific vision for what I wanted the story to be, and I could not have accomplished it without the help of so many outstanding people.

Sarah Barley, you are a true champion. I still can't believe you made time to read this book the same week that you gave birth to a baby. I am so thankful for your dedication, for the way you understand my stories, how you always push me to be a better storyteller, and your friendship.

Thank you, Caroline Bleeke, Kimberley Atkins, and Sydney Jeon, for sweeping in like superheroes when Sarah went on maternity leave. I couldn't have asked for a better team. This book is so much stronger because all of you were a part of it, and it was just so fun to work with you all.

Jenny Bent, thank you for being such a rock star of an agent, for reading the earliest version of this book, and for all your incredible support. I wouldn't want to do any of this without you. Molly Ker Hawn, Victoria Cappello, Amelia Hodgson, and everyone at the Bent Agency, I continue to feel so lucky to have you all.

So much love and thanks to my phenomenal family, to my sister, my brother, my brother-in-law, and to my incredible parents. Mom and Dad, I love you both so very much, and without the two of you, I wouldn't be doing this at all.

Huge thanks to everyone at Flatiron Books! I could not ask for a better publisher or a more outstanding group of people to work with. Thank you so much, Bob Miller, Megan Lynch, Malati Chavali, Nancy Trypuc, Jordan Forney, Cat Kenney, Marlena Bittner, and Donna Noetzel.

Thank you so much to all the wonderful people at Macmillan Academic, Macmillan Library, Macmillan Sales, and Macmillan Audio. I also want to give a huge thanks to my fantastic audiobook narrator, Rebecca Solar, for always doing an incredible job of bringing my stories to life.

Thank you so much to everyone at my brilliant UK publisher, Hodder and Stoughton, with a special thanks to Kimberley Atkins—it has been such a joy to have you as an editor, and I am so grateful you wanted to work with me and my books. Lydia Blagden, I am continually thankful for your artistic brilliance! Callie Robertson, thank you for all your terrific marketing.

Thank you, Erin Fitzsimmons and Keith Hayes, for yet another fantastic cover! And thank you so much, Virginia Allyn, for pouring so much love into another fantastical map of the Magnificent North.

To my fabulous, wonderful, incredible friends! Stacey Lee, thank you for being there for me through everything—this last year felt especially tumultuous, and I am so grateful for you and your enduring friendship. Thank you, Kristin Dwyer, for listening to me talk about this book over and over. I am so grateful for your friendship and your questions and your endless belief in my stories! Thank you, Kerri Maniscalco, for reading some of my messy first drafts and for all your brilliant feedback. Thank you, Isabel Ibañez, for your incredible friendship and for being there for pretty much everything! Thank you, Anissa de Gomery, for loving Jacks so much. Jordan Gray, thank you for falling in love with this story and for helping me make the romance even stronger! Kristen Williams, thank you for being such a good friend and such a ray of joy in this community. Thank you, Adrienne Young, for your fierce and wonderful friendship. Thank you, Jenny Lundquist and Shannon Dittemore, for all the amazing walks and talks. And thank you, Jodi Picoult, for being the first to read the finished book and for your magical quote!

And finally, I want to thank my readers! I am so glad that I love writing YA fantasy, because I think YA fantasy readers are some of the most incredible readers out there. Thank you all for reading these books, for sharing about these books, and for loving these books.

Blood will be shed, hearts will be stolen, and true love will be put to the test in . . .

A
CURSE
FOR
TRUE
★★★
LOVE

. . . the long-awaited conclusion to the bestselling Once Upon a Broken Heart series